NOBODY'S CHILD

NOBODY'S CHILD

KANCHANA BANERJEE

HARPER
BLACK

First published in India in 2019 by Harper Black
An imprint of HarperCollins *Publishers*
HarperCollins *Publishers* India, Cyber City, Building 10-A, Gurugram,
Haryana – 122002, India
www.harpercollins.co.in

1 2 3 4 5 6 7 8 9 10

P-ISBN: 978-93-5357-130-6
E-ISBN: 978-93-5357-131-3

Typeset in 11/14.1 Apollo MT Std at
Manipal Digital Systems, Manipal

Printed and bound at
Repro India Ltd.

*

HarperCollins *Publishers*, Macken House, 39/40 Mayor Street Upper,
Dublin 1, D01 C9W8, Ireland

To the voice in my head that said – rewrite the story.
Thank God I listened!

Prologue

'Finish her. I want her gone. Forever.'

'I need her alive. She's of no use to me dead. She needs to live.'

'Please! Please let me go. Somebody help me! PLEASE! I can't live like this. Please let me die.'

'I promise I will not die. I will live, and I will live by your rules. Please let him go. Don't kill him.'

'I'm nobody's child. No one wants me.'

One

Avniel. NOW.
2018

You're paying for this.

It's almost 1 a.m. when I see the message.

It makes no sense, and my brain is already dead after ten hours of staring at the computer screen.

I stretch my stiff limbs and yawn. It must have rained while I was shut inside the windowless office. The ground feels soft and wet. There's moisture in the air. Something is rotting nearby. I regret taking a deep breath. Must be domestic garbage or refuse from the nearby shops. Intermittent rain and heat has caused the rot, hence the putrid smell.

Bloody monsoons! The romance of rain is lost on me. Mumbai becomes an open gutter, an overflowing, rotting gutter, when it rains.

I walk around to relieve the stiffness; it hurts. My left knee and ankle beg to be massaged, reminding me that I haven't been exercising as per the doctor's suggestion. I walk around some more, extend my legs and flex them, and then rotate my ankles. I need to get mobility back in my joints. I also need to lose weight. My trousers have started to feel tight at the waist.

I crave for a smoke and some proper home-cooked food. Priya isn't much of a cook and I'm too busy. Meals are hastily ordered on Swiggy and delivered in disposable plastic containers. Editing thirty hours of recordings to make a spectacular thirty-minute reel for the BBC is all I have the bandwidth for. I can't and don't want to think about anything else.

I look at the other messages on my phone. Someone from college is planning someone's fortieth birthday and has created a WhatsApp group. I am in it. I have no recollection of the subject, the moron who formed the group with everyone he could remember, or those enthusiastically posting emojis, expressing their keenness to drink and dance.

Fucking shit! I detest being added to random WhatsApp groups. I remove myself. I don't have time for fortieth birthdays and I don't care for the idiots I went to college with two decades ago. No fond memories there. They never cared to keep in touch all these years because a failed reporter didn't quite make the cut. Suddenly, everyone wants to be my best friend. Everyone loves success. Sorry, suckers! Now *you* don't make the cut.

There are a few more messages I delete without opening. But I open the one from Papa. After five unseen messages, he has simply written one line.

How are you, beta? Miss you.

I have missed his pings in the last few days. He has stopped calling because I'm never able to answer. Now it's only images of sunrises, sunsets and puppies with profound philosophy scribbled over them that he sends with unfailing regularity. My response is always a thumbs up or smile emoji. The WhatsApp forwards from him and my corresponding thumbs-up emojis is how we assure each other of our well-being. In the last few days, editing has consumed every waking hour of my time. The absence of the blue ticks or a reply must have worried him. I type in a message hastily.

Sorry, Papa. Working very hard on the BBC documentary. Keeping very long hours. You okay, I hope? This is a huge deal for me. Working very hard to do it well.

I tell myself I will make the trip to see him but don't know when that will be.

I go back to thinking about the message Priya had sent earlier, at 9 p.m.

You're paying for this.

Why did she send me a picture of a wine bottle? Why am I paying for it?

It takes me a few more minutes to realize why. I curse loudly. The snoring security guard and his dog, also snoring, don't stir.

I forgot about the dinner date! Again!

This was supposed to be the make-up dinner for the last two I failed to show up for. It's too late to call now. It's 1.20 a.m. I curse myself again for being forgetful.

It's my first documentary for the BBC, on the errand boys in the studios of Bollywood. It's not every day that one gets a break like this, so I have pushed everything else to the periphery. Priya, on the other hand, plans for dinners and make-up dinners. She does everything, really.

She bought a bottle for ₹10K just to get back at me because I forgot to show up! That's a tad much as punishment. I feel annoyed, but not so much since I can afford it. It's not like before when I had to monitor every penny.

I don't wait for Kay, my assistant. I know she'll lock the office and drive herself home. I get into my car and head towards Linking Road and then Khar. It's Friday night, actually Saturday morning, so party revellers are out in full fervour. Mumbai is probably the only city in the world where one can get stuck in a traffic jam at half past one in the morning. I would have preferred to roll down my window; September nights are pleasant. With the monsoon just behind us, the days are hot and humid but late nights are cool, with just a hint of a nip in the air that dissipates ever so quickly at sunrise. But experience has taught me that it's never a good idea to keep your windows down, especially this late. Bloody eunuchs get you.

A woman – a girl, really – in a shiny dress that's too tight for her, is negotiating with those in the car ahead of me. My headlights are making her squint. She has too much make-up on, probably to hide her real age. She has a Band-Aid on her ankle; the shoe must be biting into her skin. I have seen too many of them to feel any pity. The road is dug up to my left, leaving me stuck behind the car as their negotiations carry on. I honk impatiently. I want to get home. Why can't they carry out their sex deal in the lane ahead and not hold up the traffic!

The girl leaves and the car moves ahead, as do I. She gives me a glare as though to say I'm responsible for her loss of business. I guess she needed more time to bargain and my impatient honking didn't help her case. I seem to be disappointing everyone. My dad, Priya … even the hooker on the street.

I get back home, park in the slot allotted for me. Duffy, the neighbourhood dog, opens one eye and gives me half a wag.

Sorry, dude! It's too late and I'm too sleepy to give you a proper welcome, he seems to say.

I drag my aching feet up the stairs. My left knee and ankle feel rigid, as though locked in defiance. My muscles feel knotted.

You must remember to exercise your leg regularly, else normal movement will be hampered. It was a very bad accident.

The doctor's words come back to me only when my left leg hurts and walking feels like someone has tied a 50 kg weight around my ankle. I promise myself that tomorrow will be a new day and I will get back to exercising diligently.

I promise I'll meet you for dinner.

I promise I'll visit you soon, Papa.

I just can't keep my promises.

Every time you say 'I promise', I know you'll not do it. Avniel, you're horrible at keeping promises. You know that, right?

I'm almost at the door when those words suddenly flash through my mind. Why did I suddenly think of her? She'd said them a long time ago. I fumble with my key as I try to push the thought back into that dark space in my head where I don't venture.

Priya has left the lights and fan on in the living room. Her stilettos are thrown on the rug and five wine glasses with lipstick stains, along with the said ₹10k bottle, now empty, sit on the centre table.

Did she do this on purpose? Leaving the lights and fan on. Glasses and wine bottle on the table. She knows how much I like things kept in the right place, and it's annoying when she makes a mess and leaves it for me to clean.

It's almost two in the morning and I'm cleaning up. I wouldn't get any sleep knowing the living room is in a mess. I debate over cleaning the wine glasses now or later. The lipstick marks will be more stubborn in the morning but I'm too knackered to do it now. I just run water on them. As I walk towards my bedroom, I pick up the coffee mug that has been sitting on the windowsill, enjoying the view. I make another trip back to the kitchen.

Maybe I should buy myself a Versace shirt, click a picture of it and send it to her with the message *'You're paying for this because you left the house in a mess that I have to clean up.'*

I almost chuckle at the thought. But I know I won't do it. I don't want Priya to join the club of angry ex-girlfriends. Three don't exactly make a club, but still.

We've been together for more than a year, and it's been a month since I gave her the key to my flat and emptied a closet for her things. Last I checked, it wasn't even half full. She's taking it slow. She hasn't ended the lease on her place in Lower Parel, which is closer to her office. She stays there sometimes when it gets late at work and she's too tired to come all the way to Khar.

It doesn't bother me. Slow suits me fine. I've rushed into things too many times only to beat a retreat. Slow is better.

I slide into bed and set the alarm for six. Damage control is the need of the hour. I plan on fixing her a good breakfast. I missed the make-up dinner so I settle on breakfast. I sink into a dreamless sleep as soon as my head touches the pillow.

When my phone vibrates next to my pillow, I struggle to open my eyes. It feels like I've been asleep for only a minute. I switch it off before it starts to play '*Wake me up before you go-go*'. I've been the butt of numerous jokes for having

George Michael's chartbuster as my alarm tone, but refuse to change it. I silence it before it wakes up Priya, who is softly snoring, a fact she vehemently refuses to admit.

She's just inches away from me, her new pixie haircut messy and spilt on the pillow. There are a few blue streaks in her hair that look more weird than nice. When did she get those? Her left hand is tucked under her chin and the right pushed slightly under the pillow. I don't see the charm bracelet I gave her. It was my birthday gift to her and she wears it on her left wrist all the time. I got it made especially for her, with miniature charms of things she likes. A tiny book, a bottle of wine, a sudoku puzzle, a stiletto (she loves shoes), a globe to signify wanderlust, the eternity symbol and even a tiny me, to signify the man in her life. It wasn't easy to get it done but I wanted something special. The eternity symbol was Kay's idea.

'Women love that kind of thing, boss,' she'd insisted, and she was right. Priya loved it and so did her girly gang who know everything that happens between us – from the number of times we have sex to how many times I make her come to the times I goof up and miss dinner dates. I could tell I'd scored lots of points with the charm bracelet, especially the eternity symbol. The admiring look on their faces said it all. I must have lost all those points because of my back-to-back no-shows.

She wears the bracelet all the time, but now it's not on her wrist. I need to fix this.

Have I upset her that much?

I look at her sleeping face. Laugh lines are beginning to show near her eyes. I want to kiss her there as well as on her lips. I want to slip my hand under the sheets and cup her breasts. I know she doesn't sleep with her bra on. Any other day, it would have been a good way to wake her up and start the day. But not today.

Instead, I want to wake her up with the aroma of a good breakfast. Scrambled eggs for her, sunny side up for me and some slivers of bacon to go with it. Black coffee for both of us. Nothing says *Honey, I love you and I'm sorry for being such an asshole* better than well-done eggs. Priya always tells everyone that I make perfect scrambled eggs, though I think my sunny side up is better.

I slip out quietly, closing the bedroom door behind me. I open the windows as I walk towards the kitchen. It's cool and pleasant in the morning; the sticky humid heat of the day is yet to hit us. Sticky September is my moniker for the month.

I pick up the bowl of crackers, which I'd missed the previous night. I notice the book on which the bowl sat.

She stares straight at me from the cover, unblinkingly. The photograph is brilliant and I couldn't have chosen a better one for the book cover. *I'm Nobody's Child*.

I stare back at the familiar face and smile. This book is my greatest achievement yet. I don't allow any dark thoughts to arise. When they do, I push them away. Someone had to tell the story; I was there at the right time.

It's going to be a great day, I tell myself. I'll fix a good breakfast, Priya will be happy and we will make love. Morning sex is always the best, and she'll forgive me. I'm humming a tune, confident in my anticipation.

I pull the curtains apart. It's a tiny flat, even by Mumbai standards. The owner, an elderly widow we call Sharma aunty, decided that she didn't need the three-BHK flat after her husband's demise, given that she lives alone and her children are in Canada. So she got herself an architect and put him on a shoestring budget to make two flats out of one. The part that I rent has a decent living room, an open kitchen and one bedroom. I can afford a larger flat now but Khar is close to Bandra. I know what they say – those who can't afford Bandra stay in Khar. But at least I'm close, much better than the previous dump in Kandivali that I had to call home.

I love the huge windows, which look out to leafy trees with dense foliage. The building stands in the far corner of a cul-de-sac, so it is relatively quiet. It's not a high-rise, only five floors. The owners love the privacy and often ward off greedy builders who try luring them with crores if they sign over the plot to them. So far, the largely elderly population in the complex has succeeded in keeping the hungry wolves at bay.

I stand near a window and look out. Some kids are getting ready to play gully cricket. Doggie aunty, as everyone calls her, is out with breakfast for the strays that are jumping around her in glee. Duffy is leading the pack, his tail wagging so vigorously that it might fall off. The pao-wallah has just arrived. He parks his cycle near the gate and enters with his huge jute tote. I watch the kids play. Their squeals are a welcome respite. The dogs are happily lapping up their breakfast. Duffy has finished his share and tries to take a bite from his neighbour's bowl, who responds with a snarl. He backs off and looks at Doggie aunty with a hopeful *May I have some more?* face.

She gestures a no with her finger. He understands and accepts it. She then pats his head as he rubs his muzzle against her leg. She sneaks out a biscuit and gives it to him. She clearly loves Duffy more than the others.

I stay near the window for a little longer, watching the world outside, hearing the sounds. I like the early Saturday morning sounds, wafting through the house.

I walk towards the refrigerator. It's time I start making breakfast.

A Post-it note held in place by a magnet tells me that Priya has done the weekly grocery shopping.

You forgot. Again.

My 'miss list' is getting longer. I'm forgetting too much, too often.

I take out the eggs, milk and bacon. Priya has stocked the fridge with everything I like. She's been very nice and I feel like an asshole. I hope to revive my tarnished image with this breakfast.

I place the frying pan on the stove and the bread in the toaster. I will turn it on when the eggs are nearly done. I sprinkle some olive oil on the pan and crack an egg over it; the other, I break into a bowl, add milk and start to whip. I pour it into the pan, away from my sunny side up, and then add the bacon slivers near the edge.

While the eggs are getting done, I turn the flame down, switch the TV on to watch the IKA news hour and then separate the eggs in the pan. I scramble one without disturbing the other, while allowing the bacon to fry quietly, spluttering in its fat and adding more flavour to both the eggs. I transfer the scramble to a plate for her and gently tilt the pan to place mine in another. This is when people end up disturbing the yolk and ruining a perfect sunny side up.

That's when I hear it.

'BEGGARWOMAN FOUND OUTSIDE CHURCHGATE CLAIMS TO BE ASAVRI BHATTACHARYA. ASAVRI WON INDIAN KOEL TWO YEARS AGO AND WAS KILLED IN A ROAD MISHAP.'

My hands freeze as the camera focuses on the scarred face. Who is this?

The anchor, Anindita, is speaking animatedly into the camera, saying that she found her on the footpath outside Churchgate. The camera closes in on the face of the woman, who is talking in English.

'I studied in Loreto. Shantipur.'

The face is almost unrecognizable. The skin is darker than I remember. I can barely breathe … Then she starts singing.

The pan falls from my hand as I hear the voice, the voice I know so well. I dash for the bedroom and climb into my trousers that I'd flung on the stool near the foot of the bed. I proceed to grab my mobile, wallet and car keys.

Priya wakes up because of the noise I'm making.

'Where are you dashing off to?'

'I … I have to leave. I … I will call you.' I don't wait for her to answer.

I run out of the flat. Almost comically, it strikes me that this is probably the first time in my adult life that I have ruined a perfect sunny side up.

Two

Kamini. NOW.
2018

T is calling me again.

Being a mother is like nursing a migraine. A nagging dull throb that never goes away. You just teach yourself how to manage it, how to live with it.

I've told T a million times not to disturb my only hour of peace in the morning. I like to be by myself, collect my thoughts, sip my adrak chai and prepare myself for the day ahead. But my words to her are like water off a duck's back. She always thunders her way through, disturbing and throwing my plans asunder. She arrived into this world pretty much the same way – much before the expected date, ruining my Parisian outfit and rabbit-leather shoes. Pratap had wrapped the shahtoosh shawl around me; the bloodstains couldn't be removed. What a waste! I've never quite forgiven her for that.

Tanya has remained consistent; always barging in, demanding to be heard and attended to with scant regard for anything else.

But I'm surprised that she's calling me at seven in the morning. How did she manage to wake up this early to make a call? Though 7 a.m. is hardly early, in her world it is. So if she's calling at this hour, it's either to complain, nag or negotiate. She wants something desperately. I know my T.

Of late, her constant whining and the nasal 'What the …' has been getting on my nerves, and I have resisted the urge to scream the sentence complete.

What the fuck, Tanya! Can you ever shut the fuck up and not complain all the time?

But I don't. I'm a mother – a fact I have to keep reminding myself. The seed of my womb – now twenty-two years old with long, sinewy legs, her father's sharp nose and my thin lips and wavy hair cascading over her thin shoulders – won't stop trying my patience.

In the last twenty-four hours, she has called six times to say the same thing. 'Why the ... do I have to sing all day?' She knows better than to utter the expletive in front of me. She pauses instead of using the F-word but I know she's saying it in her head. There's a line which she dare not cross but I do at will. I never hesitate to use the expletives openly with others and silently in my head with Tanya.

I have a busy morning ahead. An important meeting at the party office. I can't afford to be late and she'll have to be dealt with. I have to take her call. I think of ignoring it, but I just can't. I guess I have become the part I set out to play. After twenty-five years of playing the doting wife and happy mother, some of it might've seeped under my skin. Though I could never be accused of the former – I never pretended to be a doting wife and Pratap never wanted me to be one. Am I a happy mother? Let's save that for another day.

I swipe right to take the call – 'Good morning, T.' I've finished fifty surya namaskars and would have liked to finish the remaining fifty-seven, but if I don't deal with T right now, she will keep calling all day. I don't want that.

With my other hand, I fiddle with the cup of chai that was made for me earlier by the staff. I allow myself to sink into the large cane chair and put my feet up on the white railing, which is in stark contrast to my dark skin. Toenails trimmed short, clean and buffed. Gone are the days of blood-red nail-paint. Nowadays, it's clean and clear. Over the years, I've left behind every habit and preference of yore to fit the new cast.

'Mom! I can't do this anymore.' Her trademark nasal falsetto sounds like the scratching of nails on a blackboard. I grit my teeth. She continues, 'You promised that I wouldn't have to sing after one year and it's been almost two! My life's ruined, Mom. Ruined! My friends are going to the Bahamas and I'm stuck in this smelly, stuffy studio, belting out numbers for some dumb-shit movie. Mom! What the ...'

I hear her out like I always do, while checking my fingernails – also trimmed short, U-shaped and with no paint. I miss the long nails I used to flaunt and the insane colours I painted them. Dirty yellow. Orange with purple flecks. I miss the wild days sometimes. I run my fingers through my hair. I pull out the band that held them in place while I did yoga. It tumbles over my shoulder, letting the early-morning air caress it lightly. I know I'm tuning out what T is animatedly saying in my ear.

Sometimes, I hold the mobile away from my ear so that my head doesn't burst, hearing her rant about the same thing again and again. 'My life's ruined'. *Ruined*. Does she even know the meaning of the word? Ruin is when your father leaves you with a neighbour because there's no place else for his daughter to stay while he goes to work at Ganesh Sari Shop and you grow up making tea and pakodas for the men Asha tai let into her home while her husband was at work. I dusted and watered her plants, all the while trying to ignore the unapologetic noises from the bedroom. She didn't even bother shutting the door of her room.

Though, in many ways, people would say that ruined my childhood, Asha tai taught me things that helped me survive in the real world; stuff that no school ever taught. She taught me how to pleasure a woman. She would make me give her a massage while she lay naked with her legs spread wide apart. This came in handy when I chose to sleep with Kaveri Sharma, the PR head of Taj, because I wanted her to take me along when she joined Origin PR. I didn't want to be stuck with a front-office job. And it's not that I disliked pleasuring Kaveri. Single and much older than me, Kaveri dated men to keep up a façade but sneaked in some time with me every now and then. It was fun. Sex with her was satisfying in a way only sex with a woman can be. And the new job was worth it, for it led me to Pratap.

I usually don't do anything I don't like, and even when I do, I know how to sweeten it. For example, my landlord from when I lived in a tiny hole in Karol Bagh wanted the rent in kind. I wanted to throw up at the mere thought of taking him in my mouth. I don't think he ever used soap – he smelt of spoilt milk, garlic and mirchi bhajji. Layers of fat would trap his stinky sweat. Just the sight of him was sickening. But I found ways of making it likeable. In his case, squirting Maaza on him sweetened it for me. It wasn't like I was short on rent; I just didn't want to pay him. I needed money for other more important things, like buying clothes and shoes.

So I pleasured him whenever he wanted, I just made sure there were enough bottles of Maaza around.

One needs to handle shit in life and not complain.

Something my T, entitled-princess-to-the-manor-born-with-a-platinum-spoon-studded-with-diamonds-in-her-mouth, never had to learn.

My daughter's life is ruined very easily. In fact, it happens every week. When her Louboutins can't be found. When she wants the latest Versace products in less than a day. When her hair doesn't obey. Her life is ruined. I feel like telling her she doesn't even know what the word means. The disaster that almost completely derailed my life twenty-six years ago – *that* fits the 'my life's ruined' category. Not being able to go to the Bahamas doesn't even come close.

'Mom!' Tanya yells in my ear, breaking my reverie. 'Are you even listening?'

'Yes, T, I am.' I take a deep breath and continue, 'I'm just waiting for you to finish before saying something. Are you done talking? If you are, then I'll speak.'

I wait for her to continue. She sounds tired. Did she set an alarm to wake up and talk to me or did she just get back to the hotel from the recording studio? The first is highly improbable. No alarm in the world can wake her up. I settle for the second. She has been staying at a hotel near her recording studio to avoid travelling all the way from Andheri to Malabar Hill late at night or early in the morning. I don't like the idea of my daughter staying alone in a hotel room, but it's more practical. Dheeraj has arranged for a security woman to be with her round the clock.

Yes, security woman and not man. My T can charm the pants off a man to get her way. After all, she is my daughter.

'T, you enjoy singing. You won a contest, remember? You're the nation's favourite.'

'I didn't win the contest. I came second.' Her retort is sharp. The memory of losing to Asavri is a wound with a thin scab on it. Though I don't understand why she's so sore about it. It's not that she was holding her breath to participate. I was the one who planted the seed in the first place, gently watered it till it grew into a full fledged plant, till she realized that it would be a great opportunity.

'I became the winner only after she died in that accident, Mom.'

She really needs to stop talking like this on a call. Anyone could be listening.

I don't chide her for it. Instead, I pause before continuing, 'Tanya, life has its own way. You are the winner now and everyone loves you.' I continue before she can interrupt me.

'You love the press coverage. The magazine covers you are on. Yes, I know your gang is going to the Bahamas, but, darling, tell me how many of them were on the cover of *Vogue* or *Cosmopolitan*? How many of them were on *Koffee with Karan*? How many of them have lakhs of followers? Do they have mobs waiting to receive them at the airport like they do for you, T? How many of your friends have gone on a world tour, singing in different cities where thousands turned up to see them?' I pause again. I can hear her thinking. I have pressed the right buttons. I always do.

I walk around as I speak.

'T baby, what you have is unique! You're a star. I know it's not easy, but you have what most people would *kill* for. Just do this for some more time and then if you still hate it, I promise I will get you out of the contract and you'll be a free bird.' I need her to stay on for some more months. I really do. She can't quit now and ruin my plans. I won't let her.

'Okay. But get me a week off starting tomorrow. I'm going to the Bahamas with the gang.' She hangs up before I can say anything. I'm fuming! I want to call her back and yell, 'Did you just hear what I said?' But then I don't. Tanya is her mother's daughter. She knows how to drive a hard bargain and get what she wants. I have lost but I am not too angry. It feels good to know that my T has some of my qualities besides the thin lips, glossy hair and the ability to charm the pants off anyone.

I start punching in a message to the director. If the Bahamas is what she wants, then that's what my girl will get. The music director won't be too happy, but he'll bend … for two reasons. One, Tanya Pratap Singh, the winner of *Indian Koel*, is the best voice in the country. Okay, maybe not the best, but since the best is not around anymore, T *is* the best. Secondly, her mother, Kamini Pratap Singh, is the most talked-about MLA in the state assembly; the voice of the ruling party. The director knows better than to mess with me. I can stall the shooting of the film with a single phone call and make sure it never sees the light of day.

So after doing the needful to ensure that T can go to the Bahamas, I linger for some more time in the balcony. I walk, letting my fingers trail a lazy pattern on the film of dust on the railing. The Arabian Sea spreads out before me, as far as the eye can see – the morning sun shimmering on the waves, water gently lapping on the boulders thrown to break the waves. The sea isn't particularly beautiful. I've seen far better and more mesmerizing water-bodies than the one spread out in front of my balcony, but I know that most people would kill for what I have. Beauty isn't a word I would use to describe Mumbai. Perhaps 'struggle' … or even 'survival'.

I turn to my left. The city of Mumbai is already up and about. The Queen's Necklace is now just a dull, ordinary road clogged with traffic. It looks spectacular only at night and from a distance. So many things – often people too – look nice from a distance. I like to gaze at the city from the balcony of my sprawling seaside bungalow on Malabar Hill. I sip on my second cup of chai. Unlike Pratap and his blue-blooded family who drink bitter, fresh orange juice, I need my chai, boiled with spices and ginger, to kick-start the day. It's among the few old habits I have held on to. It serves me well when I mingle with the workers and villagers. They like that I have my tea just like them.

I don't usually gaze at the horizon and think of new ways to define the city; at least not in the morning. I remind myself of the packed agenda that awaits me.

I go back into the bedroom. The bed has been made. The sheets are tight and neatly folded into sharp corners. The throw cushions are back in place. The morning paper is next to my laptop bag that sits on the chair next to a table that faces an open window. My phone charger is on the paper. The day is waiting for me.

I switch the TV on and walk towards my closet. The flip side of constantly reminding everyone that I'm Pratap's widow and his voice is that I had to let go of my sexy, glamorous avatar and commit to wrapping myself in handlooms. Looking the part is half the game won.

I don't make it to the closet – something on the TV catches my attention.

ASAVRI BHATTACHARYA IS ALIVE. WINNER OF INDIAN KOEL, WHO WAS SAID TO HAVE DIED IN AN ACCIDENT, IS ALIVE!

'What the fuck!' I say it out loud and sit down before the gigantic TV. A scarred face with glassy eyes stares back at me; she is clearly terrified.

'Who is this? She *has* to be an imposter. Asavri is dead,' I mutter to myself. Just then, the person on the screen begins singing. That's when I know it.

She is back. She is alive.

My life is ruined.

Three

Avniel. NOW.
2018

I park my car in the first available slot and run inside. It isn't even eight in the morning and the parking lot is already full. Don't visiting hours start at ten?

'Sirji! *Yeh* doctor *logon ka* parking *hai.*' The security guard comes running towards me. I am in the wrong parking bay. I flash my press card and sprint away without further conversation. Good thing I didn't surrender the card when I resigned from *Filmfare*. It has often helped me get away with speeding, jumping red lights and parking where I'm not supposed to. I know it's not the right thing to do, but I don't mind holding on to the card for small benefits; I deserve something for sticking around in that low-paying, thankless job for years.

I didn't take my foot off the accelerator since I ran out of my house after seeing the morning news. The face I saw on TV ... I still can't believe my eyes. How can it be true? I saw her dead body on the road when people pulled me out of the wreckage. Did I really even see her? I was dizzy from having lost a lot of blood. My head had banged hard against the window, after which I passed out. But there was a dead body ... mangled, next to the driver's. I remember that much. I woke up ten days later in the hospital to the news that Asavri had died and had been cremated.

I run towards the foyer of the hospital. I want to know if it's true. *Is she really alive?*

I catch my reflection in a car window. A crumpled shirt thrown over the tee I was wearing last evening. My cotton chinos need a wash and ironing as well. Did I brush? I can't remember, though I can taste the pungent morning breath. I desperately need a mint or something. And also a comb. My fingers do a sloppy job of grooming my hair. I don't stop for anything and hasten towards the entrance.

I don't have to go far. I see Bhaskar at the entrance to the grand foyer. This is a hospital that looks more like a five-star hotel and charges similarly too. Bhaskar is surrounded by his team and some others, whom I find out later are lawyers hired by IKA TV.

Press and TV crews from other channels have arrived. There's Arunima from Zee News in her usual windswept style and a scarf tied around her neck. And Tapan ... I forget where he is currently working. He's always changing jobs. TOI and HT have sent a senior reporter each, not a junior flunky. There's a story here and the big dogs have smelt blood.

I walk ahead and quicken my pace. I know I will have to walk through the shark pit; the circle of reporters will pounce on me. I'm not ready for this but there's no escaping it.

And then it happens. Arunima spots me, walks in my direction and the others follow. They look like a swarm of piranhas swimming towards the scent of blood. I'm no longer one of them. I've crossed over to the other side and they don't try to conceal their animosity. Or is it jealousy? No one expected the floundering reporter, who didn't even have a decent column to his name, to become a bestselling author. Neither had I, though I had hoped and dreamt about it. But I had always thought it to be one of those dreams you know will never be. It's like wanting to have sex with Julia Roberts or Charlize Theron; you know it will never happen but still dream about it.

Except that I did. Not have sex with Roberts or Theron, but become a bestselling author ... and they *hate* me for it. I don't blame them. I hated other success stories when I was stuck in the pit.

I brace myself, walk towards them and it starts. I know Arunima will lead with the questions. She always likes to have the first and last word.

'You wrote a book on Asavri – *I'm Nobody's Child*. You were her best friend. Do you think the beggarwoman found outside Churchgate is really Asavri?'

'How are you feeling now? When you heard the news, what were you doing?' Another question is thrown at me before I can answer the first. *I was trying to make breakfast for my angry girlfriend, who by now must have packed her things and moved back to her flat.*

I try to keep a straight face as I answer the barrage of questions.

'I have just arrived at the hospital. I heard the news on TV like everyone else. I think we should wait for Bhaskar, I mean Mr Rai, to share other details.' I've been a reporter at press conferences long enough to know how to answer a question without answering at all.

I turn to walk away and then I hear Arunima speak again. I know her sing-song voice, which to me is nothing more than a high-pitched screech. Her voice isn't actually like that. I just dislike her and everything about her. The feeling is mutual.

'Avniel, your book on Asavri became a bestseller. You became famous because of it. Did she give you permission before her alleged death to write about her life?'

I control myself in time, before spinning around and facing the bitch. She asked the question that haunts me. But I don't want to get into a war of words right now.

'Can we please just focus on the present? Save the questions for later.'

'Whatever you say. Maybe I'll ask Asavri, now that she's alive and back. I wonder how she'll react knowing you wrote about her life,' I hear her say as I walk away from the group. From the corner of my eye, I see the smirk on her face; the kind that comes with knowing you've touched a raw nerve. I know she will pound and punch at it. That's what I would have done too.

I try to focus on what I saw on TV. I need to know if it's true. I *need* to see her. I walk towards Bhaskar, who looks like he has been having the worst day of his life. By the time I reach him, I'm out of breath. When did I get so out of shape? Just a short trot and my lungs feel as though they will burst out of their ribcage. I've pulled a muscle just under my knee; it happens every time I try to run. I try not to limp. The pain is a piercing jab. Dammit! I should have exercised!

'When did you know?' I can't bring myself to say her name. Surely the channel head knew about the story long before it broke on their early-morning news.

'Yesterday afternoon. One of our reporters was doing a story on the streets. She and her camera guy found her.'

I glare at him hard. *You knew since yesterday and I had to learn about it on TV?*

'I know … I know, Avniel. I should have told you. But there are legal ramifications to this. We had to be sure of her identity. We couldn't risk any possible leaks,' Bhaskar rambles, struggling to use legalese as an excuse for not calling me. I let it go. It doesn't matter anymore. I want to see her. What I saw on TV, the scared, scarred face, glassy eyes and trembling lips - I can't get the image out of my mind. What had happened to her? Where has she been for the last two years? I look around and see at least ten security guards hovering around, speaking into their earphones. I recognize the police commissioner and nod. *Why is he here? What's with the bulky security guards?*

The commissioner returns my nod with a grim look. Before I can walk over to him, he strides in my direction. His hand feels clammy in mine. I don't like wet, sweaty hands. They make me want to wipe my own, but I can't. Not in front of the commissioner. I let my hands fall to my trousers and wipe them on the fabric.

'Sir?' I greet him the way I always do. I've never allowed the hours spent drinking with him to lull me into forgetting who he is. I learnt a bitter lesson in my days at *Filmfare* when I allowed alcohol to get the better of me; a mistake I will never repeat. So I always address him appropriately, something he ribs me about when he is two pegs down. But I always stick to addressing him respectfully and it has worked in my favour.

'This is a nightmare. A very bad one. We had a dead body, Avniel. It was identified as Asavri's. We ran all tests and were sure of its identity. And now this ... Who is she? If she's Asavri, then whose dead body did we cremate? And where was Asavri herself this entire time?' He runs his hand over his balding head, the last few strands of hair hopelessly lying over the surface of his round skull in solitude. On his fingers, I see a new addition. Soon, there won't be any fingers left for a ring. I hope the planets align themselves fast enough to help salvage the situation for him.

'Who are these jokers?' I signal towards the security personnel with my eyes, keeping my voice low.

'Extra security.'

I don't ask why; the question's already stamped on my face.

'There's been some chatter about a gang holding her in captivity. We'll know more soon, but for now, just be careful.'

The situation keeps getting more and more bizarre. *A gang kept Asavri captive? Why? What could possibly be their motive?*

I know I'm not getting any answers right now, so I turn towards the gathered press. An hour has passed. Why is Bhaskar stalling talking to the press? It's never a good idea to keep them waiting. The sun has returned after months with unrelenting fury. Post monsoon is the worst time of the year in Mumbai, when, along with heat, humidity is also high. High temperatures, sweat and a disaster don't make a pleasant cocktail. I see people snapping, barking orders at each other and the juniors getting all the flak and scurrying around like scared mice. Bhaskar has moved to a far corner and is speaking with someone on his phone. He doesn't seem too happy about what he is hearing, since his response isn't cordial. I've taught myself the art of lip-reading. It comes in very handy. The only ones standing with a Zen-like calm are the lawyers. Bad news is always good news for them. I've yet to see a lawyer getting hassled. Their calmness worries me. This is bad. I turn to look at the gathering of reporters from various TV channels and newspapers. I spot a few bloggers. Some of them are busy on their phones. Must be tweeting about the mayhem and chaos here. I can feel the silent hum of notifications on my phone. Twitter must be going crazy. I find out later that #AsavriAlive was trending.

Even though I have no authority to do so, I decide to handle the gathered press. Neither am I an employee of IKA TV nor am I a member of the press anymore, but all the reporters and their camera crew are standing in the heat, sweating. And they're going to let out their ire in the form of nasty questions.

I have them moved into an air-conditioned room. They look relieved. I arrange for some chai and vada pao. Most of them have rushed from their homes or at the end of their graveyard shifts. None of them must have had the time to grab the morning cuppa, let alone food. They look momentarily pacified – the combined effect of AC, garam chai and vada pao. I ask for sugarless chai and get a blank stare as if I have asked for unobtanium.

'Jo hai, leke aao.'

The loud siren of the police car that accompanies VIPs breaks through the chatter.

What public figure or politician has decided to grace the mayhem?

I don't have to wait too long to find out. Kamini Pratap Singh, the reigning and ever-popular MLA of the ruling Aam Junta Party strides in as the entourage makes way for her. Moses parted the sea for his followers but here her entourage does the needful. The police commissioner scurries to her side. This explains his presence. She stops him with a raised finger.

'I want to speak with Mr Rai first, then with the doctors. After that, I will deal with you and your men.' He moves aside, looking like a pup being reprimanded for wetting the rug. The man's going to need more than a few rings to help build a suraksha kavach for protection. This is going to get interesting. I stand aside.

She has seen me. I know she has, though she pretends otherwise; she's skilled at that.

It's been a while. Our paths don't cross anymore. Not that they ever did; we just met in the shadows and ignored each other in public. Actually, that's not true. I always stared and she never even looked in my direction. If there's anyone who has mastered the art of looking through you – as though you don't exist – it's Kamini.

When Kamini walks into the room, everything and everyone else ceases to matter. Whereas some would consider her ebony skin and long hair the epitome of beauty, I've never thought so myself – but she's pure lust on two legs. I can never tear my eyes away from her. She has that effect on everyone, men and women alike. Men want her and women want to be like her. Her presence fills the room, but of course, she will look past you unless you are someone worthy of note. I'm not noteworthy for Kamini. Even when she used to summon me to her room like her very own sex slave and I readily obliged, I was still a nobody. Back then, I was just a lowly reporter stuck in a hole with no future. Now, I'm an ex-reporter who wrote a book about the girl who surpassed Kamini's daughter to become the darling of the nation. My book is a national bestseller – a fact I carry around like a halo over my head. It has sold over five lakh copies and been translated into five Indian languages. But in Kamini's world, I will always be a nobody. She ended our little dalliance as abruptly as she had started it.

Every time we come face-to-face and she is obligated to make polite talk, she pretends it's her first time meeting me. Every time, I remember the perfect spread eagle she could do with her legs while I plunged deep inside her.

Bitch. But why the fuck am I thinking about all that! Asavri is back and I'm thinking about wild sex with Kamini. I force those thoughts away and turn towards Bhaskar.

He stands ashen-faced while he explains how and where Asavri was found. I walk over; near enough to hear the conversation, far enough not to seem intrusive.

'We don't know what happened at the accident site, madam. The body that was found was proven to be Asavri's.'

'How can you be sure that this beggarwoman is really Asavri?' Kamini's voice was almost inaudible.

'We called the Aadhar authorities and did a fingerprint authentication. It is her.'

'You didn't do the same with the dead body?'

'Shards of glass were all over her arms, hands and a leg … the body was severely damaged.'

'Then how did you ascertain it was Asavri who had died?' She crosses her arms at chest level and looks Bhaskar unflinchingly in the eye.

'The car she was in … along with the driver and Avniel. She and the driver died on the spot. Her body was there in the wreckage. Others in cars behind them saw her … I mean the body. And then there were the clothes, her shoes, accessories and the blood type. The hospital had her blood type from the fire that had broken out a few days before the finale. The fire in the pub. In Juhu …' Bhaskar doesn't finish. Shefali, the PR head from IKA TV approaches. Ordinarily, she would have been admonished and shooed away, but Bhaskar looks relieved at the intervention. She looks spiffy as always – camera-ready, with her hair combed and swept away stylishly. Her smart suit and neatly done make-up form the perfect colour combination. The only time her hair looked messy was when we had a drunken quickie in the ladies' washroom of the Marriott on the night of the gala, three years prior. An incident she pretends never happened, as do I.

When the spokesperson of a channel turns up perfectly coiffed at eight in the morning and the cops have picked up some chatter about gang involvement, it means that they have known about this since before last afternoon, which is inconsistent with what Bhaskar told me. But how long have they known?

'Sir. Madam.' Shefali nods reverentially towards Kamini. 'We can't keep the press waiting any longer. It's been more than an hour since they have been here. We need to do this, sir.' It sounds as though they're discussing hungry lions. That's not far from the truth, though. Reporters *are* like hungry lions – the only difference is that one is desperate for juicy meat, the other for juicy information and gossip.

The same applies to me.

'Madam,' Bhaskar asks to be excused. Kamini turns and walks away. The conversation is over and he is dismissed. How did the girl from the dingy gullies of Varanasi learn such blue-blooded mannerisms? I have an entire folder on her. She would make a fascinating story. I had hoped to transition from her bed to penning the story of her life. But that's never going to happen. Kamini made that very clear. My job was very well defined – I was her sex slave. Not that I objected, but the story would have been awesome too!

Why she remains so cut up with me over Asavri is a mystery. She had moved on like I never happened, I met Asavri and got engrossed by her. Thereafter every time Kamini saw me with Asavri, I could tell she was pissed. Sometimes, I amuse myself by thinking that she was jealous that I had found a younger woman. After all, beneath that façade of composure, was a woman. Woman, thy middle name is envy.

My eyes follow her now. Why is she here? Why such interest in Asavri?

Before entering the hall where the reporters and cameramen are waiting, she hisses something to the man at her side like her shadow. A shadow grows and diminishes based on the sun's position, but Dheeraj is always there. It takes a mere look from Kamini and he seems to know what to do. Always in black trousers, a full-sleeve white shirt, black socks and plain black shoes; I have never seen Dheeraj in any other outfit. Ever. Be it a campaign in the dusty villages or in a factory with workers or the Ed Sheeran concert where Kamini accompanied her daughter, albeit only for a while, Dheeraj is omnipresent with the same blank expression and the same attire.

He hands a phone to her and whispers something. Kamini excuses herself, saying it is the party office calling. She walks towards the washroom. I catch only bits of the conversation before she bangs shut the door of the ladies' room.

'For God's sake, stop talking about the Bahamas. Get your … get here right now. Right now …'

This was no party office personnel. I think I know who is being yelled at to get her ass to the hospital. Tanya. I dart back to the press room. I don't want her to see that I had followed her. I stand at the back of the room and wait. Kamini arrives shortly, not a strand out of place, and refuses a place on the podium next to Bhaskar.

'I'm going to sit with the gathered press. That's where the voice of the junta should be.' She waves away her security detail, who are used to her shenanigans. Reporters make space for her and multiple chairs vacate for one shapely ass that requires a lot of work to stay that way. I know she does 107 surya namaskars every day. She once did all 107 in the nude for my viewing pleasure. She considers her options and then takes a seat in the third row, right next to a sweaty, acne-marked reporter from *Dainik Bharti*. The pimpled moron, with coconut oil dripping from his head, looks like he's living his wet dream. Kamini sits next to him and touches his wrist while speaking with her head bent towards him.

I can see the headlines flashing across TV screens and newspapers.

MLA Kamini Pratap Singh sits with reporters in the third row, demanding justice … blah, blah.

Bhaskar is going to be crucified. Kamini will see to it.

Kamini is a forerunner in AJP, the seven-year-old political party. Her daughter was declared winner of the popular singing contest *Indian Koel* after Asavri, the original winner, was found dead at the site of an accident. That was November 2016. Tanya went on to fulfil music contracts as the winner of a nationwide contest and became the most followed youngster in the country. The mother, in simple cotton saris, and youth icon Tanya, in salwar kameez and sneakers, campaigned all over the dusty villages and towns of the state. Kamini secured her position in the state political arena and became MLA Kamini Pratap Singh – the minister of state for industries. There are rumours that she is going to get the party ticket for the national election. The girl from Varanasi is headed for the South Block in Delhi.

I remember her earlier pictures just after her marriage to Pratap – travelling in a private jet with a man whose net worth was more than the economy of a few African countries combined. Fashionable, with golden streaks in her hair and a giant rock on her ring finger, she was always wearing the latest from the world of couture. Soon after her marriage, she joined Pratap in his business.

The woman in the third row, sitting next to the pimply, oily head and sipping a cup of chai, is draped in a cotton sari, pleated neatly. Hair tied in a no-nonsense bun. No golden streaks and only a few grey strands. No jewellery. The rock that used to dangle from her slim finger now hangs on a thick chain around her neck. She never forgets to touch it multiple times, especially during press conferences, when she recites the well-rehearsed lines: 'My husband gave this to me the day he proposed. A day that is so special to me.

He is no more, but this around my neck makes me feel his presence.'

The words are fake but when Kamini says it, you want to believe it. She has this ability to say the same thing over and over again and yet make you believe she means it.

Was she born with it ... this ability to play to the gallery? Or did she learn it along the way?

'May I have everyone's attention, please?' Shefali speaks and breaks my reverie. I shift my attention to the front of the room.

'Bhaskar Rai, MD, IKA TV, and the chief medical officer, Anandmay Hospital, will address you now. Please keep the questions brief and to the point. Please understand that this has shocked us as much as anyone else and we don't have all the information with us yet, but we will share all that we know at this moment.' What she says and means are two different things. She means ask what you will but you'll get only what we decide to share right now. I've been a reporter long enough to know the difference between communicated truth and the whole truth.

She steps aside for Bhaskar. Someone got him a blazer to go with his dark-blue Armani denims and also a crisp white shirt in place of the tee he was wearing earlier. My association with him doesn't go too far back. In the last two years, owing to my closeness with Asavri and all that happened during the contest, Bhaskar and I interacted numerous times. Professional association gave way to friendship. I became his drinking buddy. I have to admit, I owe my friendship with Bhaskar to Asavri. One might even say that everything good that has happened in my life since May 2016, when I first met her in the audition hall, is because of Asavri.

Bhaskar is usually never ill at ease. Confident and glib, he thinks fast on his feet and is adept at handling any shot – high or low – thrown at him. But not today. He is being torn apart by the reporters and looks like he is sinking. He is.

Reporters hurl questions, accusations and charges of mishandling at him, and he is doing a fairly decent job of answering all of them. He comes dangerously close to losing his composure only thrice, which isn't bad considering the situation.

The long and short of it is that after a reporter found her on the footpath outside Churchgate station, she was brought to the hospital. She appeared to be in need of immediate medical attention.

Why did she need medical attention?

Authorities were notified, and her fingerprint identification through Aadhar verified that she is indeed Asavri Bhattacharya. The winner of *Indian Koel* 2016 is not dead as everyone had been made to believe after the accident that happened soon after her victory.

Where was she all this time? Why didn't she come forth and why does she look … look so ravaged … run down …? Where the hell was she and what happened to her?

'How is her medical condition?' the woman from HT asks. 'The image on TV that we all saw was … that of a woman in distress. Is she … is Asavri all right?' She didn't specify who the question was meant for. Bhaskar looks at the CMO, who doesn't seem to be comfortable at all but clears his throat to reply.

'She isn't in good health. Very malnourished and … and hurt.'

The room erupts into a spate of questions. Bhaskar looks away from my glare. What had happened to Asavri? Everyone begins yelling at the same time.

'What do you mean hurt? What does that mean?'

'She looked drugged on TV. Is she now a drug addict? What happened to her?'

'Was she raped?'

'Where was she for the last two years?'

I am having trouble breathing. I want to see her now. I want to ask her these questions myself. I need to drink something but coffee or chai won't help. It's too early in the day for anything strong. I want to spit out the sickly sweet tea, but instead, I gulp it down. I keep thinking about the face I saw on TV. Why were there marks on her face? I just need to calm down a little. It feels like a tornado is churning inside me.

Suddenly, I remember a conversation. It seems like a long time ago but it was just a little less than two years back, while the contest was still going on. Asavri was crying, sobbing uncontrollably in my arms. It was after the incident in her hotel room. She'd frantically called me early in the morning and was hysterical by the time I reached.

'Why can't he just let me be? Rudra will stop at nothing till he finishes me. You'll see … one day I'll just disappear and no one will even know what happened!'

The memory of those words jolts through me like an electric shock. Is he responsible for this? No, that's not possible. Rudra is dead. He was found hanging from the ceiling with his tie used as a noose. This had happened soon after Asavri won the contest. So it couldn't be Rudra. Then who? Absent-mindedly, I take a bite of the vada pao.

I remember the breakfast I had thrown aside on hearing the news, before rushing out.

My mobile has been vibrating repeatedly for some time now. I know it's Priya. I've ignored all the calls. I try to focus on the mayhem in the room.

And then I hear someone ask the question … the one I knew was coming.

'Mr Rai, the entire incident of the road accident, Asavri's supposed death and Tanya Pratap Singh subsequently becoming the winner of the competition. Doesn't this sound odd? To me, it looks like someone wanted to make Tanya the winner. Any comments?' That's Arunima. Trust her to hit the nail hard.

I would have liked to see Kamini's face but her back is towards me, so I can't. She isn't sitting at ease anymore. She has straightened her spine; I can see from the back of the room. Bhaskar is gritting his jaws as his fingers tighten on the stand, his eyes narrow and his lips draw into a terse straight line. A seasoned professional who has weathered many professional and personal storms, Bhaskar looks like he's about to burst, but controls himself just in time.

He clears his throat, faces Arunima and answers, 'You should leave reporting and take to fiction, my dear. You'll pen the next bestseller, I'm sure, with your flight of imagination.'

Arunima, being who she is, shoots her repartee, 'No, sir, I will stick to reporting. I'll leave the job of turning real-life tragedies into a bestseller to your best friend, Avniel.' She turns to me as she speaks, smiles and sits down. Bitch.

All cameras turn in my direction and begin clicking rapidly. I stand there holding a half-eaten pao, in the eye of the storm as it swirls wildly around me, slowly sucking me in. The bite in my mouth suddenly loses its taste. I want to throw up but I forcefully swallow the rising bile.

At some point, I hear shuffling feet near the door and Tanya walks in. She looks tired but her face is scrubbed clean and hair tied in a tight ponytail that swings merrily as she walks. She has put on some weight, and it suits her. The cameras go crazy on seeing her. She is a born celeb, easy in the limelight. She has the confidence and indifference of an uber-rich kid, as though she owns the ground she walks on.

She walks up to Bhaskar and stands beside him. She isn't here as her mother's daughter. She is here as the winner of the contest and her place is on the podium, next to the man from the company that runs the contest. Tanya does a much better job than the doctor or Bhaskar. She addresses the group in a clear and confident voice.

'After finishing a gruelling schedule of recording, I was packing to leave for a trip with my friends. That's when I heard the news. I mean, I saw it on TV. I think it's a miracle that Asavri, the rightful winner of the contest, is alive. I am, of course, thrilled with the news. I just hope she's okay. She saved me from the fire ... I owe her my life. Had it not been for her, I would have died. I'm praying for her recovery. I'm sure the doctors and Bhaskar sir are doing everything to ensure she gets back to good health soon. The true winner of *Indian Koel* is alive, people! Stop being nasty and stop the blame game. It's a happy day. Here's to hoping Asavri gets well soon and claims the victor's mantle that's rightfully hers.'

She has been briefed and is flawless. She also looks relieved that she will be released from the gilded cage. I don't blame her. For almost two years now, she has either been in recording studios or helping her mother's political agenda, campaigning in the dusty Maharashtrian hinterland.

'Kamini madam, a question for you, please?' Someone in the crowd yells out. Kamini stands up and turns around to face the voice.

'As your daughter just pointed out, she owes her life to Asavri. What are you proposing to do for the person who saved your daughter's life?'

Kamini holds the back of the chair to steady herself, her face emotionless, though I think a shadow momentarily fleets by and she regains control. I remember that night and the sight of Asavri collapsing as she half carried an unconscious Tanya out of the fire. Kamini had enveloped her daughter in her arms, screaming for help. It was probably the only time Kamini has sobbed hysterically.

'I will ensure the police get to the bottom of this. It's beyond horrifying that a young girl was declared dead, then found to be alive, and that an unknown body was cremated in the midst of it all. I promise you all that I will find out the truth.' She looks at the commissioner who stands on one side of the room. He looks like he would gladly blend into the wall and stay there.

She continues, 'Of course, I remember what Asavri did for Tanya. I'm here to help in whatever capacity. The party is willing to pay for her treatment, regardless of how long it takes. Asavri is Mumbai's daughter, and I will ensure that she is well taken care of. And rest assured, I will find the person responsible for this. I am your representative – the voice of the junta. Trust me, the people will know everything.'

I'm not surprised that Kamini succeeded in turning the situation into a political opportunity for herself. Ever since her husband died in the factory accident, she has anointed herself as the champion of the masses – a role she plays to perfection.

But I will not let you use Asavri as your political pawn. Over my dead body.

I throw what remains of the pao in the nearby bin and catch up with Bhaskar as the press meet ends. We take the elevator to the floor where Asavri is kept. Kamini and Dheeraj are also with us. None of us pretend to make small talk, each staring at the screen that displays the number of the changing floors, as though that would make the elevator go faster.

The CMO meets us on the floor as the elevator door opens. He no longer looks nervous. This is his domain and his word is the last word.

'Nobody is allowed inside the room. The patient has suffered severe trauma. She was sedated but is now awake.' Clearly, there's a lot that wasn't said in the press meet downstairs.

'What is her exact medical condition, doctor?' I can't keep the tremor from my voice.

'She is severely disoriented. Very dehydrated and malnourished. We are doing a full medical on her. The results are expected in a day or two. But she has been on drugs and is displaying symptoms of going cold turkey.'

Kamini begins to say something but is stopped by the doctor. 'I'm sorry, madam, but I have to refuse. The patient's well-being is crucial. No one can go in.' The finality in his tone irks Kamini. Not one to take refusal easily, she gulps it down and remains quiet.

I can hear and feel my heart pounding. The last time I saw Asavri, we were in the car. She went to sit in the front seat because she wanted to click a picture of the rising moon.

'Look, Avniel. Look how beautiful the moon looks.' That's what I remember. My phone vibrates yet again in my pocket. I ignore it. Did the doctor really just say that? Cold turkey? As in severe withdrawal symptoms from drug addiction ...? How is that even possible? Why would Asavri be on drugs?

The CMO directs us towards a large glass window. It feels as though we are observing an aquarium. Someone has stepped inside and draws up the venetian blinds that cover the glass panel. Kamini and I gasp in unison. Bhaskar is silent. This isn't the first time he's seeing Asavri since she was brought in.

I close my eyes and stumble backwards. I can't bear to see this. What happened to her? Who did this to her and why?

Four

Avniel. THEN.
2016

The first time I saw Asavri, I didn't see her at all.

I was with *Filmfare*, doing rounds of studios for interviews no one wanted to do and I'm pretty sure no reader ever read. I was never assigned any important star interviews or trending stories. It had been four years since that moronic episode at the after-party of the annual *Filmfare* gala. I'd clearly dug myself into a hole and didn't know how to crawl out of it. I was lucky to still be on the rolls and not get sacked. I did the measly studio news watch, scraps of news from various studios and passages that were often trimmed mercilessly or removed altogether to make space for ads. I wrote about stuff that no one cared about, myself included. They had to justify the pathetic salary, so that's what I did.

If only I hadn't got piss-drunk on the night of the party and tried to kiss the leading actress. I have no recollection of the incident. The *Filmfare* annual bash is always a wild night. Everyone was drunk, me more than the others. Everyone was hugging and kissing each other, so why was it wrong for me to ask for one measly kiss? I was told later I'd screamed, 'Do me, baby, do me!' I'm pretty sure I didn't go that far and the guys at the office made it up to torment me further, but that was the nail which sealed my fate and made sure I remained crucified to the scraps column. They ensured I would never get out and make another spectacle to embarrass the magazine. I carried the weight of that one idiotic, alcohol-induced incident for the rest of my career. They wanted to sack me but I begged and pleaded. *I'll do whatever lowly job you assign me, but please don't sack me.* Those were my exact words. Film journalism was oxygen for me. I had been buying every *Filmfare* issue since I was in school, poring over the credits column, dreaming my name would be on it and eventually rise to the top. Part of the dream came true; my name featured on the magazine as 'junior features writer', but it never rose above that. I lived it for three brief years. After my debacle, I was relegated to the rank of an unknown, unnamed person who worked for the magazine but had his name featured nowhere.

I clung on to the job and the dream, waiting for a miracle to happen that would somehow resurrect me.

Little did I know that when I entered the gates of Mehboob Studios on 20 May 2016, it was going to be my lucky day. I would meet my miracle! Though when I first saw her, she looked nothing like a miracle. Her frizzy, messy hair was tied in a ponytail; she'd tried to tame it with a liberal dose of coconut oil, though irate strands still stuck out. She wore a plain kurta over denim trousers and a dupatta draped around her neck. Dull, muddy-brown skin with acne marks, Asavri looked more plain and ordinary than tap water. She was smiling unnecessarily, looking at others eagerly and expecting someone to reciprocate with a smile and a conversation. I could tell she was new to Mumbai and hadn't yet learnt Mumbai's I-don't-give-a-damn attitude.

I was there to meet the studio manager who had a few photos to give me. He wasn't there and his phone was switched off. I was in a particularly bad mood that morning. The recent issue of *Filmfare* was on the stands. The cover story was by a young and pretty thing who'd joined five years after me. Her bylines were steadily rising in importance, while I, in my eighth year with the magazine, was collecting studio news. She'd joined the team after my drunken incident but made it a point to tell me that she knew all about it and that I should keep my distance.

I'd wanted to tell her that it would take more than a drunken stupor for me to scream 'Do me, baby' to her. But I held my silence and kept my distance.

I cursed her and told myself she must have slept with the editor to get such an important story. Then I cursed the editor, my job and the manager of the studio who hadn't turned up. I cursed the weather, the traffic ... I cursed everything.

For some reason that I can't recollect now, I decided to wait for some more time that day. I ordered a lemon chai and strolled around to see why such a huge crowd had gathered.

Is some director conducting auditions? I was hoping that would be the case but if it was, *Filmfare* would have been notified and someone would've been there to do the story. And that someone wouldn't be me.

'We will begin auditions shortly. Please keep your name and number card handy for identification,' a faceless voice called out from somewhere. A young voice which sounded more important than one might think.

Huge banners and standees told me what was happening. IKA TV was conducting auditions for their hugely popular annual singing contest – *Indian Koel*. Hundreds, maybe a thousand, hopeful boys and girls had gathered to try their luck at fame and money by becoming the next Indian Koel.

Every single contestant seemed hopeful of becoming the next Shreya Ghoshal. But only one would make it and the rest would have to live with the weight of failure. For me, it was just another normal day of being disappointed and frustrated with my life.

I finished my chai and walked towards the crowd. I began chatting with some of the participants, all of whom were much younger than me. At thirty-six, I felt old and looked even older, thanks to my dirty stubble and longish hair. I spoke with Asavri, though briefly. She said she was from Shantipur, a steel township in West Bengal. I'd only heard of it. She thought I was a reporter covering the audition and began talking about how hot Mumbai is.

Why do people always talk about the weather when they have nothing to say? I'd rather they say nothing. I didn't even pretend to listen and walked away. I didn't want to make small talk or flirt with this dull-faced girl. She didn't even have perky breasts.

I recognized Tanya – daughter of Kamini and Pratap Singh, industrialist power couple in the social and business echelons of the city. Pratap's death had left Kamini as the sole heir of everything he owned, and by the looks of it, she was doing a marvellous job of managing his many businesses. She had quite the story; one worth knowing and writing about. A nobody who married Mr Richie Rich and was now the queen of his empire.

What was Tanya doing in a contest like this? Her mother could buy out an entire studio and launch her as the lead actress or singer or whatever she desired. Why was she participating in a mass junta contest? There was a story behind Tanya's participation ...

Tanya stood aside, away from the rest, like she couldn't be bothered to be near common folk. She had on designer ripped jeans and a cropped top that looked suitably grunge. On her feet, she wore ridiculously tall stilettos. Though not well versed in women's fashion, I knew that they were the obscenely expensive label that went by the trademark red sole. I once dated a girl who was a fashion blogger and learnt a bit about expensive international brands from her. That was before my 'Do me, baby' debacle, during my proverbial salad days at *Filmfare* when everyone thought I had it in me to rise up the ladder.

Tanya reached to pick out something that was sticking to her shin. Her shining, luscious mane was blowing in the wind, her lithe body bent over, one leg slightly raised above the other and her blouse sagging down to allow a good look at the purple lacy number she was wearing. People were noticeably staring at her. I looked away, stifling a yawn. Tiny breasts in a push-up bra don't interest me at all.

Where's the manager? Why is he so late? I dialed his number again. It was switched off. *He's not coming*. I'd been stood up again.

I had just turned around to leave when she spoke to me.

'Do you think I stand a chance?'

'Huh?' I couldn't remember her name. 'Asha, right?'

'No. Asavri. We spoke a few minutes back.' She looked embarrassed that someone she spoke with less than ten minutes ago had forgotten her name.

'I'm sorry. I was … just … preoccupied with something else. Did you say something?'

'Do you think I stand a chance?' she repeated, looking a tad crushed.

I hadn't expected her to start a conversation with me. She looked at me as if she was hoping for an answer that would motivate her.

'You know, they don't call Mumbai the City of Dreams for nothing. So dream the impossible. Who knows, it may come true?' That sounded so made up that even plain-Jane Asavri didn't buy it and laughed. It had a nice ring to it, her laugh. I joined in. I didn't want to disappoint her but I didn't think she stood a chance at all. These contests aren't just about pure skill, but also about one's ability to perform. I didn't see plain Jane becoming a live wire on stage.

'You know, this is my first time in Mumbai. It's nothing like what I thought it would be,' she continued, obviously bored and desperate to talk with someone. I stood there, hearing her talk. I really wasn't interested but didn't know how to walk away for a second time. I'm rude but not so rude.

'I've only sung in the colony functions, never in any competitions. Most people here have won medals in various contests. Almost all of them have trained under some guru. I just sing at home with my aunty and listen to the radio and sing along.' She twirled the edge of her dupatta around her index finger and bit her lower lip.

You must be insane to come for a nationwide contest like this without any training. I dismissed her totally. *There's no way she's making the cut. Who does she think she is, Lata Mangeshkar?*

I hung around for some reason. I kept telling myself I'd leave soon, but didn't. Little did I know the wait would change my life forever.

Her name was announced. She turned around and looked at me for last-minute words of encouragement. It was out of pity that I volunteered to accompany her into the hall where the judges sat. Others had their friends or families cheering for them; Asavri was alone. *What a peculiar name. What does it even mean?* Trust the Bengalis to come up with arty names.

So I walked along by her side.

'Don't worry, you'll be fine. Just think of something that makes you happy and then sing.' Hollow words that meant nothing. I said them mechanically. I'd planned to scoot when she went in.

Her answer stunned me: 'Singing is my life. That's all I really have.' Her eyes looked vacant, lonely and sad. I stood near the hall entrance as she walked ahead.

Asavri started singing and a spell was cast.

What a divine voice! It felt like drops of cool water on a parched throat. Like a breeze on a hot sunny day. Like the first rain after months of heat. I shut my eyes, allowing her voice to seep into my soul. Hearing her sing felt like a gentle caress. Someone managing the sound box flicked a switch and her voice reverberated all over. The gathered crowd outside fell silent. Everyone stood transfixed, almost hypnotized, wondering who the magical voice belonged to. No one had imagined that the dull-as-tap-water girl would transform into a nightingale, singing in a voice that seemed to emanate from somewhere deep inside her. She smiled while singing, as though it were the biggest joy of her life, the reason behind her existence. The judges sat stunned by the raw beauty of the voice and then everyone burst into applause. One of the judges rushed up to her and kissed her again and again. '*Beta, tumhari aawaz bhagwaan ki daen hai.*' Other contestants looked on enviously while Asavri blushed and turned a deep shade of red.

I want to know more about her, I decided before she walked out. I took her out for lunch that day. Initially, she was reluctant to go out with an unshaven man in faded jeans, a crumpled white tee and hair that touched his shoulders.

'But … eh, I don't know you … you know … I …' She was being apologetic for refusing my lunch proposal, when she had every right to do so. We'd only just met.

'I swear to you, I'm not a psychopathic serial killer. I won't have you for lunch.'

'OK, so you aren't Hannibal. But why do you want to have lunch with me?' I was impressed with plain-Jane Asavri's Hannibal reference.

But why *did* I want to have lunch with her? *Because I want to know about you and your life. You will make a fabulous story and I want to be the one to write it.*

Of course, I didn't tell her that. Instead, I flashed my best smile and said, 'Today is my birthday and I feel like celebrating.'

'You're lying,' she laughed. 'It's not your birthday.' Clearly, she wasn't as dumb as I thought. My usual pickup line didn't work.

'You're right, Asavri. It's not my birthday. That was just a joke; a bad one. I'm a writer with *Filmfare* and I think I'm standing with the person who will win this contest and become the voice of the nation. The Indian Koel. Please have lunch with a lowly reporter.' I gave her my puppy-dog look. Though I'm very much an old dog, I have mastered the puppy-dog look. It had always worked and it did with her too.

She agreed.

'Let's celebrate your win today. The judges have put you in the final twenty without making you go through the elimination rounds. That's a huge deal! Others would kill to be in your shoes.' It was just a turn of phrase. I didn't know it then that it would come true.

Kill to be in your shoes.

She said yes, but only if she could pay for her half of the meal. Careful and guarded. I liked that. I joked that she could pay my half too if she wanted.

'I'm not rich. Just an ordinary contestant.'

'Yet. You aren't rich yet. Soon you'll be rolling in riches and fame and I will be waiting outside your bungalow for an interview.' She laughed in response.

She was easy-going and simple. Yes, simple's the word. We went to an Italian place. I watched her ponder over the menu. She made a strange gesture with her hand while flipping the pages. She rested her elbow on the table and tapped her upper lip with her index and middle fingers, the rest curled in a loose fist. It looked comical and I remember laughing aloud.

'What?' she continued doing it, clearly oblivious to her nervous tic.

'Nothing. Just something I remembered. What will you have?' I changed the topic.

She'd said sheepishly, 'Please order for me. I have no clue what's what.'

She listened to my stories of interviewing stars with wide-eyed admiration. She couldn't believe that I'd been inside Mannat. I'd been there only once, that too after begging the editor to take me along. He'd agreed when I swore not to touch alcohol and stand in the background. That's where I stood throughout the entire shoot – behind the lights, holding the extension cord board, but to impress her, I made it sound like I was a frequent visitor at SRK's home. I let her think I was an important guy in the magazine.

After entertaining her with many other starry tales, I turned the conversation towards her.

'I'm an orphan. My parents died when I was a baby, and my uncle and aunt brought me up. I'm here to try and win the contest and make a career out of my singing.'

She said it in one breath, looking at me unblinkingly. It seemed too ... rehearsed. Like a practised lie she'd said out loud many times before.

I knew there was a story behind those placid lines and I meant to get to it. Something told me it would be a hell of a story.

Between chatting about popular films and how crazy Mumbai traffic was, I asked her where she stayed. I needed to know about her. It didn't take much prodding.

She told me she stayed as a paying guest with an elderly Anglo-Indian in Bandra East. She didn't know anyone in the city.

'A boyfriend or someone special ...?' I inquired gently. I didn't want to sound too nosy even though I highly doubted that there was a guy in her life. Had there been one, he would have been there for the audition or she would have at least sent out a message to him after her great performance. I hadn't left her side since the moment she came out, and I didn't see her make any calls or send messages.

'Huh?' she seemed taken aback by my question.

I immediately backtracked. 'Don't mean to intrude. Sorry if that was offensive.'

'No, no. Nothing like that. There's no one. No guy.' She tried her best to smile but I sensed something was amiss ... like she was holding her breath. She drained her glass as though to gulp down her rising emotions.

A young girl, all of twenty-three, I gathered, was a hundred miles away from home in an unfamiliar city where she knew no one, to participate in a contest and become a singer. She seemed flustered when I asked about a boyfriend. I didn't have to be a reporter to sniff out a story.

By the time lunch got over, we made plans to meet the following day. I promised to take her around the city and show her the sights.

I decided Asavri needed a friend in the city. But I would be more than her friend – I would be her best friend.

Five

Kamini. THEN.
2016

The first time I saw Asavri, I knew she'd win.

It was the evening of the *Indian Koel* curtain-raiser, 25 June 2016 – a glittering evening at the JW Marriott, attended by the who's who of Mumbai's champagne set and the cine world. All twenty participants were to present themselves and showcase their talents.

I hadn't been following the contest, having put Dheeraj on the job. He kept me apprised of T's performance. So far, I hadn't had to make any calls. After convincing T to participate and her subsequent entry into the final twenty, I focused on other important things. The year-end election was approaching and the party would soon be deciding on the candidates. I had to make the right moves. Everything needed to be timed perfectly. T needed to win the contest and assist me. The top three or four contestants hold just as much popularity as one another, but there's a certain glow about the winner. My daughter *had* to come first. First is what mattered. So far, she had been doing fine. She needed to win this on her own and become the nation's darling. If she fell short, Dheeraj knew what had to be done to fix it.

The mandate was simple.

I must win the election.

Everything had been going perfectly according to plan, but then Asavri happened.

A fortnight before the curtain-raiser, Dheeraj came to me with a file and a look that said ... well, it said nothing. His face was always blank as a wall, completely devoid of emotion. On the morning of Pratap's funeral, there was a faint tremor in Dheeraj's lower jaw. That's the closest thing to an expression I've ever seen on his face in twenty-three years of knowing him. That being said, I have always been trusting of his judgement. So when he placed the slim folder before me and said, 'Madam, there's a slight problem,' I knew it was important. He wouldn't bother me if it weren't.

'There's a girl in the contest.' That's all he said, but his silence, as always, said more.

'She's the only candidate to have gone straight from the audition to the final twenty. Everyone else, Tanya included, faced multiple elimination rounds.'

'Is she as good as they say or is it just the media going bonkers?' I flipped through the news clippings. There weren't many, but if Dheeraj was bringing it to my notice, I knew it meant something. I looked at the plain face that stared out of the article's accompanying picture. A muddy-brown complexion, bad, frizzy hair tied in a ponytail and below-average skin that was blotchy, almost patchy. There was nothing remarkable about her face except something in the way she looked right into the camera. Was it a tinge of sadness, a loss or maybe just quiet determination? The next picture was of her singing. Her entire demeanour looked different. She looked like a bird soaring up in flight. She had a smile on her face and her eyes were shining, no longer placid as in the earlier picture.

'She is very good, madam. The audio clip is in your phone.' Dheeraj had procured a copy of her audition tape.

I clicked on it and began listening.

'She's going to ruin everything.' I listened for just fifteen seconds and knew that my T was no match for her. I have always believed that everything in life can be fixed. There's no problem that can't be fixed. I wouldn't be Mrs Pratap Singh if I didn't believe that. But hearing her sing did worry me.

I looked at Dheeraj, who was standing near the edge of the table.

'Yes, madam. I'll take care of it.' I never needed to spell anything out with Dheeraj. He read the look on my face.

So I was eagerly waiting for the evening of 25 June to see Asavri in the flesh and hear her sing.

She was even plainer than in the pictures. The media loves glamour but nothing beats a rags-to-riches success story. The mystery of the slow unfolding of a story was exactly what Asavri provided the masses with. Everyone loves a butterfly but the possibility of seeing a caterpillar transform into a butterfly is infinitely more exciting. My Tanya was already a stunning butterfly; Asavri in 2016 was simple, naïve and waiting to *become* a butterfly.

My eyes sought her out in the crowded banquet hall. She was easy to spot – the most awkward person, constantly fidgeting with the hemline of her blouse, trying to pull it down and manage the pallu of her chiffon sari. Not to forget her wide-eyed 'Oh My God!' look as she stared at everyone and everything. The diaphanous designer sari and deep-plunge blouse was too much for her. In a room full of indifferent women wearing outfits that left nothing to the imagination, Asavri looked like she had been transported to an alien world and was ready to bolt if she could spot an open door.

In a strange way, she reminded me of myself twenty years ago. I looked nothing like her when I was her age. Neither was I awkward nor shy. I was in Delhi, assisting Kaveri at Origin PR – working with her during the day and pleasuring her after hours. She was my ticket out of the boring front-office job at Taj and the one who introduced me to Pratap when we pitched the services of our firm to his business empire.

Beneath Asavri's placidity, I saw a younger me, with an aching desire, characterised by the same hungry look, to win and leave behind the shadows of a past that had given her nothing. She had nothing to lose and everything to win. It was a glimpse into my own past.

It wasn't easy to keep my eye on her and make polite conversation with everyone around me.

I saw her help a girl with her hair clip and another with untangling her sari. *Eager to please.*

The reporter fellow from *Filmfare*, Avniel something – he was there too, hovering around her. He gave her hand a gentle squeeze. She looked at him and blushed a bit.

Hmm ... So the discarded newshound has picked up the scent of a story in the making. I knew Avniel. I knew everything about him. The idiotic incident that buried his career. Everyone said he was finished but something told me he wasn't. Staying on even after an embarrassing incident like that and bearing the humiliation of it every day by doing menial jobs didn't equate to stupidity in my opinion. He was biding his time. He looked like a mangy stray who'd been left out in the rain, but I knew that he was in fact a snake. Takes one to know one.

Avniel is a man with an open mind and a perpetual hard-on. It was fun while it lasted and then I got bored.

Must tell Dheeraj to keep an eye on him.

It was nice to see T mingling with some of the contestants. My T with the cattle class, a term I hated but father and daughter insisted on using. Asavri and T were laughing about something, their heads leaning in towards one another. Someone nudged T and pointed in my direction. She began walking towards me, dragging the visibly flustered Asavri behind her.

'Mom, how do I look?' She dazzled in a royal-blue Manish Malhotra that I had picked out for her. She had tiny Swarovski diamanté around her neck and a few sprinkled on the body of her dress. The colour was a perfect match for her flawless peaches-and-cream complexion. I'm so glad she inherited Pratap's ivory skin tone and not my ebony. The light make-up highlighted her best features but remained subtle. Her hairdo was simple yet casually stylish, with a few wisps of silken strands allowed to slip out. Elegant but not too made up, simple but smart. She looked the part I wanted her to play. Confident, smart and identifiable among the others. Young girls watching her from their homes in far-flung cities and towns scattered all over the country would want to dress and look like my T.

'Mom! My friend Asavri. You have to hear her sing. Seriously! We have all decided that we are vying for the second position. The first is taken.' I needed to have a session with my daughter to stoke her passion. Second position wouldn't cut it. Where was the competitive edge in her?

Asavri turned red, joined her hands and bent her head. 'Namaste, aunty. They are just teasing me. Everyone sings very well.'

'Best of luck, beta,' I said, patting her head. The frizz in her hair needed more than a wash and blow-dry to tame. 'May the best singer win.'

I turned towards T and kissed her on the forehead and touched her lightly on her perky, slightly upturned nose. 'Your papa would have been so happy today, T. Do him proud, baby. Do him proud.' I looped my arm around her waist and turned away just for a bit, knowing the cameramen would go click-happy and that the next day's papers would have our pictures splashed all over them.

I was in a cream jamdani with a simple gold border and dainty thread-work all over. My wedding ring, which I wore on a chain around my neck when I was out campaigning, was back on my finger. On my wrist, I wore a simple black leather watch. How I longed for the diamond-encrusted Longines that stayed locked away! But a people's person, championing the cause of the downtrodden, couldn't be seen flashing diamonds on her watch. I did, however, have on a heavy gold pendant with the family seal emblazoned on it. It was there for a good reason. I touched it, rubbing it slightly. I knew the press would notice and ask about it. I had my answer ready: 'It's a precious piece from the family. A traditional gift that the eldest son gives to his wife. Pratap gave it to me on our wedding night.' It hadn't taken me long to figure out that the blue-blooded old hag, my husband's mother, had given him a cheap duplicate to give to his newly-wed wife while the real thing remained in her locker. She didn't trust me – a nobody her son had married – with the family's traditional piece. Anyway, she didn't live for too long. Asthmatic people shouldn't be too far from their nebulizers as they get older – it's their lifeline after all.

It's really quite fascinating to watch a body slowly transition into lifelessness.

Since my mother-in-law's passing, every time I wore the pendant – the real one – I thought of our last encounter. The asthmatic hag, huffing and puffing, trying to reach for her nebulizer which I held in my hand. When people asked me about the pendant, I spoke about her in glowing words. How she loved me and embraced me into the family!

She was the mother I never had.

What I really thought of her: *Bloody bitch! Gasping hag!*

On the night of the *Indian Koel* curtain-raiser, I was ready with my speech. I'd planned to touch the pendant lovingly, speak about Pratap tenderly, allowing a lump to rise in my throat and then controlling it because that's how it's done. The press would have loved it. I had it all planned but Asavri ruined it.

She was called to sing. Thankfully, T had already done her number. She sang well. The gathered crowd was appreciative and I looked suitably happy, beaming like a proud and happy mother.

Then Asavri began singing.

This twit from nowhere is going to win the bloody contest. I had never in my life heard such a sweet melody. My mind turned into a whirlpool of thoughts. I still had to look as though I was enjoying the performance, which I would have except that my grand plan was dissipating right in front of me. I looked at Dheeraj. He was looking in my direction too. It's so gratifying to have someone who understands my thoughts without me having to constantly articulate them.

She has to be handled. Our eyes said the same thing.

Asavri finished her song and there was pin-drop silence in the hall. And then followed thunderous applause which seemed to go on forever. Someone decided to give her a standing ovation and so everyone stood up and continued the applause for nearly five minutes.

I was having trouble breathing. The heavy pendant was cutting into my neck and my smile was refusing to come forth, but I still managed somehow. I didn't want some annoying, camera-happy idiot capturing the look of dissent on my face. It would be all over the news the next day with the caption 'Kamini Pratap Singh unhappy that her daughter was outperformed at the *Indian Koel* curtain-raiser'.

I needn't have worried. Neither T nor I made the headlines in the paper the next day.

I sat down after the never-ending applause, forced to make polite conversation with Somnathji, minister of cultural affairs, who sat beside me. His breath smelled of onions. A tiny piece of his lunch stuck between his teeth made me want to hand him a toothpick. A rancid smell mixed with the expensive French perfume he had doused himself in made me want to throw up.

'The girl is very talented. She will surely win. She can be of use for the election campaign. What do you think?'

I gritted my teeth, tried to smile and nodded. *That's exactly my plan. But not with Asavri. With my T.*

I needed a new plan.

There seemed to be some commotion towards the back of the room soon after the applause settled down. Someone had cut his palm because of a broken wine glass. A bald-headed man. I saw him briefly. He looked more flustered than hurt. Someone took him away to have his wound bandaged and cleaned up. I wondered how he managed to get a gash, but didn't think too much about it. He returned after an hour with his palm bandaged, wearing a sheepish look on his face. He went around apologizing for the unnecessary trouble he had caused.

'He is new in the IKA team,' Dheeraj informed me. 'Rudra Chatterjee.' The name meant nothing to me, and from what I saw of him – hunched back and bony shoulders – I wasn't really interested.

But I watched him for a different reason. He moved from one contestant to another, briefly congratulating them. Somnathji was still talking but my eyes were glued on Asavri. After he spoke with her for less than a minute and moved on, I noticed her face. A sheet of white, as though it had been drained of blood. She seemed to be searching for someone in the room, her eyes looking around wildly. She grabbed her phone and made a call. It was clearly a distress call. I wished Somnathji would shut up and allow me to focus on the girl who had thrown a large spoke in the wheels that I'd set in motion. I wanted to know why she was so unsettled. She should've been walking on air after the standing ovation. The reporter Avniel rushed to her. He looked dishevelled, like he was caught with his pants down. *Wonder who he was romping with.*

He was running his fingers through his hair as she whispered something into his ear. He draped his arm around her and together they walked away. Asavri seemed unsteady on her feet, like she would collapse if Avniel didn't hold her.

'Madam, Somnathji is asking ...' Dheeraj whispered in my ear. He noticed I wasn't paying attention to the minister and that my eyes were elsewhere. 'Madam,' he nodded in the direction of Mr Smelly Onion Breath, reminding me that I was there for a much larger purpose than to just support my daughter. His unblinking stare told me something else, which I noticed too: *Asavri and that bald man. You focus on the minister and I'll do the needful.*

What would I do without Dheeraj?

The morning after confirmed my worst fears. Tanya and I got a tiny box on page four. The press had found a darling to swoon over and it wasn't my T. It was Asavri all over the newspapers, Twitter and TV channels. It was all about her. The girl from nowhere with the sweetest voice ever. The one who smiled while singing, as though it were the reason for her existence.

Everyone was calling her 'the girl from nowhere'. *The girl from nowhere.* That's what Pratap's family called me when he had announced he was marrying me. They'd thought I'd be a one-night stand or a sleazy kept woman that he would tuck away in a luxury pad somewhere. I know for a fact that his mother had suggested he do that with me. A convenient fuck at his beck and call.

Everyone is from somewhere and everyone has a story – a past. A past they either want to run away from, hide or erase. Like me.

You have a story too, Asavri, and I will find it.

Six

Avniel. NOW.
2018

I can't leave her alone in this condition.

Why did this happen to her? Who did this to her?

I compel Bhaskar to get me an all-day access pass. It's for family members only, the hospital authorities say, but I'm the closest thing she has to a family. Bhaskar backs me up.

I'm not allowed to go inside the room.

'Please allow her to settle down. You see, she gets very agitated, so she needs to be sedated most of the time,' the attending doctor tells me when I request repeatedly.

I've started visiting the hospital every morning. I wait outside the glass panel, watching her. Sometimes, I stand at the door with my ear pressed against it to try and hear what's happening inside. There are times when she starts mumbling. Sometimes I hear her scream.

Last night, she began screaming because she was worried that someone was at the door. She yelled for Monty.

Who is Monty? And why did she scream when the nurse turned off the lights in the room? Asavri always liked the room pitch-black while sleeping.

The hospital is now my home. I'm here all day, often well into the night. I try to snatch away a few hours as and when to work on the BBC documentary, but Kay is taking care of it for the most part. I need to be at the hospital. I *want* to be here. I try to get information out of the doctors and nurses.

'How is she? Is she a bit better today? Can I go in?'

The answer is always the same: 'No, you can't go in. The doctor will speak with you when it's time.'

My breath forms a hazy circle on the glass panel; it is dotted with my fingerprints. I feel like pounding my fists on it. Who did this to you, Asavri? Who would hurt you like this?

Kamini and Tanya also make frequent visits. The latter looks distraught as she peers through the glass panel. She asks the doctor a lot of questions but gets no answers either.

'Why is she in so much pain, doctor? And why do you need to strap her to the bed like that? Let me at least go in and talk to her, please.' Tanya is trying to hold back her tears as Dheeraj leads her away.

I can understand Tanya's reason for visiting. She got the victor's crown, music contracts and fame, all of which was rightfully Asavri's. They were close during the contest, perhaps even friends. And Asavri had saved her from the fire. But why is Kamini here? She never does anything without a reason. I wonder what it is this time …

My head hurts with all these thoughts running amok. I'm worried about the documentary, to which I'm unable to give a sufficient amount of time and attention. There are just too many tangled knots that need to be untied, but I need to set them aside for now.

It's been five days since the press conference. Five straight days of standing outside her room, watching her through the glass panel and not knowing what the hell happened to her.

Finally, the CMO calls me to his room.

The room has a spectacular view of the bay, with the Sea Link clearly visible in all its glory. It's a beautiful iron bridge with suspensions holding it in place. The office is on the seventh floor – the administrative floor – and is as plush as one would imagine. The carpet is so soft that the soles of my shoes practically sink in it. Healthy, leafy plants lining the corridor gleam in the light. Expensive paintings adorn the walls.

But today, I neither see nor admire any of it. I *can't*; I'm barely sleeping. My days are spent in the hospital, outside Asavri's room, and at night I'm usually editing the documentary. *Trying* to edit; I can barely focus. My mind returns to the dark, scarred face with eyes in sunken hollows, arms riddled with scratches and needle marks and the incoherent mumbles that often turn into piercing screams.

I wish the doctor would just hurry and not keep me waiting. I hear the door open and turn around to greet the CMO.

'Hello … doc –' I stop. It's Bhaskar.

I give him a cold hello and don't bother to get up as he drops himself on the chair beside me. He looks like he hasn't slept since the whole ordeal started. I look in the opposite direction. I'm in no mood to forgive. He should have called rather than let me find out about it from the news.

'I know, Avniel … I know you are upset. I should have called. But you can now see—'

'You bloody well should have,' I cut him off and glare at him.

'It's a fucking bloodbath outside, in case you haven't noticed.' He lowers his voice and whispers, 'The company board is tightening the noose around my neck. Do you know ... can you imagine how this reflects on the channel? The winner who had the nation in a frenzy dies within days of her victory and then turns up alive, that too in *this* condition, after two years! You have no idea what's happening. The questions that are being asked. Our reality shows are taking a major hit, our sponsors are exiting. Not to mention the onslaught of the media. We are being crucified.'

'How comforting to know that what worries you the most about it all are the optics!' I don't bother to edit the venom in my retort.

'Oh! So your moral and ethical compass just suddenly started working then! How convenient, Avniel. Let me remind you that it was *you* who wrote the fucking book on Asavri, exploiting her entire life for public consumption,' he throws it right back at me, exactly where it hurts the most.

We both fall silent and look in the opposite direction.

Thankfully, the CMO arrives before we bludgeon each other.

'Good morning, gentlemen.' He sounds and looks cheerful; more cheerful than he should, but then again, he heads a hospital, where death and disease are commonplace. A catastrophe means business for them. Still, I wish he didn't sound so ... normal. I'm pretty sure he doesn't have good news. Nothing about Asavri seems to be good news at the moment. Even my non-med eyes can tell that.

He opens a big folder that he walked in carrying. Her name is written on it with a thick, bold red pen, underlined thrice. It would stand out when stacked with other folders.

I guess she is an important patient. I wonder who is responsible for determining something like that. Kamini? Bhaskar? Or is it her condition?

I decide to stop thinking and look at the CMO for answers.

'I am afraid I don't have good news. She has been abused. Severely. Drugged and raped repeatedly. She has been severely traumatized and is delusional. She is afraid of everyone and drifts in and out of awareness. She will take months to recover. Even if the drugs are flushed out and the medicines heal her, the mental trauma can take months, maybe a year … or more.'

'So then the rehabilitation process must begin immediately,' I try to suppress the tremor in my voice. Bhaskar has his head in his palms. I know what he is thinking.

'Of course it will, but it's not that simple. There's more to her condition,' the doctor replies, adding to my confusion. 'Yes, she has been sexually assaulted, but not recently. The wounds in her vagina are more than a year old. They seem serious but have healed. She hasn't been sexually active in the recent months. The drug abuse stopped sometime back, about a year ago. But someone was giving her a dose every now and then.'

'What does this mean, doc? What are you trying to say?' I get the feeling the doctor is trying to make a point.

'It's a very strange case, Avniel. It seems like she was in captivity, where she was assaulted severely for a while but then it stopped. Maybe someone decided to step in and protect her. So the assault stopped. The drug dosage also reduced considerably but a small dose was still administered about once a week.'

My blank look tells the doctor that I don't quite follow what he is trying to imply.

'Someone has been taking care of her but still wanted her to be incapable of being totally drug-free. He was protecting her but wanted to keep her prisoner and have control over her.'

'How do you know it's a he?'

'I don't, Avniel. It is a manner of speech. All I know is that she needs a lot of care. More than medicine, she needs care and rehabilitation. She needs to be in a safe environment and needs to understand and realize that she is no longer in any danger.'

'I hate to be the one to ask you this, doctor,' Bhaskar clears his throat as if removing the phlegm of hesitation, 'but when do you think Asavri will be able to sing and perform again?'

The doctor doesn't seem surprised by the question. 'She will need therapy sessions before she goes back to being normal. Normal is far away right now. I don't see her doing any public performances soon. She's in no state to even talk to anyone she is unfamiliar with. It took us a few days to assure her that we don't mean any harm. We have the same doctor and nurses attending to her every day to ensure a sense of familiarity for her.'

I'm trying to process everything I just heard. It feels like a bad nightmare.

The CMO speaks again, 'I hate to sound insensitive but I need to know who is going to be paying for her stay and treatment. It is going to be long drawn out and expensive.'

I control the urge to punch his mousy face. Trust him to discuss finances and Asavri's condition in the same breath.

I'm disgusted but also understand that it's a hospital, where care is the trade.

'Don't worry about money. No expense should be spared in her treatment, doctor. IKA TV will pay for it all.' Bhaskar redeems himself slightly with this proclamation.

'Kaminiji's office has been in touch about the same. Offering to pay. She'd announced at the Press meet …'

'Asavri was a contestant in a show hosted by IKA,' Bhaskar interrupts him. 'It's no consequence who said what, when. She is our responsibility.' The tone of finality in Bhaskar's voice is enough to close the discussion.

'I want to meet her, doctor.'

'Yes, Avniel, you may meet her today, but don't expect anything. The CMO seems relieved at the change of subject. Money matters out of the way, he is back on safe, firm ground. He continues. 'The person in that room is not the woman you knew. You know and remember her as your friend but she may not remember you that way. She may not remember you at all. So go easy, very easy.'

Before I walk away, Bhaskar grabs my hand. 'You and I need to talk. Soon.'

As I enter the room with the attending nurse, Asavri is looking towards the large window. Sunshine floods the room; there's too much of it. It almost hurts the eye. Why doesn't someone lower the venetian blinds?

The nurse whispers something. I don't hear her. I'm staring at the thin, almost shrivelled figure lying in bed at the centre of the room.

Her skin is burnt to a dark shade of brown. Lots of boils and marks on her face. Her hair is lank and sticks to her scalp. It appears thinner than before, and so does she … a malnourished kind of thin, almost gaunt. What I see before me is a ghost of the woman I knew.

I'm tongue-tied. I have been rehearsing this moment for the last five days. Saying it in my mind, saying it to myself in front of the mirror while shaving, saying it aloud in the car while waiting for the traffic signal to change. But standing inches away from her hospital bed, I am completely lost for words.

On her arms, I see multiple needle marks. The skin on both her wrists is puckered, as though an unpractised hand stitched up a gash. Who cut her wrists? Or did she ...? I can't even complete the sentence.

I find my voice. 'Asavri. It's me, Avniel.'

She turns away from the window and looks at me. Our eyes meet. I can tell she knows who I am. She tries to sit up, managing to go as far as the restraints allow.

'You said you'd take care of me. You never came. I thought you would.' It takes me a few seconds to realize that she's talking to me.

'I thought you were dead, Asavri. There was a body.'

I'm standing next to her bed. I'm unable to keep my eyes on her scarred face. I touch her gently on the arm. She winces and shifts further into the bed.

'Don't touch her, sir, please.' The nurse who is standing near the door rushes forward. 'Please don't touch the patient. She reacts very violently when touched.'

I get to see that in seconds.

I stand in silence, trying to find the right words. The speech I had prepared just dissipated. I keep staring at her. She shivers slightly. I think she's weeping.

'I'm here, Asavri. I'll take care of you. You'll get well soon.' My words sound so hollow to me. I hope she doesn't feel the same way.

'Go away. I don't want you. You can't take care of me. No one can. Only Monty can. Go away, all of you!' She tries to pull her arms out of the straps. They hold her tight and secure. As she continues to struggle, they bite into her skin, leaving a red imprint. I step back. Her sudden outburst takes me by surprise.

'Please call Monty. He is looking for me. He will be very angry. Please call him. He shouldn't get angry. They will hurt him. He will hurt them.'

I stagger back even more at the impact of her words. Who is 'they'? Who will hurt whom? And Monty … She's said that name before …

There are questions galore, answers to which lie within her and she is in no state to talk. She is now thrashing her head wildly on the pillow. The nurse punches a large red button on the wall and I hear a siren go off somewhere. She pulls me back and glares at me.

'I warned you! Told you not to touch her! If I get into trouble, it's your fault.'

I stand aside, watching doctors rush in, injections being administered. One of them holds her and pushes a wad between her teeth so that she doesn't bite herself. She keeps thrashing her legs wildly for some time and then her body goes limp.

'You need to be very patient. Allow her to get used to your presence. She will be asleep for some time now. Come back later,' the attending doctor tells me on his way out.

I pull a stool and sit on it, a few feet away from the bed. I whisper to the nurse, 'There's too much sunlight in the room. Lower the blinds.'

'No. The patient gets agitated if it's dark. I need to step out for a minute.' There's a warning in her eyes: *Can I trust you not to do anything rash while I am away?*

'Don't worry. I will keep my distance. I'll stay till you return.'

I can see Asavri slowly sinking into sleep, softly muttering, 'Monty'.

How did she end up like this? Why would anyone brutalize Asavri? She isn't a politician's daughter or someone who would be worth a lot in terms of ransom. Not that anyone ever asked. So who stood to gain from her disappearance?

Tanya?

It's beyond reason to think Kamini would do something like this just to make her daughter win. Kamini likes to win. Always. And Tanya was of great help during the election campaigns; she was a massive crowd-puller. But would Kamini go so far just for an election? From what I know of her, she's capable of anything. But this?

I need to find out where she was held captive. If I can find the place, that could lead me to the people behind this. This couldn't have been a one-man job.

My phone vibrates in my pocket. I step out.

'Yeah?' I answer without seeing who it is.

'What do you mean *yeah*?' Priya sounds annoyed.

'I'm sorry, baby. I was just busy and didn't see—'

'I know, I know. I'm going to Shibani's dinner.'

'It's today!' I blurt out and regret it immediately.

'Yes, Avniel. Some people have normal lives to live.' She doesn't tell me how many times she reminded me of the dinner and yet I forgot. I don't offer apologies; we are past that. I don't think she even expected me to turn up.

'I'll try to make it. I promise.' I mean it when I say it, though my eyes are glued to the glass panel through which I can see Asavri, who is now peacefully sleeping.

'OK.' She hangs up and moments later I get a WhatsApp ping. It's the address to Shibani's house.

I stuff my phone in my pocket as I see the CMO speaking with the attending doctor outside Asavri's room. I catch up with him. I need something and I hope he can get it for me.

'Let me see if we have it. Meanwhile, please wait in the visitors' room.' He directs me towards the lounge that is now empty as visiting hours are over. Pictures of sunny beaches and snow-covered peaks with useless philosophical quotes on them adorn the wall. Another wall has a huge poster of the latest cosmetic surgery facilities that Anandmay offers. On the centre table are magazines with healthy, cheerful faces showcasing how Anandmay saved their lives. The recycled air has a certain antiseptic smell to it ... the smell of a hospital. It's the smell of dread, disease and death. I don't smell any hope. The room feels stuffy or maybe it's just me. I pace around the tiny room. I don't know what to do or think.

The attending doctor comes in carrying a plastic bag. 'I don't know what you hope to find in the clothes the patient was wearing when she was brought in. Anyhow, lucky for you, the cops haven't asked us for them yet. I'll need them back, but I don't see why you can't take a look.'

Thankfully, he leaves immediately. I empty the contents on the centre table. A pair of jeans, a kurti and her undergarments. I don't know what I'm looking for. I thought of it while sitting in the room, watching her shiver and mutter 'Monty'.

Maybe the clothes she was wearing when she came in can tell me where she had been.

Dirty, mud-stained and with a few tears along the leg, the denim is flimsy. It has a glossy finish. Not expensive at all but not very cheap either. A reasonable and practical purchase by someone who wanted to buy something nice but didn't have money to splurge. I look for the brand tag. There's none. I pick up the kurti. The neck is a deep V; Asavri 'is' a prude. Her small-town upbringing stopped her from wearing anything that clung too tight or had a deep neck. Clearly, someone had decided for her and she complied. I hope the kurti has a tag at least. There was one but it has been torn off.

I keep staring at the heap of clothes.

Few things are certain. She wasn't in the hills or somewhere cold. So the plains. Possibly hot and humid. The kurta is cotton.

But hot and humid is most of the country. That hardly narrows it down. I consider taking the clothes to a lab to find out if there's any salt residue on the fabric, to find out if she was anywhere near the sea.

Next, I turn to the innerwear. I hesitate touching them. A pungent smell surrounds me. Touching the bra and panties worn by Asavri seems like an intrusion. We were close and this won't be the first time I'd be touching her undergarments, but it's different now. I pick up a pencil from the table and use it to turn them around. The panties are a local make and the bra is by Triumph.

I lean my head on the sofa. The clothes lie in a tiny heap. Something strikes me as odd but I'm unable to put my finger on it. The doctor's words play in my mind.

Someone has been taking care of her but still wants her to be incapable of being totally drug-free. Someone who, probably in his or her own way, cares for her but wanted to keep her prisoner.

I run the details in my head. He abused her, raped her, then stopped. He bought her decent undergarments but continued to give her small doses of the drug to control her.

What kind of a hell have you been in, Asavri? What on earth happened and who is behind this? What a mindfuckingly amazing story this will make.

That last thought runs through my mind like a lightning bolt. I get up and start pacing around again. I want to shake it away. It's so wrong. So very wrong to be thinking about a story when she's lying battered and restrained in a hospital bed.

She needs help. Asavri needs help. You are her only friend. I almost scream to myself. I pick up the clothes and stuff them into the bag they were in. As I stuff the denim inside, something rustles in my hand. I touch the pocket and feel something inside. It feels like paper. I put my hand in and pull it out.

It's a folded paper napkin, almost crushed, but the letters are clear.

'Madhubala Biryani House. Paha …' The rest of it is badly smudged. A few grains of saunf remain in the scrunched-up napkin.

I can't believe what I'm looking at. The paper napkin tells me Asavri must have eaten there. The place couldn't have been far from where she was kept. I fold it carefully and put it in my wallet. It's just the weird name of a restaurant with the rest of the address erased. But at least it tells me something. I think about what I have gathered.

Someone hurt her, abused her, drugged her, bought her clothes and took her out for biryani. Asavri loves biryani. But he kept drugging her so that she could be controlled. I'm going to find out who the motherfucker is. And I'm going to see to it that he rots in hell.

It will make a great story.

I curse myself at this recurring thought.

Stop it, you bastard! Stop it. She needs help. She really needs your help right now.

The thought stops but I know it's not gone; just silent for now. It will soon become tough to avoid, I know that.

I return the bag of clothes to the doctor and walk to the elevator. As I wait for it, I make a few calls. The first is to Kay. I need her to do some digging around. About Madhubala Biryani House. She isn't going to be happy, already buried in work for the documentary. But if there's anyone who can dredge up information from anything and anywhere, it's Kay. Though I don't really expect Madhubala Biryani House to have a website or call-on number to book tables, at least I have a name.

Then I make a series of calls to the few news reporter friends I have. I select those who cover crime beat in different regions across the country. Madhubala Biryani House could be anywhere.

I forget about Priya, her WhatsApp message and the dinner party I promised to try and attend.

Seven

Kamini. NOW.
2018

The day isn't going well.

I'm with the commissioner. I make it look as though I'm concerned about the Asavri issue and that I want an update on the investigation. What I'm really interested in finding out is if there are any suspicions pointing in T's direction. Bhaskar and Avniel's TV interview two days ago was incredibly disconcerting, to say the least.

'Avniel and Bhaskar were on at prime time,' says the commissioner. He has watched it too.

'Yes, they were.'

'Everyone is asking questions about Asavri. The police department is being accused of mishandling the case. It is not like it was before. Today, social media and TV channels can make any issue a national issue.'

'The truth needs to be known, don't you think? What happened to that poor girl? Who did that to her? Have you seen her?' I play it safe. 'It's horrifying to see someone in that condition.'

'Yes, I have, but the police department isn't at fault here, madam. IKA TV swung in after the accident and managed it. They identified the body as Asavri's. So why is my department being hung out to dry now?' His eyes bore into me. The man is playing games with me. I can sense it. He is on to something.

Bhaskar and Avniel are doing a good job of stoking the fire. That's what the TV interview was all about. Very carefully planned and executed.

'We're not blaming anyone, but this was *done* to her,' Bhaskar said. 'Her condition is very critical. More than physical harm, it's the mental wreckage that's so heart-breaking. A spirited young girl who sang her way to victory has been reduced to a bundle of nerves.'

Avniel adds, 'I'm with Mr Rai on this. Unimagined horrors have been inflicted on my friend. I will not rest till I find the person responsible for doing this to her. Whoever she or he is, I will get justice for Asavri.'

Bastard! Who says she or he? Common usage is always he or she. Clearly, the filthy fucker is throwing a veiled hint at my Tanya. Bhaskar and Avniel have kissed, made up and worked out their differences. Their bonhomie that was absent on the day of the press meet is undoubtedly back. Social media hasn't shown any slack on the Asavri subject.

Avniel was sporting his carefully cultivated messy style, like he hadn't slept for a while. The TV cameras zoomed in on him and then the screen broke into two. The other half showed a scared and trembling Asavri in her hospital room.

Bloody vipers! These reporters and TV channels! They know how to whip up a frenzy. Whoever she or he is ... Not taking any names but pointing in my direction. Actually, in T's direction. And this idiot child of mine is merrily drinking, posting pics on social media and throwing tantrums about going to the Bahamas. I have to protect her. I can't let these wolves get to her.

The public outcry – courtesy social media – which makes everything an issue of national importance, has compelled cops to investigate the case of the accident that led to her alleged death.

Twitter has given birth to an entire army of self-appointed custodians of the truth, and the case of a wronged woman, shivering and trembling as shown on TV, has become a case too juicy to let go of.

'To start with, we are poking around with the gangs of Mumbai to find leads … if any of them were holding Asavri as a prisoner or if they have any intel.'

Why would any gang keep her as a prisoner? There was no demand for a ransom. Whoever kept her as a prisoner meant to use her when the need arose. This isn't a case of money. It's a much larger play. But how is she alive?

'We will know soon, madam, and I will keep you posted,' the commissioner interrupts my thoughts and looks at me as though he's asking why I'm so interested.

How can I not be? Asavri can ruin everything.

'I'm a mother before anything else. Asavri and Tanya were very good friends during the contest. Asavri is like a daughter to me. She is Mumbai's daughter. She came here and won the contest. It's unbearable to see her in this condition. We all know that her family has severed ties with her. The poor girl has no one. Tanya is very upset to see her friend like this, as am I. We should work together to help her.'

'Tanya beti is looking good. I saw her on Instagram last night. No, no, I'm not on Instagram. My daughters are.

They follow her. They showed me.' He leans back on the chair and looks at me.

The man looks like an idiot. Big eyes bulging out of his sockets, flicking and staring at me. Greasy skin with folds of fatty layers on his neck. He is likely to have a cardiac arrest if he's forced to run.

But he isn't an idiot. He wouldn't have risen to where he is had he been one. Also, he has dealt with enough criminals to know what's amiss.

He continues to look at me after telling me about my daughter's Instagram post. The flab on his neck moves as he swallows his saliva. He looks like a frog waiting to stick out his long tongue and catch an unsuspecting fly.

He just informed me very casually that he is aware of my daughter's shenanigans. While I was trying to portray her as a concerned friend, he told me he knows she is out partying, drinking and posting on social media.

Can this day get any more thorny?

As I take my leave, the man clears his throat and says, 'Tell Tanya beti that my wife and daughters love her songs. The new album that was just released. They would love to meet her. Any time that suits her. She's here right now... right?'

'Of course. Where else would she be? Let Dheeraj know when and he'll arrange it. Tanya is very much here.'

I understand the message behind this. The commissioner, in a seemingly normal way, just told me that Tanya should be around and not leave the city. His parting comment isn't exactly an accusation. Yet. But there's a hint of it.

Everything that I painstakingly built is falling apart! How could things go so wrong? Dheeraj was supposed to take care of it all.

Can things get any worse?

Yes, they can. Things can always go further south than one imagines. Who knows that better than me? Just when I thought I got rid of them all – all the bloody skeletons – she turns up alive.

I'm fifteen minutes from home and my phone buzzes. It's Dheeraj.

'Madam, Tanya is insisting on joining her friends in the Bahamas. I can't reason with her.'

'Take her passport and hold on to it. I'm reaching soon.'

She can't leave the country now. She absolutely can't go anywhere on holiday. I'm trying really hard to keep my head calm but it really annoys me that my daughter fails to see the enormity of it all. How can she be so clueless? The cops can issue a warrant in her name. She can become a person of interest in the ongoing investigation. The commissioner made that clear without specifically saying it. How has my idiot daughter not caught on yet? Has her privilege made her daft?

I'm furious with Dheeraj, too. He was supposed to handle this. Asavri and the whole mess. I'm supposed to be focusing on my candidacy and the election.

Dheeraj meets me at the door of my living room. 'She has posted pictures of her packing a suitcase,' he says, handing me his mobile. He has a fake account to keep track of my daughter's digital footprint.

What is T thinking? Is she mad? I see the picture of an open suitcase with string bikinis of all colours strewn, a straw hat, sunscreen and sandals.

'This has to stop,' I snap at Dheeraj. 'What the fuck is all this?' I throw the mobile at him and he catches it before it hits him. Experience has taught him.

'Madam, it will be handled.'

'You said that before too, Dheeraj. Then how is this shit exploding in my face?' I don't bother lowering my voice. 'Elections aren't far, Dheeraj. The party will be deciding on candidates and campaigning will start soon after. How do I manage this? Tell me … how?'

'Madam, you focus on the party. I will handle the rest.'

'If you'd handled everything, why am I still dealing with the same shit again? These are the national elections, Dheeraj, *not* the state elections like last time.'

'Madam, I will fix it.' His brevity, which can be reassuring at times, can also be extremely frustrating when I need detailed assurances to calm me down. I glare at him.

'Madam, when have I let you down?'

What is happening right now is the biggest let-down I could imagine. I don't tell him that.

I fling my Birkin, knowing that Dheeraj will pick it up and put it in my study. I march towards T's room. I need to speak with her before I leave for work.

I walk towards the ear-splitting music.

I usually knock before entering her room. Today, I don't bother with niceties. I don't have the time or patience for it.

'Mom! What the hell happened to privacy? You can't just barge in,' she screams.

My daughter, in her tiny denim cut-offs that barely contain her butt cheeks and a stringy vest with a magenta bra underneath, her silky hair messily dropping on her thin and bony shoulders, looks younger than twenty-two. Her room looks like a candyfloss machine exploded in it. So much pink that it hurts my eyes. There are more clothes and shoes than one could possibly need, scattered everywhere carelessly. I sigh.

This is the sole heir to the 2,000 crore empire Pratap built. When he inherited it from his father, it was merely 100 crore. He and I worked to make it the gigantic enterprise it is today. All of it will be Tanya's responsibility. It will be in the hands of my daughter, whose life begins and ends with posting on Instagram, and whose sole aim in life is to be Paris Hilton 2.0.

'Sit down, Tanya. I don't have much time so I need you to pay attention.' I seldom address her as *Tanya*. When I do, she knows it's regarding something serious; something she won't like and, more importantly, won't be able to wriggle her way out of.

'I am going to say it once and you will follow. No questions asked. You will not be going to the Bahamas or anywhere else for that matter. No late-night partying and drinking with your gang. No more posting pics. No more tweets. As of today, in fact right now, Dheeraj will have someone manage all your social media accounts. You will make an appearance at the hospital. Every day. Spend an hour there, speak with the doctors, inquire about Asavri's health and then leave. Yes, I know you've visited the hospital twice. Do more. Show people that you care.'

'But, Mom! I can't bear to see Asavri like that. It's so scary. I ... Mom ... it's awful, just looking at her in that state. I just need to keep my mind away from it. There's nothing I can do. I thought it would be best to go away for a while.'

There's no getting away from this.

'Tanya, listen to me. You aren't going anywhere. There will be two security guards with you at all times and they will hold on to your mobile phone till I instruct otherwise. They have my permission to literally pick you up and bring you back home should you disobey. Are we clear?'

Her bony shoulders sag under the weight of my directives. I am not happy doing this but if she doesn't mend her ways, I have to force them on her.

And then I inch in closer for the final blow and whisper, 'The cops are wondering if you were responsible for what happened to Asavri. Don't give them a reason to think you are insensitive.'

She seems terrified. I don't like what I just did but it had to be done.

Dheeraj waits for me at the door.

'Tanya's social media accounts will be managed by us. Only posts about recovery, life, wellness ... shit like that. Find out what happened with Asavri before the cops do. There's some chatter about the gangs. Get on it. There is no scope for error now. I am winning the fucking elections, one way or another. Am I understood?'

I don't wait for him to answer.

Having dealt with Tanya , I set forth to tackle the storm that's brewing in the party office. It takes me an hour to reach the party office in Matunga from Malabar Hill.

Located on a dusty street clogged with traffic, the AJP office in Matunga is a three-storey building that can be passed off as any other decrepit Mumbai building. The outer-wall paint is peeling off and is stained from people spitting pan. But it's the nerve centre of the party. Inside this seemingly neglected building are rooms that are swept clean by the hour and walls freshly painted. The corridors are encased in fibreglass so that every inch of the building is centrally cooled. The ambient temperature is almost chilling. I often carry a pashmina. The temperature helps to soothe the frayed nerves and rising temperatures among the inhabitants. Several heated discussions have taken place in these rooms. Many political fates decided and destroyed. Today is my turn and by the end of our discussion, I will know which way I am headed.

'Kamini,' Rathod clears the ever-present phlegm in his throat. He looks like a poodle who hasn't been groomed in a while but likes to believe he's a Rottweiler. Small in size, he sits on a cushion during meetings and has a raised platform to stand on during public meetings. I always wear tall stilettos when meeting him. It's his Achilles heel and I know how to make good use of it.

Today, however, I'm wearing flats. Dheeraj insisted on it and surprised me by taking out a pair from the boot. I was a little confused when he did.

'Madam, today is the day to look pliant and amenable.'

'I think you mean apologetic, Dheeraj.' I'm neither, but I need to come across as humble when combating politicians, so I slip into the flat Kolhapuri chappals. Didn't know I had a pair in the shoe closet. Turns out I didn't; they feel new, raw and unworn.

It's only noon and I feel exhausted. My shoulders ache. My head is throbbing. The Bahamas wouldn't be such a bad idea.

It's a hot October day. Steaming hot. Mumbai has the worst weather. No time of the year is bearable. It gets somewhat pleasant during monsoon but city life becomes a nightmare. Anyway, if everything goes well, I will be in Delhi soon. Then the weather will be good for at least half the year.

'Yes, Rathodji,' I choose to add the little suffix of reverence to his name to remind him to do the same.

It has the desired effect. 'Kaminiji, this is most unfortunate,' he says, looking at the two idiots who flank him for support. The moron can't even say what he wants to without their support. Wonder if they rub his prick to help him get an erection. I know for a fact that he finds it difficult to rise to such occasions and I almost grin at the thought of it, but control myself in time.

As if on cue, Palgaonkar adds, 'Kaminiji, elections aren't too far away and all this attention is proving to be rather negative. You are one of the most visible party members in the state. There's too much talk about you in the media right now.'

He reminds me of a Doberman. Sleek, thin and aggressive. He sits erect, as though someone replaced his spine with an iron rod so he can never relax. His eyes are narrow slits and he never speaks more than what's necessary. It's like he has to pay out of pocket every time he speaks. I don't like him and the feeling is reciprocal. I know it. He thinks a woman is best suited to the kitchen. I've seen him at home with his wife. She's more like a kitchen maid, always serving him at his convenience. This is a man who cannot be changed. Sex, money ... nothing will work on him. He dislikes me because I'm a woman. Because I'm popular and the fact that he can't do anything about it. Till now. He has finally found a bone to pick with me. He was waiting for me to stumble and make a mistake. And I'm enraged that I gave him the opportunity.

I have to make an effort to keep my composure, considering I feel like spitting on the three idiots in front of me. I decide to address Rathod, who is the head of the tripartite committee.

'Rathodji, before we continue, I wish to bring to your notice ... and, of course, to that of the committee,' I add, looking at the Doberman and the fat Boxer who flank the Poodle, 'that the workers' union has been rallied. We have solid support from that end. The safety measures that have been made mandatory at all workplaces show the party in a very positive light. As you all know, that in adherence to my late husband's wishes, medical facilities have been opened throughout the state. As promised, they are run in the name of the party. My heart is in the right place, Rathodji.'

The Doberman starts to speak but the Poodle silences him with a raised hand. That's a good sign. The Boxer, I know, is inconsequential. He was put on the committee by the Poodle as his yes-man.

I know what the Doberman is going to say. Timing is critical here. I don't wait for too long before I proceed.

'Rathodji, I know the party isn't too happy about the media attention my daughter and I are getting. The media just likes to spin yarns. Of course, I didn't have anything to do with Asavri's disappearance. It's ridiculous to even suggest that. Hypothetically, even if I *was* that desperate to make Tanya the winner, I would have done something before the finale. I wouldn't have waited for Asavri to win and then stage a road accident. And, yes, I've decided to pay for her treatment. She has no family. She's no older than my daughter. She saved my daughter and now it's time to repay the debt. It's the right thing to do. Perhaps you don't know, but I have announced that the Party will pay but it will go from my pocket. Party comes first. Always.'

I don't tell them the hospital has refused to accept my payment. Not once but multiple times. It's an IKA matter, I was informed. This has Avniel's stamp all over it. Bastard!

'Oh! Is that so? You intend on saying the party is paying?' The Boxer decided to wake up, but then crouched back as the Doberman gave him a look.

'Of course. I have already said that and will continue to reiterate it. Asavri is the voice of the nation and the daughter of the State. Yes, I know she isn't from here but it was in Mumbai that she met her destiny. If I am … I mean if the party is seen as being responsible for her recovery, that would be great for the AJP. After all, we represent the common folk.

'And, of course, Dheeraj will apprise you on the status of the new factory that Pratap & Sons is opening in Nashik. It will increase employment by a great deal.'

I'm done. I can now watch the Poodle and the Boxer salivate. The Doberman has receded. He knows he has lost this round, but I'm sure he will return with more and this time, I will be prepared.

The three-member committee has been placated regarding the Asavri issue. The meeting's over. I'm standing in the corridor and looking out the back of the building. I look at the dirty, narrow, slush-filled lane between two buildings. Grimy pieces of cloth hang as curtains on the windows. A few of them even have plants; earthen and cracked plastic pots that hold something green. Some of them are dripping water and leaving a stain, not that the exterior wall was clean in the first place. It has patches of moss all over. It reminds me of a neglected urchin who hasn't had a bath in ages.

And just like that, without any warning, my mind decides to take a trip down memory lane. I think the Kolhapuri chappals started it. They always chaffed my skin, with its colour leaving a hue on my feet. That's what I used to wear in Varanasi.

And I've been transported back. The cramped two-room house Baba and I lived in. Kachori Gully. That's what the road was named and famous for. Ma was nothing more than a stern picture on the wall. She died when I was too young to have any recollection of her. Baba worked long and hard hours. At Ganesh Sari Shop. Showing reams of shiny, gaudy silk to women. Sometimes he would drape them around himself to display how beautiful the silk was. The world-famous Benarasi silk. Ganesh Sari Shop didn't really sell any authentic stuff; only cheap imitations of the best. The customers knew what they were buying but that never stopped Baba from praising the counterfeit goods to the sky and beyond.

Everything about my childhood home disgusted me. I never thought of it as home. It was a pigsty. Small, smelly, sunless and, most of all, poor. Everything in life has a smell. The rich have a rich smell, like the best French perfume money can buy. Similarly, poverty has a stench ... of sweat, neglected dirty gutters and, worst of all, of failed dreams or the lack of dreams altogether.

Our two-room home, if one should even call it that, was on the ground floor. It was impossible to open the windows – not that there was anything to look at – just to air out the room. The sun found it difficult to skirt past the buildings leaning towards one another, colluding and conspiring like nosy neighbours. The open gutters ran along the narrow lane on which we lived, and even the closed windows couldn't keep out the stench of rot and filth. The rooms felt cold and miserable, a musty, dank smell in everything. I don't know which was worse – winter, during which the rooms felt like ice chambers, or summer, when it would become a hot oven. I preferred being upstairs with Asha tai. She had a water cooler during the summers and a heater in the winters.

Baba never had any dreams, or at least he never spoke of ever having any. He had just resigned to penury and told himself it was all right.

Next life, I'll do it right.

Everyone in Varanasi spoke about the next life as though it were next year or next week. Or they spoke about moksha like it was the best starboard suite on a Mediterranean cruise.

Bloody idiots. That's what I thought about them. All that mumbo jumbo they rattled on about. I lived in Varanasi and dreamt of Venice, Vienna and all things fancy. I had no intention of waiting till my next life to make it happen. It would all come true in this life, including bloody moksha or whatever it was. I was sure of that.

I stayed with Asha tai after school till Baba returned from the shop. She lived alone on the floor above us. Her husband worked somewhere far and came home once every few months. She fed me and, in turn, I did odd jobs in her house like dusting, watering her plants, ironing her clothes, cleaning the water cooler and, of course, massaging her. And sometimes on the weekends, Baba spent the evening and night with her. Between father and daughter, we paid her for babysitting me throughout my childhood.

'Why, tai? Why must I change my name?' I must have been no more than fourteen then.

'Moon – that name will take you only to cheap bars and sleazy bedrooms, my dear.' She turned around on her stomach and instructed me to oil her buttocks. She looked like a whale that had washed up on the beach.

I never got to know why my father had chosen to name me Moon and I never asked him either. We interacted very little. I was the plant he brought home because it was handed to him and he didn't know how to refuse. So he left it on the windowsill, hoping for sun and water to keep it alive. In my case, sun and water came in the form of Asha tai.

'Change your name and get as far away from this hole, as soon as you can.'

That evening, we sat munching on kachori and jalebi while watching the latest episode of *The Bold and the Beautiful*. I told myself I wanted a Ridge Forrester in my life. I knew I was more Brooke Logan than the hoity-toity Caroline Spencer, who got everything in life on a gilded platter. Many saw Brooke as the gold-digging opportunist but to me she was smart, knew what she wanted and made sure she got it. That's who I wanted to be.

'What would I call myself?' I could barely tear my eyes away from the TV screen. Brooke was walking down Fifth Avenue in New York City. She was constantly on my mind. The impossibly tall heels, thick jacket, furry collar around the neck and a bag dangling on her arm. Confident, smart and rich. I'm sure she smelled good too.

Yes, I was going to be that and much more.

'Kamini. Call yourself Kamini. That's a name that'll take you places. Far, far away.'

'Kaminiji.' The voice seems distant. Dheeraj gently touches my elbow to snap me out of the thoughts of my not-so-glorious past.

'Huh!' I turn around to see Rathod standing near me.

'Yes, Rathodji. Sorry, I didn't hear you.' I gather my thoughts and focus on the present.

'I just want you to know, Kaminiji, today's meeting ... it uhh ... it shouldn't be seen ...' The man is stalling. But I know what has happened since I sat across the three dogs. He must have reported back to the party high command in Delhi about everything I just said regarding the crores being spent in the new factory, new medical centres, etc. In turn, they must have issued the clear directive to make nice with me. If I decided to take my money, the factories and the clout some place else, that would cause serious damage to the AJP.

I decided to save him the trouble of hopelessly stuttering through that one sentence. 'Don't worry, Rathodji, I'm a humble servant of the party. After all, we are here to help the aam junta and do good.'

We both have a hearty laugh and leave it at that.

As I step outside, my uniformed driver is waiting by my Mercedes S7, holding its door open. I kick the Kolhapuri slippers off as soon as I get in. I wipe my feet with baby wipes soaked in avocado oil. I get mine from Saks. Only when I'm sure they are clean, do I allow them into the comfort of my Jimmy Choos.

I let my head sink back, close my eyes and relax.

Moon, Asha tai or Baba in Ganesh Sari Shop – they are too far behind for me to think about. And the ten-minute reverie I had was more than what any of them deserved.

Today, Moon is Kamini Pratap Singh. Asha tai has been taken care of. She will never try to slink her way into my life.

And Baba passed away with his face buried in his stinking pillow, in the sunless room that reeked worse than sewage. My train to Delhi was supposed to leave in two hours and he decided to have a paralytic stroke. How could I have stayed back and helped him? I had to get away. I knew he wouldn't have got any help anyway. Tai was away, visiting her husband and it would be a week before she was back. The shop was closed for a few days, so no one would notice his absence.

I actually did him a favour. I helped him get to the next life he always spoke of.

Eight

Avniel. NOW.
2018

Kay hasn't been able to find anything on Madhubala Biryani House, neither have any of my reporter pals. I tell her to keep trying and message my reporter friends to spread the word.

I've been at the hospital all day, every day. I keep attempting to have a conversation with Asavri but get nothing in return.

I almost always begin with 'Did you sleep well?' followed by 'What do you want for breakfast? You liked the egg fries I used to make … Want that?' I know there's no chance of that in the hospital, but I say that for the sake of conversation.

I get no response.

I just wish she would speak with me, answer my questions or at least make eye contact. Almost every day I ask her, 'Do you remember where you were for two years?' I get only silence. She looks away and slinks under the covers. I sit with her throughout the day in uncomfortable silence. I tell her about Tanya and how great she has been doing. 'You know, she wore your victor's crown with ease, Asavri. Today, she is the most popular singer in Bollywood. She took your place.' I add the last bit with the faint hope that it may elicit a response. There's none.

It's not that she doesn't recognize me; I know she does.

She scratches the needle marks on her arms and the badly sewn gashes on her wrists. I offer to apply lotion on them to ease the itchiness. She doesn't let me. She does it herself. When I ask her about them, she turns away, sinks into her bed and pulls the sheet to cover her face. She often lies like that, on her side with the sheet almost up to her nose, as though she's hiding. Her eyes go blank and she stays like that for a long time.

When the nurse arrives with the food tray, she stares at the food in front of her and takes a few bites sometimes. I munch my store-purchased sandwich and wash it down with sickly sweet coffee from the vending machine outside. We eat in silence. We sit in silence. She leaves the yoghurt untouched every time. I take it. I ask before taking it from her lunch tray, hoping to get some response. There's none. Not even a movement of the eye.

I put up a few pictures in the room of her from the contest in simple photo frames. She doesn't look at them. She has slipped into a blank state. Doesn't talk, only mumbles in undertones. It's always about Monty. I wonder about the deep, dark pit her mind has slipped into and how to get her out of it.

Who is this Monty? Is he the one who abused her or is he the one who protected her?

I start spending my nights in the hospital room, on the sofa bed that stands in one corner. Something stops me from leaving her alone in the hospital room. Priya is understandably unhappy with this and doesn't seem to fathom why I am doing this.

'This is just too much concern for a friend. You've told me about all the others who came before me but you don't like to speak about Asavri. Every time I ask, all you say is that you wrote the story of her life. But what you're doing now ... spending days and nights in the hospital ... Were the two of you a couple before the accident?' she asked me a few nights back.

She waited for a reply, but all I said was, 'We weren't a couple.'

It's the truth. We weren't a couple. I didn't see it that way, though I know for a fact that Asavri did and I never addressed it. I let her think so. In fact, I encouraged it. It got me what I wanted.

'She has nobody to take care of her, Priya. Her family has abandoned her. She's all alone and she needs help. I can't just leave her there, can I?' I tried to reason with Priya.

She made an effort to accept it and wanted to make love. I wanted it too but I couldn't.

'I just don't get it, Avniel. I understand humanitarian feelings and wanting to be there for a friend, but when you can't have sex with your girlfriend because your mind is preoccupied with her, then that's a sign.' She pushed me aside and left the bed.

After a week of sleeping at the hospital, as I am getting ready to leave again, she stops painting her toes and says, 'You're going again. Today is Sunday. Let's spend some time together, Avniel. It's been long.'

'I can't, baby. I need to be there.' I know she doesn't understand. I don't understand it myself. I just need to be there next to Asavri. All the time. She may say something.

As I leave, Priya stays silent and continues painting her nails.

When I return the next morning to shower and change, her closet is empty. Priya is gone. A yellow Post-it note is stuck on the fridge door. It's not really sticking too well; it could use something – maybe a magnet to hold it?

'I'm going back to my flat. It's closer to the office and more convenient. No point staying here if you aren't here.'

It's not a goodbye note. It doesn't say much and yet it does. Convenience has taken precedence for now. I know where this road leads but I still don't take the right steps to fix it.

I can't tell Priya the true reason I need to be with Asavri. I haven't even admitted it to myself.

I load the washing machine and set it to 100 per cent dry. No one will be home to put the clothes in the dryer. The house is a mess. There's a thick layer of dust on everything. I don't bother. I rush back to the hospital.

It's been a month since she was found on the pavement and brought to the hospital.

'Good morning, Asavri.' I try to sound as cheerful as I can. Sunlight floods the room. I notice all the lights inside are still on. I switch them off.

'Good to see you walking around.' For the first time, I see her taking a few steps, though she refuses to step outside. She sips from a steaming cup.

'What's that you're drinking?' She doesn't turn in my direction nor does she look up. When I get no answer, I walk over to see what the cup holds.

It's tea. Asavri loves coffee, or used to love coffee. That's the Asavri I remember.

I hate tea. That sugary, milky thing that people boil with spices. I don't know how people drink that yucky stuff. I would throw up if I had it.

That's exactly what she's sipping now and she seems to be enjoying it, hugging the cup with her entwined fingers, allowing the heat to permeate. Milky, boiled with spices and sugary (must be, I don't taste it). I stare at the woman before me. She only looks like the Asavri I know, albeit darker, sunburnt and a lot thinner than her earlier self; she could easily be someone else.

My mobile vibrates. I look at the number that's flashing. It's a call I've been waiting for but am still not excited to receive. I tell Asavri I'm stepping out for a bit. She doesn't respond. I might as well have spoken to the wall.

'Yes, ma'am. Thank you for calling back. I'm sorry to have bothered you with so many messages and calls.'

'No, that's OK.' The voice on the other end has a heavy Bengali accent. She doesn't seem too comfortable speaking in English but since I can't speak Bengali, it will have to do.

She continues before I can say any further, 'Mr Avniel, I have spoken with other family members and we all feel the same way. Asavri isn't part of this family. She never was. Dada … I mean my older brother …' Her voice trails off and I can sense that she's trying to control her tears. 'Dada didn't tell us … any of us about her … that she was adopted. It was only later that all of us found out. She's responsible for everything that has happened.' The last bit comes out as an angry, venomous spat: 'She ruined us all. We can't step out of the house because of her. She isn't one of us. We have nothing to do with her. Please leave us alone and never call again.' The line goes dead.

This is Asavri's aunt in Shantipur. I thought that maybe having some people from her family could help jog her memory and make her feel safe. Soon she'll be discharged from the hospital. Where will she go?

I know the answer to the question even before it pops into my mind.

I can see her through the glass panel. She's standing near the window that looks out to a bunch of shanties and a few tall buildings. The usual Mumbai cityscape. Not a worthy sight at all. Even from her bed, I've seen her stare towards the large window, looking outside. What does she see? What is it about the view of dirty slums that she likes to stare at? *What are you thinking, Asavri?* There are times when I want to shake her and yell the questions till she answers: Who is Monty? Why do you keep asking about him? Was he the one who hurt you, drugged you?

She likes to sleep with the lights on. She starts shivering if I switch off even a few lights. She says nothing. Just looks terrified and begins to shiver uncontrollably, crying and uttering the same name again and again.

'Monty. Please, Monty.' Not a scream but a slow mumble; more of a scared plea.

'I love being in the hotel room. The curtains are so thick. They block out all the light,' she'd once said. Everything she was has been replaced by a contrasting trait.

I sink into one of the plastic chairs outside the room, thinking about what to do. My mobile vibrates again. It's from the police commissioner's office. I take the call, wondering what could be the reason.

It's his secretary. 'Sir asked me to call you. We have got something from the CCTV footage in VT station. You should come and see it. Are you free right now?'

I tell him I am and walk back into the room to pick up my backpack. I tell Asavri's motionless back that I will be gone for a while. I don't expect any response but she turns her eyes towards me as though she heard what I said. This is the first time she has turned and looked at me. I stand still, holding my breath, to see a flicker of something in her eyes.

'Have you found Monty?' Her voice is almost a whisper. I can barely hear her, so I move closer. She shifts slightly towards the bed and I stop in my tracks. Do I frighten her? I take a step back so as to reassure her I mean no harm.

'No, we haven't, but where and when did you see him last?' She has already slunk under the sheets and is in that faraway zone where she can't be reached. I stand looking at her.

Talk to me, Asavri. Tell me. Let me help you.

I keep standing there, hoping she will turn towards me and say something. She makes no movement, so I leave. I don't want to keep the commissioner waiting.

I decide to leave my car in the hospital parking lot. The train will get me to the police headquarters in downtown Mumbai faster than a car.

An hour and a half later, I'm in the two-storey Victorian neo-Gothic structure, now considered a heritage building. This should have a state library like the National Library in Kolkata. Every time I visit the police central command and see cops, most of who are unfit and need to go on a strict diet, I cringe a little.

This building would make such a fantastic library. Instead, portly men and a few women who look equally uncomfortable in trousers can be seen walking around. It's not that I have a great aversion to or affinity for the police force. They are as useless as they are useful. They decide what to be when it suits them best and they do it with full fervour. But right now, I need their assistance. I'm drawing a blank with Asavri. I need to find out where Madhubala Biryani House is. And who is Monty? If I can find out where she was kept, maybe that will lead to why this happened to her. I'm thinking I'll share the bit about Madhubala Biryani House with the commissioner.

'Avniel, come in.' The police commissioner shakes my hand. His is sweaty as always and I control the urge to wipe mine. As always, I let my hand hang near the top of my khakhi pants and discreetly wipe my palm on the side of my trousers.

'You know, my men aren't as useless as all of you seem to believe.' He leans back, his head touching the pristine white towel that drapes the head of the chair. I have never understood the purpose of that towel. Is it to ensure his oily hair doesn't stain the chair head? But then he hardly has any hair to oil.

'I watched you on TV, Avniel. Bhaskar and you. What did you call it?' he pretends to not remember. I know him too well to fall for his theatrics. I keep silent and appear to be more interested in a glass paperweight on the huge bare desk. The man is either super-efficient or he simply delegates everything. I settle for the latter. He still hasn't finished playing the I-have-forgotten-the-name game. There are four other men in the room apart from us. One of them replies.

'What happened to Asavri, sir?'

'Yeah! That's right. Smart title, huh? Avniel? What happened to Asavri? And both of you … Bhaskar and you didn't spare us. Nahin, nahin, don't protest. It was very clear from your words that, as always, we messed it up.'

I'm in no mood to discuss the efficiency rate of the police force. In fact, it isn't a discussion I would ever have with him. So I just ignore his comment and continue looking at him with a slow smile.

'Sir, your secretary called me.' I want to get to the part where he tells me why I have been called to his office. Surely it isn't because of the TV programme Bhaskar and I did.

'Yes, I have valuable information to give you. We found something on the CCTV footage that will be of interest to you.'

'Checking the CCTV was a great idea, sir.' I try to make nice with the man. 'To try and trace where Asavri was and what she was doing before she was found on the pavement.' I can't believe the cops thought of this on their own. I'm more surprised to learn that CCTV cameras in the city actually work.

'This one wasn't working so we didn't check till recently thinking there would be nothing recorded. Someone checked and found it had been working earlier. It must have stopped working only recently.'

The commissioner clicks his pudgy fingers and one of the men in the room hurries over to his desk and punches a few buttons on his computer. Wonder who wipes his ass after he's done the job. I wipe the grin off my face. The image from his laptop is projected on a large TV screen in his office. Another cop steps in and begins talking.

'This was on 4 September. The day of the final visarjan. It's 10 a.m.' A grainy picture appears on the screen. 'This is VT station.'

'That's Asavri!' I exclaim.

'Yes. Keep watching.'

She seems to be holding on to someone. Almost clinging. She looks scared, very scared. Her eyes keep darting at people rushing by and then looking down. An arm goes around her shoulders, pulls her and she moves in closer.

'Who is she with?'

'Wait and watch.'

The face appears on the screen, though barely visible. It's hidden behind a pair of large glares and a cap pulled low. He has a thin build, almost bony. A hurrying passerby knocks him over. The cap and the glares fall. That's when I get a good look at his face. My gasp is loud.

'Who the fuck is that?' I don't bother to mind my language.

The face is white like a sheet of paper. A long and deep scar runs from his right temple till his lip. An unshaven, scraggy beard is visible. He pulls out what appears to be a penknife.

He wants to knife the man who pushed him accidentally! What kind of a man does that!

Asavri stops him and he puts it away. She picks up the goggles and cap for him. He seems to be slightly unsteady on his feet. As she places the cap on his head, they seem to have a moment, sharing a tender, loving look. She huddles closer to him as they stand in the camera's line of focus. The man touches her face, tucking a strand of hair behind her ear and she smiles and bends her head towards his chest. Then they walk away.

I'm now pacing around in the room. I need a minute … more than a minute to process what I just saw. They almost look like a couple in love. Asavri actually looks okay ... more than okay with him. The smile, him tucking her hair, her body moving towards him – it indicates closeness. Almost love. It can't be. How is it possible that Asavri is in love with such a vile-looking man? It doesn't make any sense!

I forget where I am and yell, 'How is this possible? How can she be with such a man ... a man who looks like that? Who is he? He ... he looks like a ...'

The commissioner completes the sentence for me, 'Like a thug. A low-life gangster.'

I throw myself on the sofa and hold my head in my palms. It is burning.

'There's more,' the commissioner speaks. I look up and his face tells me it isn't going to be good.

'There's more CCTV footage?'

'Not on the CCTV but something else.' He reaches for a file and opens it; it consists of a few photos. He summons me near his desk, wiggling his index finger.

'Do you recognize any of them?' He pushes the open file towards me.

I sift through the pictures. I don't recognize any of them but I'm guessing they are all wanted men. The commissioner leans over and points to one of the pictures. An ordinary-looking man who could pass off as just another administrative officer in any government office. He's wearing a blue checked shirt, hanging loose over trousers.

'This one is called Bhai. No one knows what his real name is. He was the right-hand man of a small-time goon called Pilot. It is rumoured that Bhai killed Pilot and now rules the roost. He controls a drug and prostitution ring on the outskirts of Pune, in an area called Pahargaon. He is a small-time operator – nothing huge – but we have never been able to pin any charges on him. His followers are staunch or maybe too terrified. They prefer death over telling on him. He runs a small, tight ship.'

Hearing the name of the place Pahargaon completes the half-erased word on the paper napkin. *Madhubala Biryani House, Pahargaon*. I don't say anything to the commissioner. I want to know more before I do.

'Now look at this picture. This was taken about two years ago at a wedding of a real estate tycoon. Look at this man carefully. Do you recognize him?' He points to a short guy standing next to the one called Bhai.

It's the same white face I just saw on the CCTV recording. I look at the screen and then at the picture on the table. It's the same man. The face in the picture is clearer than the one on the TV screen. He has a deep scar on the right side of his right chin, a nasty leer pasted on his face and his hair heavily gelled and combed back. It's the face of a man I wouldn't want to be in the company of. A man I wouldn't trust. A man I would never associate Asavri or any woman I know with. A sigh escapes me.

'He is Bhai's shadow. Some say he is Bhai's younger brother while others say he isn't. He has a skin disease. An albino. His white skin looks sickly, marked with spots. He has a bad limp. See ... he is leaning on a stick. Due to his disability, he isn't included in most jobs but he is very much part of the gang. When the other men rape the hapless girls they lure into the ring, this *suar* records it on his mobile and then sells it. Some say he is psychotic, with an awfully cruel temper. He takes advantage of the fact that he is close to the gang leader. Whatever be their relation, this white guy is untouchable in the group.'

How did you land up with these people, Asavri? How? Why?

I pick up the glass of water on the table. I know it's not for me but I'm not in any state to bother with niceties. Nothing makes sense to me. Not after the image of Asavri looking at the man lovingly and then finding out that he is an integral part of a drug and prostitution gang.

'Do you know his name?'

'Monty,' the commissioner replies as he gathers the pictures back into the folder and snaps it shut.

Nine

Kamini. THEN.

2016

I walked away from the counter at Starbucks, Bandra Kurla Complex. I was distracted, reading a message on my phone. I stumbled and almost tripped on a table. Spilled my coffee and also knocked over the cup on the table. There was hot coffee everywhere – on the table, on the shirt of the man sitting at the table, some of it also on his laptop.

I apologized, 'I can be so clumsy. I'm awfully sorry.' I grabbed paper napkins from the adjoining table and dabbed the spill. The man was irritated but looked at me and smiled.

'Please allow me to buy you another cup.' I looked sheepish and suitably apologetic. He agreed. His eyes were fixed on the pallu dangling at the edge of my shoulder, barely concealing my breasts and giving him the view I knew he didn't mind.

This wasn't happenstance. Rudra fell for the oldest and most common hookup trick. A woman knocking over a man's coffee. It's so clichéd that it's ridiculous but sometimes that is what one needs. We moved to another table, away from the window but not too close to the corner. I wanted it to look like just a coffee meet. It was anything but that. When I walked to the counter to pay, I knew his eyes were on my hips. The good thing about being draped in cotton handloom yarns is that they accommodate the proportions of my body as per my liking. My narrow waist and full hips are even more accentuated in a cotton sari.

When the coffee arrived, he emptied two sachets of sugar in his cup. I offered mine. I like mine bitter and black. He grinned and took it.

'I like sweet. Bengali, you know.'

I smiled and sipped mine. On the evening of the gala night at the Marriott, I hadn't seen him properly. Now I could. Tall-ish, lean-ish. I could tell he would go bald soon. The front of his head was already smooth and hairless. He spoke with a nervous laugh and some remnants of his Bengali accent that he had been working to get rid of.

He knows who I am and was flustered to be sitting with me and having coffee.

'Do you come here often?'

'Yes, often. My office is right next door.'

'You mean, the companies you own ...'

'Yes. My companies. But I still drink tea, coffee and water like others.' I allowed a tiny smile. I enjoyed his flustered demeanour.

'What's your name?' I had a folder with his picture and some of his history in the car. Dheeraj had been quite thorough. Pretence comes easy to me.

'Rudra. Rudra Chatterjee. VP, media planning, IKA TV.' He handed me his card as though he were meeting me for a job interview. I put the card carefully in my purse and would toss it in the bin on my way out.

I wasn't the only one agitated by Asavri's sudden rise to stardom. The breaking of the wine glass on the night of 'Meet the contestants' was no accident. He was shocked to see Asavri on stage. I needed to know why a man was so perturbed by Asavri that he crushed a wine glass in his palm. Lucky for me, Rudra turned out to be more stupid than I bargained for.

We talked till we finished our coffees. I made inane conversation about the TV industry and the kind of shows that are being aired. Then we exchanged numbers. I told him I was interested in the industry and was planning to be a part of it.

'I'll be putting together a team soon. Good that we met.' His eyes shone with hopeful excitement. 'I'm going to keep your card, Rudra. Who knows …' I completed the sentence with a smile as I got up to leave.

At the door of the café, I paused and said, 'Do keep in touch. It's always nice to meet dynamic and enterprising young men like you.'

What followed was exactly as I'd anticipated. A stream of messages about ideas he had and news clippings from around the world. I waited for three days before sending him my first message.

Do you exercise? You look very fit. I so badly need to start. The idiot had a paunch and looked like he had never seen the inside of a gym.

The reply came promptly. *I've just joined. Too early for results. You must exercise, not that you need to. You could do yoga …*

I yawned and threw the phone on my bed. I wondered if the soon-to-be baldy started running and bought a gym membership after my message. Telling me to start yoga … bloody idiot. Some of the postures I can twist myself into, he couldn't do them even in his dreams.

He messaged me all day, while I took time with mine. From the coffee shop to my pad in Bandra took about three weeks. He was willing, eager and mad as hell, maybe a little horny too.

I had texted: *Let's meet for a drink. I promise not to spill it on you.*

He agreed immediately and arrived sharp on time. In a pale orange shirt with a sheen that hurt every aesthetic sensibility. He really needed a new wardrobe. I could smell him even before I opened the door. He had embalmed himself with a perfume that smelled expensive. No one had taught him that less is more. He didn't make as much as he would've liked others to think he did. He needed better shoes. Most people on a limited budget splurge on clothes, watches and perfume – things they think will be noticed. Shoes show class and money. Baldy Rudra had neither.

I could tell he was disappointed to see me in jeans and a comfortable white shirt. *Was he thinking that I would answer the door in a negligee?*

For him, not in a million years!

'Oh! You're on time. What a delightful trait, and especially in someone so young? Kids today don't have any sense of time.' I let him close the door and walked ahead as I gathered up my hair and made a bun that barely held up. Silken strands of my hair were slipping out. My hair is too straight and silky to be held in a bun without a tight band. But when the bun gives way and the tresses tumble over my shoulder, they look sexy as hell. I wasn't planning on seducing Baldy.

I was having fun. It had been a really long time since I did. It's fun to send a man home with a boner.

'I'm not really a kid … and you aren't that old.' He gave out a nervous laugh.

'Aren't that old … hmm, that means I'm old but not so much.' I turned around to look him straight in the eye, pushed up my elbow against the bar table and leaned back. My breasts rode up against the cotton fabric. Rudra was trying his best not to look.

'No, no, that's not what I meant, Mrs Singh.' He turned to the view beyond the balcony.

He was nervous and also a bit excited.

That's good. I wanted him nervous and excited.

We were on the twenty-second floor with the sea on one side and the cityscape of Mumbai on the other. It was dusk. The twilight zone between day and night. The sky was a riot of colours. The fading glow of the sun over the horizon was mesmerizing.

'Kamini.'

'Huh?'

'The name is Kamini. Not Mrs Singh. I think you're old enough to call me by my name.'

'Yes, I'm old enough,' he said and then added, 'I'm old enough to do a lot of things.'

I let his comment pass. Indifference is a better retort than a response sometimes. I stifled a yawn. I'm past the age and stage in life when such games would excite me. I'd played so many and so many times.

'Let's have a drink, shall we?' I walked to the bar and pressed a button. Though no one could hear anything, I knew that my staff in the pantry would spring to action.

Rudra was taken aback when two men appeared almost magically.

The look of surprise on his face told me he had expected the flat to be empty. That my invitation for a drink was a covert invitation to my bed and body.

What an idiot!

We sat in the balcony. I sipped a Glenfiddich rare collection, a fifty-year-old single malt Scotch, with the customary two rocks, while Baldy mixed Coke with his. I should have thrown him off the balcony for that. Someone who mixes Coke with a Glenfiddich rare should die a slow and painful death. I ignored his drink and tried to look interested in his monologue about how he landed up in Mumbai to work for IKA.

I asked him the question after he was on his fourth glass, while I was still on my second.

'So this contestant … Asavri … she's really good, isn't she?' His fingers tightened around the glass as though it were her neck. I swirled my drink and the ice cubes tinkled as they tumbled along the sides and against each other. I looked at the sea which had turned into a dark black blanket. Mumbai skies are usually starless.

'I don't want to talk about her.' He took a large gulp from his glass.

I let it go, stayed silent, breathed in the night air and did nothing. I knew he would talk sooner or later.

'You have no idea how cheap, low and disgusting she is.' He was breathing heavily and raised the glass to his lips, when I stopped him.

'Give it a break, Rudra. You've had enough.' I gently prised the glass out of his hand and placed it on the table.

My hand returned to his clenched fist and I let my finger trace a lazy line over it. His fist opened. I could see the bruise of the gash from the crushed wine glass. I stroked it with my thumb.

'That's a nasty cut. Don't let people see your anger, Rudra.'

'I know her truth. She's a bitch. A dirty, used rag.'

I was all ears and I whispered quietly, 'You can tell me if you feel like. It's nice to take the load off one's heart, you know.' I continued touching the wound and slowly massaged his palm.

Rudra spilled everything faster than I'd expected.

'Can you believe that woman had sex with someone while in college? She got drunk and woke up naked in bed the next morning with no recollection of how she got there. She didn't even remember his name.' He looked disgusted.

I tried to look shocked while suppressing my own thoughts. *How many times has that happened to me? Too many to remember.* I focused on looking horrified.

'That's awful, Rudra. Beyond horrible. Girls, today, I tell you.'

In my head, I was impressed. I didn't think Asavri had it in her to have drunken sex. Maybe I underestimated her. Maybe she wasn't as dull and boring as I had thought? I shook my head like a nun and tried to look stunned by what Rudra told me, all while trying not to think of the countless times I'd had drunken sex. With many men and women, sometimes both at the same time. Drunken sex followed by absolutely no memory of how, where and who!

Those were the wonder years! I almost sighed but stopped myself in time.

'I come from a family of chaste Brahmins. Our family tree traces back six generations. Till sometime back, women in my family didn't step out of the house, and this randi ...'

I stopped him. It became impossible to hear his moronic rant any longer. Chaste Brahmins ... If he'd studied history, he would know about the not-so-chaste activities his Brahminical ancestors indulged in. But I wasn't there to give him a lesson in history or upgrade his thinking to modern times. I was there to stoke the fire and make him my pawn.

'Now, now, Rudra. Let's not sully our mouths with dirty words.' I placed a finger on his lips.

A sigh escaped him. 'You can't imagine how devastating it was to find that out during our honeymoon. To find out that the woman I married wasn't a virgin. Which self-respecting girl does something like that? Did she really think that I would take her home and make a life with her? Never!'

'I know it's horrifying. So what did you do? You poor man!' I wiped the beads of sweat from his forehead with a paper napkin. I was starting to get a migraine and needed to wrap up the charade fast.

'I did what any self-respecting man would do. I took her back to her home in Shantipur and revealed to the entire family what she had done. They looked shocked. Of course, it was an act. I'm sure they knew about it and were only pretending. Her father fell at my feet, begging that I forgive his daughter and not leave her. Of course I left her there! That was two years ago. And now ... look at the shameless bitch. She is here in Mumbai, participating in *Indian Koel*.

How can a woman with such loose morals be the country's favourite? I feel like vomiting.' He pretended to retch.

My ear caught the most important part of his rant. 'Her father? Family in Shantipur ... but Asavri told everyone she's an orphan ...'

'She's a liar. She's saying all this to get pity votes. She's no orphan. There's a family in Shantipur. A big fat Bengali family.'

Later that night, after I instructed my driver to drop the much-inebriated Rudra back home, sleep eluded me as I lay in my bed. I went over everything Rudra had said. Few things were clear.

Baldy is a moron and can be used as and when I please. Asavri has skeletons in her closet that need to tumble out at the right time. My T will become the next Indian Koel.

With that final thought, I slept.

The next morning, Dheeraj met me for breakfast and we went over the blue-print of the plan. Rudra would sing like a canary and do anything I asked. The plan was for me to entice him and get more evidence and proof of Asavri's former life.

I played it slow and easy with Rudra. No point in making a hurried move. I didn't want him to think I wanted the information. I made it seem as though he was offering it to me and Baldy played along just as I wanted him to.

To prove what he was telling me was true, he gave me a copy of their wedding card and pictures from the ceremony with the whole smiling family.

'So not only is she not an orphan, but she's also married. Hmm. Still waters run deep, huh, Dheeraj?' The plain middle-class face hides a lot.

'First, let's go with the family angle to bust the orphan story. Then we can decide how and when to use the rest.' Dheeraj wasted no time. I've always liked that about him.

'I'll leave it to you. Do it at the right time to cause maximum damage. She must get thrown out of the contest, Dheeraj.' I rose from the chair. I had a busy day ahead and couldn't afford to spend more time than I already had on Asavri.

Sometimes, the best-laid plans turn turtle. I kept meeting Rudra on and off; just enough to keep him salivating and at my beck and call. I was beginning to tire of him. Dheeraj and I'd decided to leak the news in a few weeks' time.

But before I could, I woke up to every TV channel screaming that Asavri was a liar. The article and the pictures that had made their way from Rudra's Gmail to my dining table were on every news channel.

Did the moron do this in a fit of anger? Dheeraj called me before I called him.

'Ma'am, it's not Rudra. I checked. It's someone else.'

'Then find out who it is, Dheeraj!' I didn't like the way the morning had begun.

I left the TV on as I carried on with my morning yoga, barely able to focus.

If there's another person who knows the truth ... who could it be? Obviously someone who wants to malign her. Someone who doesn't want her to win. Who could it be?

I followed the news all day on Twitter and the news app. I tried to be discreet. I had a meeting with the execom members. After Pratap, I had placed the companies in the hands of qualified professionals. I needed to free up my time to focus on my own goals. Before going in for the meeting, I called T. I needed to tell her to keep her mouth shut and not make any comments on social media.

My angel greeted me with the usual I'm-bored-why're-you-calling tone: 'Ya, Mom? Wassup?'

'Good morning, T.'

'Morning, Mom. Whatcha doin?' Whatever happened to full sentences, I wondered.

'T, I don't know if you've seen the news. See it now if you haven't. Not a word or comment from you. Absolutely nothing, am I clear?'

'Huh?' T sounded clueless. I wasn't surprised at all. Anything other than news about the launch of new haute couture had never been of the slightest interest to my daughter.

'Watch the news and stay silent,' I told her and walked into the meeting.

The meeting went on for longer than I'd anticipated. It was almost lunchtime when I got out. I walked out to be greeted by Dheeraj, who looked like someone had drained the blood from his body. The last time he looked like that was when he had broken the news of Pratap's accidental death to me.

'Tanya. Is she okay?' My heart almost stopped.

'She's fine, ma'am. It's something else.' He was barely audible. He made a feeble attempt to smile at the people I was in the meeting with. I realized it was something he couldn't say in their presence. I excused myself and we walked to my office.

'What is it, Dheeraj? Why are you so ashen? What's the matter?' I was irritated. Without a word, he shut the door firmly, walked up to the gigantic TV screen and switched it on.

A newsreader was animatedly speaking, with the 'breaking news' banner running below.

'ASAVRI IS AN ORPHAN. SHE DIDN'T LIE. SHE WAS LEFT AT AN ORPHANAGE IN SHILLONG: HOME OF MERCY.'

It felt like someone had sucked out the oxygen from the room. I couldn't breathe. I stood there feeling the walls close in.

Ten

Avniel. THEN.
2016

My mobile had been ringing for a while before I finally came to my senses.

The night before had been a wild, drunken party that threatened to never get over. I'd planned to make an exit after an hour but one drink led to another and that hour became five or six. I staggered back home at four in the morning. I had to ask the Uber driver to help me till the door. I chose to leave my car at home, reluctant to be seen in my beat-up Santro while my friends got into their Audis and Mercs – cars that cost more than what I made in a year.

When the phone rang, my first instinct was that it was a dream, but when it didn't stop, reality broke through. In an alcohol-induced haze, I opened my eyes and tried to locate it. My eyelids felt like lead, lips dry and throat parched. I desperately needed to hydrate myself. I answered the phone without seeing who was calling at what felt like a dreadful hour.

'Who's this?' I sounded far from my usual welcoming self.

'Have you seen today's paper, Avniel? Have you seen the morning news?' The shrill cry hurt my ears.

'Who is this?' It was difficult holding my head up, let alone a phone conversation.

'Huh?' I got an annoyed reply before the yelling continued, 'What do you mean who is this? This is Asavri. Are you drunk? What's wrong with you, Avniel?'

I bolted upright in my bed on hearing her name and rubbed my eyes with the free hand. 'Asavri! Sorry, had a very crazy night. What happened?'

'Please come to the hotel, Avniel. Rudra has made his move. I don't know what to do.' I can tell she is crying. 'Please come quickly. Please.'

It felt like a hammer was banging the inside of my head. The sunlight streaming in through the windows told me two things – it was way past the time I usually woke up and the light was hurting my eyes. I could barely keep them open. My head was pounding and splitting into half while she was sobbing incoherently on the phone.

I staggered out of bed with the phone plastered to my ear. 'What happened? Tell me quick.' It still hadn't registered. This wasn't the first time she'd made a distress call. I had become her go-to person for every little thing that upset her. Of late, she seemed to be losing her music sheets, mixing up her schedule and arriving late for practice sessions. Every time something went wrong, I was the one she called. It annoyed me. I wanted to be there for her but she didn't seem to realize that I had a life and a job. If she couldn't sleep, she called me. If she was bored, she called me. One time, she called me to say, 'I just want to hear your voice.' I almost banged my head on the wall.

The previous week, she called to say that someone was trying to poison her. I wanted to shout back at her to shut it with her never-ending ranting and attention-seeking tactics. Her failed marriage and getting thrown out of home had made her insecure, but she was just too fucking clingy and needy. I had to keep reminding myself that she made for a great story and was my ticket out of the hellhole I was stuck in.

Of course, I was going to go … scurrying to her side to soothe and pacify her every time, dropping whatever I was doing.

The things I did for a story!

'What happened this time?' The sunlight hurt my eyes. I needed water, a darkened room and no screaming.

'It's all over the news. About my family. I told you all about it, remember?' She whispered, 'Please *jaldi aajao*, Avniel. Bhaskar's secretary came to meet me. Bhaskar wants to meet me in an hour. Please *jaldi aao*. They will throw me out of the contest for this.' She hung up.

'Holy fuck!' I screamed and clicked on the IKA news app. The running headline hit me like a cannonball.

'ASAVRI LIED ABOUT BEING AN ORPHAN TO GET PITY VOTES. SHE HAS A FAMILY IN SHANTIPUR.'

Pictures of Asavri with her family – father, mother, aunts and uncles – were splashed all over. The entire nation sat glued to their TVs and mobiles, watching the story unfold. Some lines had been highlighted to add emphasis.

'I'm Baba's favourite girl. He loves to hear me sing.'

'My Maa makes the best fish fry and mutton chop.'

'It was Baba who named me Asavri. It's the name of the morning raag.'

'Holy fuck!' I cursed loudly again. I couldn't believe my carelessness. What I was attempting to do needed careful orchestration and I couldn't possibly afford a slip-up. I really needed to stay away from alcohol.

I needed to reach her before Bhaskar took action. I felt like hell and knew for a fact that I looked no different. My mouth reeked of alcohol and my eyes were bloodshot.

I pulled my hair hard and slapped my face a few times as an alternative.

'Wake up! Wake up!' I couldn't slur while speaking to Bhaskar. I had to make the call. It couldn't wait till I was sober.

I made the call. He didn't pick up. The MD of IKA TV was busy handling the controversy that had hit the leading contestant and the show. What he didn't know was that the breaking news was stage-managed and thrown in their path by me.

No one could ever find out, especially Asavri.

I punched in the message, which I hoped he would see. I needed to get to him before he made a decision and announced Asavri's dismissal from the contest. If I'd had the sense to not drink myself into a stupor, I would've been at the IKA office with the documents ready to counter the story I myself had leaked. I wouldn't have been dealing with an ugly hangover, a pounding headache and eyes that couldn't bear streaming sunlight.

I knew the story. She told me everything, and I didn't just take her word for it. I did my due diligence as always. She wasn't lying. She was an orphan. She had known nothing about it till Rudra dumped her back home and humiliated her father.

'Asavri isn't lying about her parentage. She's an orphan. I have the proof.' That was my message to Bhaskar. Having done that, I placed the phone on the little rack near the mirror, with my shaving foam, toothpaste and toiletries. I wanted to hear the notification of the incoming message when it arrived. It didn't.

How could I be so careless and drink till the wee hours, when I should have been home, bright and sparky, to tackle the situation? I really need to be more careful. Alcohol always leads to disaster, like the fiasco at the Filmfare *party. And now ... Don't fuck this up, Avniel. This is your last chance.*

I stood under the shower and turned the knob, bracing myself to be hit by cold water. Instead, a pathetic little trickle landed on my head. I stared into the shower like everyone does, as though staring into the bloody faucet would magically make water gush out.

Why is the universe conspiring against me on the day I need things to be in order? Because I allowed myself to get drunk and pass out!

I badly needed a cold shower. I tried the tap. It had nothing to offer either. The basin tap was no different.

I knew the reason. It had happened many times before. Six times that month. The landlady liked to watch reruns of TV series and ended up sleeping in, through the alarm that's supposed to wake her up in time to switch on the pump at 6.30 a.m. Water would fill the underground tank from six and in half an hour, the pump needed to be switched on to push the water to the overhead tank. If she forgot, which happened often, my mornings began with a dry wash. I wanted to yell at her. To walk to her door, pound my fist on it and quarrel with her. The low rent and the frequent Parsi meals she sent over had stopped me from yelling at her in the past, but that day I was in the mood to pick a fight ... but there wasn't any time.

I decided not to waste any more time. I squeezed toothpaste on my brush, grabbed the phone and headed to the kitchen basin. Bhaskar hadn't replied yet; I checked. I began rinsing the foul taste of alcohol from my mouth using a bottle of drinking water. I took out two bottles of chilled water from the fridge. Desperate times called for desperate measures. I emptied the bottles on my head as I bent over the kitchen sink. The chilled water soaked my hair and calmed my burning head. The pounding stopped for a while. I cursed the landlady again, as well as the Mumbai municipal corporation for the scarcity of water.

Water was running down from my head, drenching my naked torso. I stood shivering in my flaming-orange tiger-print briefs, washing my head over the kitchen sink, when the phone rang. It was Bhaskar. I didn't have a towel to wipe my wet hand to take the call but didn't want to risk missing it either. I swiped right with my knuckle and turned the speaker on to be able to speak without soaking the phone.

'Are you sure, Avniel? Are you absolutely sure of the fact?' Bhaskar usually began conversations with pleasantries. Always very formal and proper about such things. But that wasn't the day to bother with niceties.

'Yes, Mr Rai. I know for a fact that she is an orphan. There's a story behind all of this. I know it and I have the necessary proof.'

I said the magic words: *There's a story behind all of this.* If there's anything the TV world needs more than air and water, and wants desperately, it is a story. Give them a story that grips the audience, increases the TRPs and makes the cash registers ring, and their life is made. Asavri was an amazing story.

'I'm reaching the hotel in an hour. See you there.' He hung up and I made a hurried dash back to my bedroom, ignoring the little puddle that had pooled near the kitchen sink, on the floor. I didn't have the time to tend to my OCD for cleanliness and order. The head bath seemed to have accomplished what the shower was meant to. I felt kind of fresh, my eyes hurt less and the pounding in my head seemed to have abated for the time being.

I changed hurriedly, grabbing the first clean shirt and trousers I could find. I towel-dried my hair and ran a comb over it. I really needed a haircut. It was almost touching my shoulders. I tied it in a messy man bun. A shave would have been nice but there was no time for that. I dabbed some cologne on my stubble, sprayed some deo on my body and prayed I didn't reek of alcohol. I couldn't find my breath mints. Bloody hell!

I'd crossed my daily quota of cuss words and it wasn't even ten.

Thankfully, the necessary papers were already in a folder in my backpack. I slung it on my shoulder, took a deep breath and walked out to play saviour after having wreaked havoc. I had one hour to reach Juhu from my pad in Kandivali, pacify Asavri and then meet Bhaskar. Traffic was at its worst then. I checked the time. It was 9.15 a.m. *Train to Santacruz and then auto. That should be the quickest route.* I flagged down the first auto I spotted outside my building gate and hollered, 'Station. *Jaldi*. Extra *dunga*.'

It was 10.40 a.m. when I reached the lobby of Juhu Centaur. She was there, waiting for me. I could tell she had been crying, her eyes red and swollen. On seeing me enter, she gave a small cry of relief and ran towards me. I stopped her in time from falling into my arms. Though I didn't spot any camera crews from newspapers or TV channels, I kept in mind that everyone nowadays was a photographer with camera phones. I wasn't ready to have my picture plastered in every newspaper with Asavri sobbing in my arms. She's already something of a national celebrity, and the contest is only halfway through. My office didn't know about my Asavri connection, yet.

'Let's go to a coffee shop. I've spoken with Bhaskar. Everything will be all right.'

'Why can't Rudra leave me alone? All I want is to sing and make a life for myself. Why does he care what I'm doing?' She was sniffing. There are some women who look pretty when they cry; vulnerable and soft. Asavri wasn't one of them.

People passed us by, staring, whispering and pointing in her direction. Some walked slower as they approached, trying to eavesdrop on our conversation and pretending to be busy on their phones. If there's anything people like more than adulating and hero-worshipping, it's digging out dirt on those same people. Everyone loves a scandal; dirtier the better. She was a known face. Asavri was getting more than enough publicity since her audition and was placed in the final twenty without having to compete in the elimination rounds. She began as the darling of the contest, and still was, but of late, she had been slacking – missing the schedule, losing her music sheets, etc. There had been a few stray comments about her tardiness. She needed to stay on top all through. That's why I had decided to leak the adoption story.

When she had told everyone that she's an orphan, sympathy mixed with love for her voice made for an intoxicating cocktail. The article I leaked anonymously showed her with a loving family; it made her look like a scheming liar. It had only been a few hours, but that was enough for the fire to spread. People were spitting venom exactly as I knew they would. Exactly as I had wanted.

The surge of pity after a shaming hits like a tsunami. When the truth would be revealed, there would be a tidal wave of sympathy for Asavri. I knew how these things worked. Film magazines thrive on scandals, and my job had given me a ringside view of it all. I knew what I was doing. It was a well thought out strategy and it couldn't go wrong. I wouldn't let it go wrong. There was too much at stake.

She's your ticket out of this hole, I kept telling myself when she got on my nerves, which was often.

Everything was going as I'd planned. The revelation after the news leak would work in her favour and she would ride up the popularity lists. I sat with a cloud of fake worry on my face, trying hard not to look excited.

'I knew you didn't believe me when I said that someone was deliberately misplacing my music notes and my schedules. I landed up late for the practice sessions more than twice and got scolded for it. I didn't have the music notes before going up for the performance in the last round. Thank God I didn't fumble, but I told you and you didn't believe me.' I hadn't believed her. I still didn't. I needed to sit her down and drill some sense into her. She couldn't afford to misplace her music sheets, not know the schedule and continue being so sloppy. I planned on having that conversation with her soon, but right then, I focused on doing a good job of looking sorry.

'I also told you then that Rudra is behind it all. I know it, and I am not wrong. These pictures are from an email I sent to him before our marriage. It's him, Avniel. That man isn't going to rest till he sees the end of me. I'm telling you, someday he is just going to kill me. He won't stop till he finishes me off. Till he wipes me off completely.' She stifled a sob. I covered her hand with mine. A slow throb began to start at the back of my head. I ordered a strong black coffee and a croissant.

'Don't worry, Asavri. This adoption issue will blow over. You didn't lie. You just didn't tell them the whole story. I am here to handle them. Don't worry.' I felt a little sorry for her, that I did everything without taking her into confidence, but she would have never agreed to it in the first place. She wasn't smart enough to play games. It could only be done without her nod and that's what I did. What I did would make people want to hug her and adopt her as their own. It would erase her negative reports and push her up in the contest. The public would show their love and sympathy with votes and make her win.

We waited in the café. Asavri looked sullen and scared. She slipped into her nervous tic again. Tapping her upper lip with her middle and index fingers, almost touching her nostrils. 'Don't do that, Asavri.' I pulled her hand away.

'You are a star and can't be seen making such strange gestures.'

When Bhaskar arrived, we were called to see him in Room 101.

Security personnel were crawling all over the hotel. Everyone, the staff included, had ear microphones on and were speaking in a terse tone. They made way for Asavri. I thought about the day they would do the same for me.

Someone muttered, 'She is here.'

Another yelled, 'The press has arrived.'

Someone replied, 'Get them to sit in Hall B. Serve them something cold and fresh.'

'Is Bhaskar ready?'

I could feel her stiffen next to me.

'You have nothing to worry about,' I assured her. 'I have the original papers.' I patted the backpack that was slung on my shoulder. Since she had no place of her own, when she moved in to the hotel for the contest, she left a suitcase full of valuable papers with me. All her adoption papers and a small suitcase of memories was what she had carried with her when she left Shantipur. She didn't bother to lock the bags when she left them with me. Why would she? She was leaving her belongings with a friend. What she didn't know was that I was the kind of friend who would read her private diary and sift through her stuff. I'm nosy that way; a writer needs to be nosy and curious, for how else would we get our stories! I don't give a damn about anyone's privacy except mine.

'Don't worry. I'll do the talking. Believe me, everything will be OK.' The morning had begun badly but I was back in control.

Bhaskar didn't need too much convincing. These contests are all about TRPs, just like several other reality shows. That's where the money lies. And it's always been about money.

'Mr Rai, these are the original adoption papers from Home of Mercy, Shillong. It clearly states that a four-month baby girl had been adopted by Amol Bhattacharya. It states further that he named her Asavri.'

'So then how does she explain the pictures and the story printed in the article?' Bhaskar's question was a valid one.

Asavri had shown me the newsletter while we were packing her stuff for the hotel where all contestants would be staying for the duration of the contest.

'This is my family, Avniel.' She had handed it to me with tears brimming in her eyes. 'Or at least I thought they were my family.'

I'd suspected since our first lunch that there was something fishy about the I'm-an-orphan line she said in one breath.

It was an article done for her father's company newsletter. A long one with many pictures of her with different family members. The kind companies do under the section 'Know your colleague'.

'It's my family and yet not.' She'd told me the whole story – how she always believed she had a loving family till the day Rudra brought her back and shamed her and the entire family. How her father yelled out the truth of her adoption later one night and had a stroke. We stayed awake that entire night as she told me everything about her life – her fairy-tale childhood, playing in the lawns, her sweet, innocent life in a small town away from the chaos and grime of a big city, discovering her talent for singing, becoming the darling of the colony and, finally, her marriage to a man who looked nothing less than Prince Charming. She also told me why Rudra brought her back from their honeymoon. She sobbed in my arms, crying bitterly, cursing her fate for how she'd lost everything and that the only thing left in her life was music. I held her as she wept and said soothing words, but in my mind, the story was starting to take on its true form.

Thank you, God, for dropping this in my lap! I couldn't believe my luck was turning.

Soon after, I had the entire plan chalked out and started writing the outline of the story. The story of an orphan who was given a home and a fairy-tale childhood by a loving childless couple. She was married and subsequently humiliated by her husband, after which she was cast away by the family. Following this, she comes to Mumbai and becomes a singing star! I didn't need to be a reporter to know that it was bestseller material and it had dropped right into my hands. *There is a God!* All she needed to do was stay focused and win. She needed an ally who would help her steer her way, and I would be that person.

As I sat across the table from Bhaskar, I spoke as though I was Asavri's spokesperson. I was already seeing myself in that role. 'Asavri wasn't privy to this information at the time of the interview. She found out the truth only a few months before coming to Mumbai for the contest. She grew up believing that she was the natural child of the family.'

'She could have ... should have shared all of this with us when she joined the contest.' That was Rudra standing behind Bhaskar. Prince Charming seemed to be balding really fast and needed to do something about that paunch. Someone should've told him it's not cool to wear tight trousers; his ass was sticking out. Prince Charming looked like an idiot.

I chose to ignore him and looked at Bhaskar instead. Rudra was done playing his two-minute role in her life; he wasn't going to get any more.

'Please try to understand how traumatic it was for Asavri to find out after twenty-three years that she is an adopted child. It's not the kind of story one goes around narrating at will. And she did say she's an orphan. Why is it important to narrate the entire scenario that led to her finding out the truth?'

It was a valid point, and Bhaskar nodded his head.

'Yes, but what was the reason for her adoptive parents to spill the truth they had kept from her for years? Did something happen?' Rudra probed and I knew exactly why. I just didn't want the conversation to go there. Yet. The story had to be revealed bit-by-bit. It was too early to give the full picture. Asavri shuffled her feet and clutched her palms. I placed my hand over her clenched, entwined fingers, in full view of both Bhaskar and Rudra. A muscle tightened on Rudra's face.

'Asavri is the favourite of the show. I'm sure you'll agree, Mr Rai. She's the best thing to have happened to your show. Let's not ruin her chances for something that's not her fault. She didn't lie. She *is* an orphan.' Bhaskar didn't need to hear any more. Rudra started to say something but was stopped by Bhaskar's raised hand.

'I've heard what I wanted to and I'm assured. Asavri didn't do anything wrong. She will continue on the show as before. We will keep a copy of the original adoption certificate, of course.'

'Asavri,' Bhaskar rose from his seat and came towards her with an outstretched hand. 'My sympathies for all the muck that has been thrown at you. You are our star performer. Today, there's an important performance, am I correct?'

'Yes, sir, there is.' She was choking. 'I ... I don't know what to say, sir. All I want to do is sing.'

'That's exactly what you should do. Sing, and may you win.' He patted her head as though he was decades older, though he was probably less than ten years her senior. 'I will make the announcement and we will release a copy of the adoption certificate to the press. That should quell the storm.'

Once back in her room, Asavri couldn't stop crying. 'I can never thank you enough for everything you're doing.'

'Now, what did I do?' I tried to sound modest.

'You're a friend I can trust, Avniel. You are the first and only person I think of when I'm in trouble. In fact, you are also the only person I think of when I'm happy.' I could see a slow blush spread over her face. She looked away, embarrassed at having let out more than she had wanted to.

'Hmm.' I was working hard to become a friend, a confidante, maybe even her manager if I did things right. But being her lover didn't feature on the list.

She threw her arms around me.

'I don't know what I'd do without you, Avniel. I have nobody in my life who cares about me anymore.' Asavri was very emotional that day. She feared she would be thrown out of the contest. I needed to tread carefully. Too much had happened in her life and she was desperate to find someone, be with that someone – someone she could call her own. In her mind, I was that person.

When Asavri hugged me and held me tight, I reciprocated with restraint. My hangover was under control but I still had a lot of alcohol in me. It had been quite a while since I had made out with someone and I didn't want to ruin it by being hasty. I have ruined enough things already with my impulsive behaviour. Not anymore.

'I'm always there for you, Ri, you know that, right?' I said with my face buried in her coarse, frizzy hair that smelled of coconut oil. *Why the fuck did she use coconut oil to smoothen her hair? Does she know nothing about serums and hair gels?*

'Ri? So you decided to give me a nickname, huh?' She looked straight into my eyes, smiling, her arms wrapped around me.

'No, I didn't mean to ... it just... I'm sorry, I shouldn't have,' I fumbled on purpose. The shortening of her name had the effect I knew it would. She was so vulnerable; she believed anything and everything. I disentangled myself, turned my face away and combed my hair with my fingers, pretending to be embarrassed.

'I like it. Ri. I like the sound of it.' She looped her arm around mine and pressed her body against my arm. I could feel her nipples. They were hard. An urge to grab her, push my hand up from under her tee and rub my thumb across her nipples rose somewhere deep inside me.

I didn't do any of that. Instead, I freed my arm, draped it around her shoulder and affectionately rubbed her shoulder bone. 'You have a session to go to. Or have you forgotten about that?'

'No, I haven't. But I feel like spending some more time with you. We hardly get any time together.' She turned around and buried her face in my chest.

I needed to stop it before the alcohol got the better of me and I lost control. I needed to do it fast. There was only so much I could control. I didn't want us to end up naked because that's exactly where it was heading. It would ruin everything. I knew that. She wanted physical intimacy but if we followed through with it, she would regret it later. Because she would then discuss it with some of the contestants with whom she was thick. They would make her think reasonably, which she would be incapable of, given the sex haze she'd lapse into. She would then distance herself from me. I know how girl packs work, having been at the wrong end of them too many times. I couldn't let that happen. If word got out that the *Filmfare* reporter was sleeping with contestant numero uno … well, I didn't need imagination to understand how that would play out.

The way to douse sexual fire was to play cute, I decided.

I pushed her away tenderly, cupped her face and said in a mockingly stern voice, 'Asavri Bhattacharya, focus. You have a contest to win.' I then kissed the tip of her nose. 'Believe me, when this is all over, you and I will have lots of time. Together. Tell me, where do you want to go?'

'Stop pulling my leg.'

'No, no. I'm serious. *Batao*, where do you want to go? Imagine us taking a holiday. Where would you like to go?'

She answered promptly, as though she had already thought and imagined it. 'Kausani. I love the hills. The cold, crisp air that hurts your nose as you breathe in … and the Himalayas. Silent, dark and just there … forever. Yes, I want us to go to Kausani. Can we?' she asked the question more with her eyes than with words.

'Of course we can, and we will. Promise.'

'Every time you say promise, I know you won't do it. You're horrible.' She gave me a fake punch and smiled.

'I promise. *Sachi.*' I stared deep into her eyes as my lips hovered inches away from hers; a hint of the promise I had made about the future.

A promise I had no intention of keeping.

Eleven

Avniel. NOW.
2018

'Hey, go ahead and pour yourself a glass.' Bhaskar points towards the bar. 'I need to be on this call,' he whispers and slips back into his study.

I don't hesitate to pick up the Talisker. I am used to the good things in life now. No more Officer's Choice for me. Only Talisker, Laphroaig and such others. I have also taught myself self-control. Never more than two pegs. Gone are the days of moronic behaviour. But Bhaskar's home still makes me nervous. Too many expensive things strewn around; things that cost more than I will possibly ever make in my life. Being new to money, I'm still awkward around it.

Opulence makes me uncomfortable. Like the Amrita Sher-Gil that hangs on the wall. I sit ramrod straight, lest my head touches the painting. I've been at the hospital round the clock and haven't had the time to wash my greasy hair. Thank God for the man bun.

There's a gigantic Murano vase near my elbow, its colours seductively swirling into each other in a passionate dance. It's beyond beautiful and I'm terrified of being anywhere near it. I don't want to knock it over with my elbow. The upholstery feels like rich silk. I want to dash into the washroom to clean my hands; my grubby fingers might leave a stain. Gigantic lilies bloom in a crystal vase; lilies of different hues. These are bloody expensive. I know this since I buy them every time I get too busy with work or have an argument with Priya. But all that's in the past. Now she's in her Parel flat. I don't have the time to buy lilies and land up at her doorstep. I don't think any number of lilies will make her return.

Bhaskar is still in his study and I'm alone in the company of Amar, Akbar and Anthony –a shih-tzu, golden retriever and boxer. His babies, as he calls them. I don't understand why people have dogs *or* babies – slobbery, needy and just plain annoying. The canine trio eye me. They never liked me. They loved Asavri. It was a sight watching her with dogs; rolling on the floor, hugging them, and they'd returned her love with the same gusto. She is a dog person. Or at least she was. I don't know her anymore. The present Asavri is a very different person; she likes very different things. She likes to sleep with all the lights on. She likes sugary sweet tea. She looks at a lame gangster with love in her eyes.

I can't shake off the images I saw at the police commissioner's office. The CCTV footage, Monty's picture and everything else I learnt. I'm tired; more mentally than physically. I take another sip of the Talisker and roll it in my mouth before allowing it to slide down my throat.

I wish Bhaskar would return. I'm uncomfortable being left alone with my thoughts and the canines glaring at me.

You look worse than the street-side mongrel, dude. How did they let you enter the premises? They seem to say as they cock their heads in unison and stare unblinkingly at me. They all have collars with sparkling stones – I won't be surprised if they are diamonds! I'm sure the collars cost more than my watch. I know for a fact they make frequent visits to an expensive salon for their grooming. I even can't remember if I bathed today. My denim looks like it needs a wash. My shirt is crushed. I came directly from the hospital when Bhaskar called.

Shut up, you dogs, go find a bone and chew it. I reply with my eyes as I take another sip of the exquisite single malt.

We are champion breeds. What are you? They seem to ask. Thankfully I don't have to answer. Bhaskar returns. He doesn't notice that his canine trio has been giving me the silent treatment. He pours himself a Laphroaig and adds an ice cube.

'Avniel, we have a big problem on our hands.' He takes a large gulp from his glass as he walks towards me.

'Asavri.' I know it before he says it.

'Apart from the ongoing investigation about what happened to her, where she was for the past two ... nearly two years and how she became such ... such a ...' He's grasping for the right word.

'Psychological mess.' I haven't told him about what I saw and learnt in the commissioner's office.

'Yes.' He sits with his face grim, staring beyond the glass doors. The dark city glitters at night, it's ugly reality hidden. From the fifteenth-floor apartment, facing the sea and the city beyond, it is indeed a pretty sight. We both stare out but don't see any of it. We are thinking about her. Asavri.

'You don't understand, Avniel. What happened is only part of the problem. What happens from here on is my concern. Music directors are calling up. Every day. They want Asavri's voice. There's a lot of money riding on her.'

Bhaskar is leaning towards me and gesticulating. He looks tired. Doesn't look like he has been sleeping well. The board of directors must be pushing him hard to repair and restore the channel's image. Their 2016 winner was declared dead after a road accident but then she resurfaces all messed up two years later. Stories are great on the TV screen and in books, but when they come alive, it's a nightmare.

What he isn't telling me is that apart from the money IKA stands to make from her assignments, if Asavri isn't reinstated to her original glory, heads will roll and Bhaskar's would be the first to go. And then there's the legal case. Asavri could recover and press charges. The list of horrors seems endless.

'There's a lot of public outcry. It's a good thing her family wants nothing to do with her. They could have sued us. The channel. With them out of the picture, it's one less thing to lose sleep over.' He puts his glass down on the centre table with a careless thud. It doesn't matter to him if the table cracks or the glass spills the uber-expensive whisky on the God-knows-how-expensive rug on which the Amar Akbar Anthony trio lie supine.

I feel like pointing out that it may be one thing less to worry about but it essentially means she's alone. No family. No one is with her. I keep quiet.

'Everyone wants Asavri. She has become the face of the tortured and tormented. Public outcry is colossal. She has to get better and stand before the public once again.'

'She's in no shape to be presented to the public, leave alone singing,' I add.

We both need another drink. This will be my second, then no more. I'm keeping a count. Bhaskar does the needful.

'Her safety is of utmost importance. Whoever kept her and abused her like this could make a move and try to nab her again,' I speak up while Bhaskar is fixing the drink. Monty doesn't look like a person who would sit quietly on his prize catch gone missing and neither do Bhai and his flunkies.

'She needs to get better and get better fast, Avniel. This can't drag on.'

'In the past month, I've been with her every day, sometimes during the night too. She's in a very bad state. She barely speaks. She is lost in some faraway world that she can't seem to get out of. I'm trying … trying really hard to communicate. I'm there all day, every day.'

'I really appreciate it, Avniel. You have gone the extra mile to help her. You really have.'

'She's very fragile. Needs a lot of care, maybe psychiatric treatment and continuous supervision. She will be discharged soon. The doc told me today. Where will she stay once she's out of the hospital?'

'Avniel, there's a beautiful place that IKA TV owns in the hills, up in the Himalayas. In Kausani. You take her there. I will arrange it. IKA will pay for everything. We will send a therapist along with you for daily sessions. What do you think?'

'Me? I … How can I … You think I can help?' This is a preposterous suggestion. How can I go away and stay with her till she recovers? That could take months.

'She trusts you. I mean, she trusted you. Right now she's in a confused state but soon she'll trust you again, Avniel. You can get through to her like no one can. You can slowly draw her out of the black hole that she's slipped into. You can help her get better.' He looks expectantly at me.

'Hmm. This is quite a task, Bhaskar. I don't think I could just go away like this.'

'Buddy, please bail me out. Anything you want and need. Just name it and it's yours. Asavri needs to recover. That's all.'

Silence punctuates our conversation. Bhaskar is staring hard at me and I'm staring at the ice cube in my glass. I finally speak up.

'First of all, the location must remain a secret. We'll tell people she's in the hills but I have a different place in mind. I don't want the press following us. And keep Kamini away from this. I don't want anyone getting political mileage out of her.'

'Done. I agree with you. Kamini and her people have been visiting the hospital regularly. I will handle them. The last thing I need is politicians getting involved. You don't worry. Consider it handled. Anything else?' Bhaskar finishes his drink.

'Yes, I need security. Very good and reliable security. The kind of security that can discharge firearms if needed.' I can see a question mark forming on Bhaskar's face. 'Those who kept her captive, raped and drugged her repeatedly must be looking for her. She needs protection. If she's kidnapped, we will never see or hear of her ever again.'

This is much more than a gang job. Why would a drug and prostitution ring leader keep her? Someone powerful enough wanted her gone but kept her alive for some reason. I intend to find out the who and why of it.

'Whatever you say, Avniel ... you got it. Consider it done. Just get her back to normal. And you can have your sequel. You want another one?' Bhaskar gets up and walks to the bar.

'What do you mean?'

We look at each other for a few minutes and then Bhaskar smiles a little.

'Let's not kid each other, brother. Okay? We've known each other for too long to bullshit each other. This is your sequel screaming to be written.'

'You think I'll use a helpless, tormented woman's life and make a story out of it. What kind of a bastard do you think I am?'

'An opportunistic one. Come on, Avniel, why the fuck are you getting upset? It's not the first time you'd be using Asavri.'

The reality of the words pierce me hard and deep. 'I should go now, Bhaskar. I'm brain-dead.'

'Okay, okay, don't get upset. Don't make a story out of it. Do it from the goodness of your heart. She's your friend and needs help and has no one in her life but you.' That last bit sounds snarky and is accompanied with a smile.

'Come on, have another drink? Let's drink to Project Asavri, shall we?'

I stare at Bhaskar and want to yell, 'Stop calling her Project Asavri!' I stay silent.

I decide to break my two-peg rule. I need the extra alcohol now. After we clink glasses, Bhaskar puts his down, holds my hand with both of his and shakes it hard. He looks happy and relieved. 'You don't know how much I owe you, Avniel. Buddy, my neck is on the block. Thank you for saving it and agreeing to help with this Project Asavri. I owe you big time.

Big time.' Bhaskar is smiling and shaking my hand. I want to punch him every time I hear him say Project Asavri, but I don't.

'Anything for a friend,' I mumble.

Which friend am I talking about? Bhaskar or Asavri?

I drain the glass and tell him I need to leave. We are near the elevator. The canine unit has followed us and are resolutely looking at me as though they know what's on my mind.

Some friend you are! And they call us dogs.

Bhaskar thanks me again as the elevator door closes. Why do they have mirrors on all sides inside elevators? My reflection, in multitudes because of the three mirrors around me – some law of reflection and refraction in physics I studied light years ago – stares back at me with many faces.

When was she not a project? Even earlier ... all you wanted from her was the story.

You cosied up to her, made her believe you were in love so that she'd feel comfortable enough to spill every detail of her life. Don't you deny it, you newshound! It's almost yelling now.

You haven't changed. You're still using her for a story. Pretend all you want. She's a story. That's all.

I hold my head in my palms, pressing hard against them, as though I can squeeze away these thoughts. Stop the voice that's screaming inside me.

The door opens and I rush out ... almost running. Away from the multiple reflections, the questions galore and the truth of it all.

Twelve

Kamini. NOW.
2018

I'm sick of this bitch! And everything else. Nothing has been right since she returned.

I'm back in the hospital foyer. Asavri is getting discharged today and there's a press conference. Of course, there is. Avniel and Bhaskar can't possibly let go of the opportunity to show how scared, tormented and broken the singer of the nation is. Makes me sick. *She* makes me sick.

The bright November morning mocks me. There's a nip in the air; a few months of decent weather in the usually hot and humid Mumbai. It could have been a pleasant morning. Clear blue sky, bright sunshine and fresh air that feels good on the skin. It's not the Delhi kind of cold where you need to stay wrapped in woollens, but the kind that allows the skin to breathe, be happy and smile.

But I don't enjoy any of it. The bright and sunny day, the blue sky or the nip in the air.

Dark grey clouds swirl in my head and follow me everywhere I go. I keep hearing whispers of things to come. They say, 'Kamini is over.'

It's not over till I say it's over. I have overcome far bigger hurdles than Asavri and won. This time will be no different. I keep telling myself this over and over again, but of late, I've been finding it difficult to believe in myself. The ground below is shifting and I do not like it at all. It's all because of her; because she couldn't stay dead.

'Madam, how did your meeting with Mr Patil go yesterday?' I don't hear the question. When he repeats it, I turn towards the person that asked it. He isn't important enough for me to remember his name. He is a correspondent with *Nayi Subah*. I can see the name tag dangling around his neck. His name is printed on it. I don't bother to read it. I know the likes of him – reporters who attend every event for the free food and booze. I do notice one thing about him, though. There's dirt under his nails; remnants of trying to get his grimy paws anywhere and everywhere.

I know that he knows I was unable to meet Patil. I waited for more than two hours only to be informed that he had to change his plans last minute. It was deliberate. A year ago, this wouldn't have happened. I would have been the first meeting on Patil's agenda while in Mumbai. But now it's different.

I decide to deal with the reporter standing next to me. 'Are you here to get political bites or report on Asavri's condition? I'm not a politician here. Today I'm just a mother of a contestant, here to support my daughter's friend – the rightful winner of *Indian Koel*. Have a heart ... or at least pretend to have one.' I walk away without giving him a chance to reply or react.

Dheeraj hurries over to my side. 'Madam, maybe it's not the best move to get tough with the reporters.' How he hears my conversations from wherever he is standing, which is always at a distance, is beyond me. He whispers while pretending to show me something on his mobile.

'Maybe you should leave politics to me, Dheeraj, and handle the job that's been entrusted to you. A job that you haven't been doing well at all.' I'm losing patience with him. For the first time in twenty-three years, he is slipping up. I should be able to overlook one slip but this is too big to ignore.

'There! There she is,' someone yells out. The gathered press – cameramen, TV reporters and the rest – rush towards the raised voice and where his finger points. From the far end of the main foyer of Anandmay Hospital, Asavri steps out of the elevator. Security guards restrain the surging reporters, forming a body chain.

'No one is to step ahead of this area! Please maintain order,' one of them, a short, thin and bespectacled pint of a man, speaks up loud. He reminds me of lanky, thin-boned half-naked boys who control herds of buffaloes using just a stick. Power is certainly in the brain and never brawn.

From where I stand, alongside Bhaskar, some other key IKA TV personnel and Tanya, I can see Asavri clearly. She is trying to hide behind Avniel, who seems to be whispering something to her. Where else would he be if not right next to his little bitch? He is touching her elbow and leaning towards her.

There's a nurse and another woman whom I don't recognize. Asavri is dragging her feet. Seems unwilling to make an appearance. She looks terrified, like she'd rather have her teeth drilled out without anaesthesia than be here. She looks very thin, almost bony. Her clothes hang on her, limp. Someone got her a dark blue palazzo, white kurti and an indigo dupatta that hangs around her neck. It's rather cold in the foyer. The AC is at a chill temperature but she is sweating. Her face looks shiny.

'Mom. She looks awfully beat up. She looks like she's been in a mental hospital.' Tanya leans over and whispers in my ear, 'What happened to her?'

'I don't know, sweetie, but I will soon.' Good thing I convinced T to dress conservatively. In dark blue denim and a shapeless white shirt that conceals her curves, with her hair carefully tied with a band. No make-up. Tanya looks like an ordinary college girl. I didn't want her to look glamorous next to the ravaged Asavri. Their pictures will be splashed on all the TV channels and newspapers. That's the whole point of today's gathering. Avniel has been doing a great job of stoking public interest in Asavri and keeping it alive. Otherwise, she isn't worth more than half a day's media space. And here she is, after three months of being found on the streets of Mumbai, still creating a frenzy. Seeing the size of the press gathered, one would think a Bollywood celebrity is being discharged after treatment for a terminal ailment.

Avniel started the prime-time programme on IKA TV a while back, strategically titled *What Happened to Asavri?* The half-an-hour programme shows rushes from the past, video recordings of various sessions and interviews, with the past and present fantastically juxtaposed. And images of Asavri now in the hospital room, anxious, scared and scarred. The camera zooming in on the scars on her arms and wrists. She may have had a seizure or two but that image is shown in every episode, freezing as she cries out in agony, her mouth open in a big O, eyes wide open in horror and saliva dribbling out of her mouth. Such a dramatic picture! How can it not make the public cry out in sympathy? Every episode ends with the lines 'WHAT HAPPENED TO ASAVRI? WHO DID THIS TO HER?'

Some of the episodes show personal recordings of Asavri with fellow contestants, doing her morning riyaaz, walking on the beach with a pensive look as if she was among a crowd but in a world of her own. I've seen them all. Every episode. It's almost as though someone had been collecting footage that could be used at a later date in a situation like this.

Oh my God! I can't believe I never thought of this before. It just strikes me now. Of course it has to be. It *must* be.

I see him walk closer towards the press. His dirty, messy man bun is so disgusting. Being a bestselling author put him in the spotlight, gave him status and money, which I sometimes see traces of when he presents himself in decent attire ... but his hair is always greasy and outright disgusting. Why can't he trim it, wash it and keep it clean? His hair didn't bother me back when I dug my fingers deep into it and pulled him closer as I rode him hard. Now I find his hair and everything about him disgusting. I wonder if he's fucking her again. The horny bastard can't keep his pants zipped for long. Anyway, Asavri doesn't look like she can give anyone a hard-on. She never had that kind of potential.

He is handing out the press kit that I'm sure contains details of her condition, what she went through and what is being done to help her rehabilitate. The person who has always benefitted the most from Asavri and her life is Avniel.

She became the winner and then died … almost … and he went on to publish a book about her. The book came out in less than three months after her alleged death. It was an instant bestseller. The failed movie reporter who shot himself in the foot while drunk, the guy who everyone had written off, rose like the proverbial phoenix with the book *I'm Nobody's Child*.

And now, after almost two years, it's time for a sequel.

How did I not see this before? It has to be him. But how did he manage it? He was badly injured in the accident too. And where did he manage to keep her hidden for all this time? There are many loose threads but Avniel seems like the perfect candidate to play mastermind behind it all.

What a swine! Will do anything for a story, huh? I dislike him so much that I almost start to like him again. I'm strangely aroused by the thought.

I tell myself to focus on the now. How is it that Dheeraj didn't consider this?

I touch T's elbow, who has disinterest plastered on her face. When will she understand how delicate all this is?

'Go to her, stand next to her and hug her.'

'Why? Last time I did, she pulled away like I was a leper,' she hisses back, nearly audible.

'Just do as I say, T.' I can see some of the reporters are looking in her direction.

As T walks towards Asavri, the security men stop her.

Bhaskar calls out, 'Let her pass.'

T stands next to Asavri, who is more interested in the mosaic pattern on the floor. She does more than I asked her to. She is saying something to Asavri, who finally looks up at her as though they are meeting for the first time. T is holding

Asavri's listless hand and speaking. Doesn't matter what she's saying. The cameras are going crazy. After a while, T returns to the empty seat next to mine.

'She's seriously creepy, Mom! I spoke with her but she just mumbled something. She doesn't even look you in the eye when you talk to her. What happened to her? Why is she like this? I wanna go home, Mom. She creeps me out.'

I'm not the least bit concerned as to why she is the way she is. The question now is *how* did Avniel do this all? I'm pretty certain he is involved. Who else stands to benefit from the return of the girl who refuses to die or stay dead?

'Madam.' Dheeraj's voice is almost inaudible as always. I turn towards him and he tells me with his eyes that I should be standing next to Bhaskar and the others. The optics, yes! I walk over to him.

'Bhaskar, you know my Alibaug bungalow is at your disposal. For Asavri, I mean,' I say, loud enough for a few reporters to hear. I want them to. 'Or any other place that you deem more suitable for recuperation. Up in the Himalayas, maybe, if the cool mountain air is better. Though November would be very cold.'

'Madam, you are most gracious as always. I know we can count on you and you'll be the first person I call should I need assistance in this matter. But, really, Asavri is my responsibility. IKA's responsibility.' His extra polite speech basically translates to 'Fuck off'.

I begin a conversation with Shefali, the PR head of IKA. I stop listening to her and instead look at Avniel, who is standing alone. He is observing something. T is sitting in the front row, where I left her a minute ago. Avniel is staring at my daughter ... I follow his gaze.

I can tell T is disturbed. Seeing Asavri like this is unnerving for her. She had seen a few episodes on TV too. They had become close during the contest. And Asavri saved T from the fire. The sight of my T, unconscious, as Asavri hauled her out of billowing smoke, is etched in my memory. T could have died that day had it not been for Asavri. I don't think I ever thanked her properly. My anger had given way to relief. Anger because I'd categorically asked T to stay at home and not be at the pub.

Almost two years have passed since that fateful night. Every time T gives me a migraine, I remind myself that I almost lost my baby.

Why is that mangy stray dog staring at her? Is he planning to make a move on my T? I'll have him roasted on live coals if he makes a move on her. Bloody bastard!

Wonder what he's thinking. Why the hell is he staring at T? What's cooking in that crafty head of his?

'Tanya looks more and more like Pratap with every passing day, doesn't she?' Avniel strolls up to me after a bit. He's in a pale yellow linen shirt and dark blue denim. Messily rolled up shirt sleeves reveal his thin arms with scraggy hair. He's wearing the shirt untucked.

The denim is by FCUK, the linen shirt is also an expensive fabric; I can tell. But for some people, no matter how much they spend on their attire, their middle-class upbringing is stamped too noticeably on their demeanour. Avniel is like that.

I raise an eyebrow and just as I'm about to turn away, he speaks again.

'Who did you expect her to look like?' It nauseates me to have a conversation with him.

'Genes have a funny way of expressing themselves, don't they?' A smile, almost a leer, takes over his face as he allows his eyes to linger on my face and gradually drop to my breasts. I'm annoyed with myself when I feel my nipples harden.

'Chewing nails is a bad habit.' I point to his half-eaten nails.

'I know. It's a very bad habit; one that was passed on to me from my father. Such traits are often passed on from parents to children. Quirky habits are shared by the family, eh?'

'Trivia and reporters!'

I hear the announcement and begin to walk away, but not before giving a parting shot. 'Focus on your sequel, Avniel. You seem to have another winner on your hands.' I signal towards Asavri with my eyes.

The shameless bastard doesn't even make an attempt to look shocked or embarrassed.

Soon the press conference begins and Bhaskar addresses the gathered group. 'Asavri will stay in the company guest house in the hills. She needs some more time to recover fully.'

'Where is she being taken?' multiple voices ask.

'I'm sorry, but I will not reveal that. She needs solitude and therapy to get better. But she will return soon. I promise.'

'How long will she take?'

'Can we speak with her? Can she address the group?'

Questions pour in as Bhaskar addresses each of them.

'She'll take as long as it takes. Time isn't of the essence here. Her well-being is the thing to focus on. And, no, she isn't going to interact today. Please respect her need for privacy. Anyhow, we have invited all of you here today to share a rather grim piece of news.'

Tension takes over the gathering and it becomes silent as everyone sits up in anticipation of the news that Bhaskar is about to share. He really is the TV guy; he knows drama and uses it well.

'The ever-helpful police force of Mumbai has intel that has led us to believe that Asavri was held by a certain gang ...' A collective gasp skims through the foyer. I'm intrigued too. This is news, indeed!

'Please allow me to finish. Yes, she was held captive by a gang for reasons still unknown. But rest assured the police will get to the bottom of it. As you can imagine, this makes her security and safety a matter of concern and priority. Asavri must be kept safe at all costs. She isn't nobody's child, she is Mumbai's daughter. She is IKA's responsibility, my responsibility ...'

I stop listening after hearing the gang bit. Avniel did a good job with speech writing. The 'nobody's child' line and repeating the bit about IKA and Bhaskar's responsibility. My eyes find Avniel, who looks all serious and then suddenly winks at me.

You are really a piece of work, aren't you, Avniel? Enjoying the poor girl's plight and using it for your next book. I'm totally certain that all of this is your doing.

I look at her. She is staring into empty space, lost in a world far from where she stands. Poor girl doesn't know that the person she thinks is her best friend is a bloody viper.

Someone yells, 'We love you, Asavri. Everyone is waiting for you to return. We love you.' It catches on like a chant and soon the foyer is reverberating with 'We love you, Asavri'. I try to identify the person who shouted it first. It's difficult now that almost everyone is chanting the same. I wouldn't be surprised if Avniel prompted someone to do this. He is getting better at the game. It's a pity we parted. He would have been a good ally.

I seek out at Dheeraj. He seems to be looking elsewhere. I follow his gaze. He's looking at Avniel, who in turn is staring someplace else. Avniel is staring at T again, who is nervously fidgeting with her hands. Meeting Asavri upsets her. Avniel's eyes move back and forth from T to Asavri. Dheeraj is following Avniel's eyes.

After a while, Dheeraj looks at me and as our eyes meet, we have the same question.

Is it possible?

I can't focus on the press conference anymore.

Someone requests a photo op. It's denied. 'I promise you, Asavri will return shortly and then you all can ask her all the questions you want. Please pray for her safety and good health.' Bhaskar is politely emphatic.

'Can you tell us where she is going?' someone asks again.

'I told you, someplace in the hills which will not be disclosed because she needs complete privacy to heal. Please respect that.'

'Is it Kausani? Asavri had spoken about Kausani in the past. She wanted to go there.' The reporter is unrelenting. Bhaskar ignores him. I'm sure Avniel will take her somewhere else, someplace unknown. I wouldn't be surprised if Bhaskar finds out later that she isn't where he planned for her to be.

I need to find out a lot of things. What is this gang angle that has been thrown at the press? Why would a gang keep her captive? Is this Avniel's work? Is he on to something? Where is he taking her? I'm certain he will be with her.

Suddenly, I notice Asavri and Avniel aren't here anymore.

'He knows.' Dheeraj is behind me.

'I think he suspects it.'

'Madam, when a reporter suspects something, it's not long before he knows.'

Thirteen

Avniel. THEN.
2016

She bit me when I called her Suzie.

'Ouch!' I yelled. 'That hurt!'

'Good,' she muttered, almost inaudible considering she had me in her mouth. 'I'm not Suzie. I'm Angie.' Thankfully she wasn't the kind who cared, so she went back to what she was doing.

My phone rang. I knew who it was. I didn't need to see the name since I'd assigned a different ringtone to her. Nothing creative, no famous song. Just a loud and piercing tone to break through clutter, chaos, deep slumber and awesome sex; a ringtone that couldn't possibly be missed or ignored.

'Sorry, sex goddess.' I forgot her name again. 'Duty calls.' She didn't complain.

'Yes, Ri. *Bolo?*' I tried hard to sound normal. I signalled the naked what's-her-name, who was getting out of bed, to be silent. She was very understanding and quietly tiptoed to the bathroom.

I could tell something was wrong, very wrong. Asavri could barely speak. She was choking, trying to talk.

'Ri? What happened? Why are you crying like this, baby?'

'Please come quickly, Avniel. It's Rudra again. Please *jaldi aa jao*. Please.' She hung up. I was standing stark naked next to my bed.

'You need a cold shower to fix that.' Angie was already dressed in her butt-clinging jeans and breast-hugging tee.

'Yes, I know.' I looked down and rued the fact that I would need a cold shower to calm my aroused nerves when the better alternative stood right in front of me, albeit all dressed up.

Angie laughed. 'One in bed and another on the phone. Lucky fucker!' I didn't offer an explanation and luckily she wasn't the kind to ask or want one.

'Damn you, Asavri!' I cursed her for making me leave paradise. I was sure it wasn't anything serious. I took my time in the shower.

The phone rang again while I was in the shower. I knew it was her and let it ring. When it rang for the third time, I picked it up.

'Are you on your way?'

'Yup, I'm coming.'

When I reached her room, she was a mess and could barely speak. She looked like she'd seen a ghost. It'd been two hours since she called.

'What took you so long?' She was hiccupping and crying.

I pulled her in my arms and ran my fingers through her hair. 'Shhh. First calm down. Don't talk. Just calm down, Ri. I'm here now.'

'I've been waiting for you. What took you so long?'

'I missed the fast train.' The lie came out easily, without hesitation, and it didn't bother me in the least. I was way past that. 'Now tell me what happened.'

She pointed to her bedroom slippers that were kept in the far corner of the room. Then she took me to the bathroom and pointed at the toothbrush holder that was kept near the WC on the floor.

'That's weird. Toothbrush holder should be on the slab next to the washbasin.' I looked at her puzzled. 'That's strange. What's it doing there?'

'There's more. Come here and see my closet.' She slid open the door. I didn't know what I was supposed to notice. Neat arrays of clothes, folded and piled atop each other.

'I don't get it, Ri. What are you trying to tell me?'

'Avniel! I'm the messiest person on the planet. I never arrange my closet like this. It always looks like a tornado hit it. It's that messy. Who made this neat pile? And ... and how did the toothbrush holder land up on the floor all the way near the shit pot? How? And my slippers? I take them off near the side of the bed before going to sleep, not in the far corner of the room.'

Is she losing her shit? She has been through a lot but now she is just being weird. Except for the toothbrush under the WC, nothing else struck me as odd.

'You think I'm going cuckoo, hai na?' She looked like she was inching towards a meltdown, I could tell. I didn't want that to happen.

'Let's calm down, Ri.' I led her out of the bathroom and we sat on the bed.

I went over everything she just told me. Anyone could keep slippers in the far corner of the room and forget.

The toothbrush holder near the shit pot was odd, I had to admit. Her closet … I'd never seen her closet before so I didn't know how messy or organized she was. She looked at me while I sat thinking.

'There's more, right?'

'Yes.' She handed me her mobile.

'What am I supposed to see?'

'Look at the wallpaper, phone book and gallery of pics.' Her fingers were cold, almost icy, as my hand brushed against hers when I took the mobile.

When I saw what was on it, I felt a cold shiver run down my spine. She wasn't being hysterical. Rudra was out to get her.

The wallpaper was a picture from her wedding. The phonebook was totally erased. In the gallery of pics were shots of Asavri from her honeymoon. Half-naked, under a quilt, with smudged vermillion in the parting of her hair; another of her wrapped in a towel. Pictures newly-wed couples take while on honeymoon. I put the mobile on the nearby table.

This wasn't on her mobile. The wallpaper was an image of her singing and the gallery contained pictures of her sessions and others clicked with the contestants. Someone erased the pictures and uploaded these!

'Someone entered the room while I was sleeping, Avniel! And rearranged everything in the room while I slept.' I began shivering. It was a creepy thought.

'When did you last check your phone?'

'Last night before going off to sleep. I checked the alarm. Everything was normal then.' She was still shivering.

How do I prove that it's Rudra? The man is going to such lengths just to get back at his ex-wife? It seems too far-fetched. But who else stands to gain from this?

Tanya. The name occurred to me like a lightning bolt.

She'll do all this just to win a contest ... well, people have done far more for far less. Her mother... Kamini stands to gain a lot if Tanya wins.

The food I'd ordered arrived but both of us had lost our appetites by then. Asavri sat on the wide windowsill, deep in thought. She began doing that thing with her index and middle fingers, tapping them on her upper lip. She was sure to win the contest if she could sustain her sanity, but someone seemed to be hell-bent on messing her up. She wouldn't make it to the top five if she went cuckoo, and that was dangerously close to happening. She *needed* to win. There would be no book deal without a win, the publisher had made that clear. I needed to salvage the situation and come up with a plan, but I was drawing a blank.

We both sat in silence. I had two cups of coffee and took a bite of the cheese sandwich. Asavri didn't touch anything.

'I need to get dressed. Today is an important event. Pandit Dayaram Joshi is doing a classical session with all of us. Just twelve days to go till the finale. Rudra sure has his timing perfect.' She gave a wry laugh. I wanted to say something but words failed me.

'I'll be outside.' I paced the corridor, thinking about how I could prove Rudra or Kamini were behind it all. I decided Tanya was innocent. She's too much of an airhead to plan and execute something of this magnitude.

This has to be Kamini or Rudra. Both of them stand to gain if Asavri loses or leaves the contest in fear. Tanya is sure to win if Asavri abstains, which in turn will benefit Kamini's political ambitions, and Rudra wants his revenge. The two must have teamed up … but how do I prove that?

When Asavri called me back in, she was dressed for the day. Well, almost. Her eyes looked tired. There was a tremor in her voice as she spoke. She was trying to smile. In fact, she was smiling too much to hide what was on her mind. She stood near the mirror, applying eyeliner. Her hands shook too much and she was unable to do it.

'Let me do it for you.' I didn't know I could apply eyeliner on a woman so well. I did the rest for her too. Touched her lips with gloss, finished with compact.

'You're supposed to apply compact first.' There was a hint of an actual smile on her face.

'I'll do it right the next time.' She put her arms around my hips and buried her face in my crotch. It was awkward and we both laughed at it.

'Can you stay back today?'

'Yes, I will. Don't worry, I'm not leaving you alone.' I wrote a message to my editor. Everyone at the office knew about my Asavri connection. Of course, they tried to ruin it and get me ousted, but I didn't allow that. Actually, she didn't – Asavri told my editor that she didn't want anyone other than me from *Filmfare*. So my status in the office was somewhat revived, though I knew the bastards were betting on me to fuck it up. But I knew I wouldn't.

'It's done, Asavri. I'll be here all day. You focus on the session today.' She walked into my arms and we hugged each other tight. I could feel a sob starting to rise.

'No. No more tears, Asavri. You've cried enough. I'll think of something to tackle this and you win the bloody contest. The only thing that will silence everyone is your victory.'

It was past 5 p.m. when her session ended. I hadn't moved an inch from the chair outside the hall where her session was on. I wanted her to see me when she stepped out.

'How was it?'

'It could have been a lot better if the day was a normal one but I think I was fine.'

'Let's grab some food. I haven't eaten all day.'

She dropped the bomb after we ordered. We sat perched on chairs in the far corner of the terrace garden outside the coffee shop, an unhindered view of the sea and the faraway horizon before us. The evening walkers were heading home. The hawkers were wrapping up, the day's business done with as it was a weekday. Few strays were strolling around, expecting some crumbs. They would soon go towards the main portion of Juhu Beach where the crowd throngs. Few lovers walked aimlessly, in no hurry to get anywhere, hopeful to stretch the aimless meandering and pointless dreaming of a future together which both knew wouldn't fructify. Some of them would take advantage of the approaching darkness and touch each other.

'I've been thinking all day, Asavri. I—' She didn't allow me to finish, not that I had a grand plan to unveil. What she had thought of on her own was indeed ingenious.

'How soon can you arrange a TV interview or a press conference?'

'Huh? Why a press conference?'

'I want to tell the whole world what Rudra did. He's threatening me with the truth. I will tell the truth. I'm sick of being scared and terrified, Avniel.'

I couldn't believe what I was hearing. The look on my face said it all.

'No, I'm serious, Avniel. I don't want to be scared anymore. I don't want to live in fear. I just want to live my life, and if Rudra thinks he can threaten me then he is bloody mistaken.' She glared at me. She looked angry.

'Let's not be hasty, Asavri.' I wondered if she had considered the consequences of what she was suggesting.

'I'm not being hasty. I have been thinking about this all day. You know, when I sing, everything becomes clear. I want to do this, Avniel.'

Something had changed inside her. It was almost like she had shifted gears. Whatever Rudra or Kamini or Tanya had hoped to achieve by terrifying her, it had had the opposite effect on Asavri.

'Can you do it, Avniel?'

'Yes, I can.'

I got it organized by the next morning. Bhaskar was briefed in advance and he was unable to contain his excitement. Asavri was an ace singer with a raw, untutored talent that was last seen in Kishore Kumar. And there was so much drama in her personal life that the public was already hooked and the growing viewership couldn't seem to have enough of her. Money was rolling in. Bhaskar, who is always proper, speaks with carefully considered words and displays just the right amount of excitement, looked deliriously happy. I'm pretty sure he could see the TRPs shooting up and hear the cash registers ringing.

At the press conference, Asavri sat like a statue. Cold, distant and resolute. Our eyes met once. I thought I would see tears in them. They were dry. Her jaws were set tight, almost clenched, as though she were biting into her gums. She was holding herself tight like one does before an injection. Her palms were clutching her knee; I knew she was trying to stop them from trembling. She kept them away from the glare of the reporters and cameras as she spoke about how Rudra had slut-shamed her.

'I told my husband on our honeymoon that I got drunk and had sex with someone while I was in college. It was a stupid thing, what happened between me and the other guy. It meant nothing. It was nothing but a huge mistake. But it was too much honesty for him. He wanted a virgin wife, which I wasn't. So he took me back home, humiliated me and my entire family, called me a whore and left me. My father suffered a stroke because of it and my mom sank into a state of delirium. I was asked to leave home. I was told I had shamed my family and that I wasn't one of them because I was adopted – a discarded rag my father had picked up.'

The room erupted with questions, but Asavri held her calm.

'Tell me, why did I pay such a big price for a mistake? Yes, I admit it was stupid to get drunk and have sex with a stranger. My bigger mistake was being so honest. I should have kept quiet and none of this would have happened. Now that I'm trying to make a life for myself as a singer, my ex-husband, unable to bear my success, is threatening me. What have I done to deserve this?'

I stood aside, watching plain-Jane Asavri turn into a fiery woman demanding justice. It was like watching a dormant volcano explode. It wasn't a hasty outburst of angry words. Quite the contrary, actually. It was a steely, determined voice, motivated by anger and pain, sending out a clear message: 'Don't mess with me.'

She's really got balls.

For the first time since I'd met her at Mehboob Studios, when I'd dismissed her as a nobody, I was impressed with her. I knew it then that she would win ... not just because she had a God-gifted voice.

She has nerves of steel. She's a born winner. She's lost everything ... and when one has nothing more to lose, that's when they become fearless and unstoppable.

But I wasn't prepared for what she said next.

'My ex-husband's name is Rudra Chatterjee. He works with IKA TV.'

Shefali stepped in to control the spate of questions. As expected, a tsunami of hatred for Rudra was unleashed.

Social media exploded within minutes. #ImWithAsavri began trending like wildfire. Rudra was beaten up by women outside a café in Andheri. Subsequently, Bhaskar made two announcements: Asavri would have a 24/7 security detail and Rudra was sacked with immediate effect.

Asavri stayed quiet, almost aloof. I stayed with her all day but we barely spoke. She didn't say much since the press conference.

'I have burnt all my bridges, Avniel,' she told me after two days of near silence.

'I can never go back now. When I left Shantipur, I promised Pishi I wouldn't tell anyone about what happened. When Rudra brought me back within three days of our honeymoon, humiliated Baba, left me at home and went away, Pishi had said that they would cook up some story about Rudra being in love with someone else. Even when I left home, she reminded me to never tell anyone what had really happened. Now I've told the whole country. I can never go back. Ever. I'm truly alone in this world.'

I couldn't bring myself to utter yet another lie and tell her I'd be there for her always. I just slipped my hand into hers and held it tight.

Later that night, I wrote down everything she'd said. I didn't want to miss anything. I added some of my thoughts to it.

She just wants to belong. A family to call her own. She hoped that if she won the contest, the family would accept her back – the winner. She'd win their hearts by winning the contest.

It was shaping up to be a kickass book. All that I needed to do was make her agree to the idea of the book. I knew that wouldn't be easy.

But then something happened a week before the grand finale. All the contestants were invited to a party at Vodka-Tequila. It was the latest pub and dance bar in Juhu that everyone wanted to be seen at. For all Mumbaikars, VT stood for Victoria Terminus station. The pub gave 'See you at VT' a new and fun meaning. That gathering was only for contestants but I snuck my way in.

Things got a little crazy that night when a fire broke out. Not a huge inferno but a fire nevertheless. All of us got out safely when suddenly someone started yelling that Tanya was stuck inside. How did she even get there? I hadn't seen her all evening. Someone had said that she wanted to be at home with her mom before the finale. So how did she land up at VT? Before anyone could react, Asavri dashed inside and came out within minutes, dragging an almost limp Tanya out of the flames.

The fire made the next day's headline but what no one could stop talking about was how Asavri saved Tanya. The picture of a coughing Asavri half carrying Tanya out of the fire remained etched in everyone's memory. I had the good sense to click many pictures with my phone. I knew they would come in handy for the book.

A week later, Asavri sailed through the finale, singing with a smile, her trademark style by now. She was declared the undisputed winner of *Indian Koel* 2016, winning by an unprecedented margin of five lakh votes between her and Tanya, who was the first runner-up.

I think even Kamini accepted the results. She even tried to make one last attempt to get her political ropes around Asavri in the public rally. A few days after the win, thousands gathered in Azad Maidan to see and hear their favourite participant. Never before in the country had so many people, young and old, turned up for a singer who had just won a contest. Everyone just wanted to hear her sing and see her in the flesh. The orphan girl who was abandoned by her birth mother and adopted by a childless couple only to be discarded by her newly married husband who slut-shamed her. Homeless and alone, she came to Mumbai and won the contest against all odds. She had the country in a hypnotic frenzy.

Kamini addressed the crowd and said, 'Asavri is Mumbai's child. She isn't alone. She's our girl—'

Asavri didn't allow her to finish. She stepped up, took the mike and said in an unhesitating voice, 'I'm nobody's child. I'm an orphan. I'm alone and I'm okay with that. All I want to do is sing. I'm here to sing and entertain you.'

She then began singing her winning number and the crowd exploded. It was past dusk. Everyone lifted their mobiles with the flashlights turned on. As thousands of mobile screens shone across the maidan, it seemed like stars from the sky had descended on earth.

I'm nobody's child. Just like that, I got the title of the book.

The darkness of the approaching night descended upon us. Kamini retreated into the far corner of the stage. I saw the look on her face.

She looked like she could kill.

A month later, while on a road trip to cities around the country, our car smashed into a lorry and Asavri, who was in the front seat, died on impact.

Fourteen

Avniel. NOW.
2018

I'm in the car with Asavri. Again. After two years. Road journeys have made me nervous and sick ever since the accident. I take the road only if I absolutely must, if other modes of transport are not an option. The few times that I do, I knock myself out with two tablets of Domstal. I sleep through it. Anything to avoid seeing the approaching trucks race by. But today, I can't afford to be knocked out. Asavri is with me and I have to be in my senses.

The AC in the Innova with dark windows is very effective but beads of sweat form on my forehead regardless.

Once again, I tell the driver to drive slowly. I have said it four times already, this is the fifth.

'He isn't driving fast. Are you feeling unwell?' she suddenly speaks. It's the first time in two months that she has spoken to me. I don't want to remind her of the accident. 'You haven't recovered since it happened? The accident...?' She sees me clutch the side of the seat and maybe also notices how I'm holding my breath.

I'm surprised she's talking about the accident. I can't decide whether I should admit it or not ... While I'm considering my options, she answers, 'The accident … It was very bad.'

'Is that when Monty took care of you?' The therapist has instructed me to casually ask questions. *Just weave in small queries as part of a normal conversation and wait for her to reply. Don't push*. I remember her words.

Asavri turns her face away. I don't repeat my question but watch her closely. She's scratching the upholstery on the sidebar. Her nails leave an impression on the leather. Though the therapist has given me detailed instructions on how to deal with her, I'm nervous. I feel ill-equipped to handle her delicate situation and don't press the subject. I don't want her to have a meltdown in the car. Both of us retreat into silence. I close my eyes to avoid looking at the road and thinking of the accident. The moment I shut my eyes, I see Asavri in the front seat, holding her camera phone out of the window.

'See, Avniel, the moon is so beautiful tonight.' That's the last thing I had heard her say. Next, I saw the blinding headlights of a truck smashing into our car, and everything went black.

I wake up with a jump. I'm drenched in sweat and my heart feels like it's going to burst out of my chest. I can't breathe. I need water. I need air. I try to move but can't. My legs are twisted, mangled and in a bloody mesh. I'm sitting in a pool of blood, some gushes out of my mouth … I try to scream but the blood gags me.

'Sirji, sirji … *kya hua? Aap theek ho?*' The voice sounds faint, as though it's coming from far away. I open my eyes to see the driver next to me.

'Huh?' is all I manage to mumble. I take the bottle of water the driver is holding and step out of the car. I splash the cold water on my face. It feels good against my burning skin. I stay outside for a while, take a few steps to breathe in gulps of air and steady my pounding heart. We are well into the Western Ghats, which is no longer the lush green carpet it turns into during the monsoon. The green is already a burnt yellow and brown. But the air is fresh; much better than that of the city. Though there's some traffic on the expressway, it's nothing like the traffic-clogged Mumbai streets. The cars zip past us, blatantly ignoring the speed limit. Who can resist the temptation to push the accelerator on a road like this? Most give in, but speed terrifies me. Even the sound of whizzing cars makes me nervous. I want the road journey to get over.

I look at Asavri through the open door. She is unaffected and distant. Staring out of the window, lost in her world of thoughts, of Monty or whatever it is she thinks about. I feel stupid for allowing a nightmare to feel so real. I get back into the car in the seat next to the driver and force myself to talk with him.

We aren't far now. Scenic Valley is about four hours from Bandra. About another hour and we should be there.

Scenic Valley is beyond Lonavla. Fifty acres of luxury and state-of-the-art private security. Surrounded by the verdant Western Ghats and away from the tourist mayhem of Lonavla, this sprawling resort is tucked away like a well-kept secret. Funded by a Dubai-based business tycoon and designed by world-class architects and designers, it's a place for the rich and the famous to get away from public glare or when they want to recoup.

I'd met the owner at a book event in Dubai. The semi-literate buffoon collected art, books and everything else that had a hefty price tag to merely move up the social ladder. He liked to befriend authors, only bestselling ones, to brag about in his parties. He loved *I'm Nobody's Child* and commissioned a book on his own life. I ghostwrote it and was paid an obscene amount in return. He printed one lakh copies and kept them in his offices across the world and in every room of every hotel he owned in Europe and North America. He told everyone he wrote it. The idiot can barely string together a sentence in English.

Delighted by my work, he gave me a lifetime free pass for checking into Scenic Valley anytime, for as long as I please. He also readily agrees to my request that no one be allowed in while I am there. I tell him that I'm working on my next book and need complete solitude.

He doesn't need to know about Asavri. Besides, the book bit isn't entirely untrue. I *am* writing my sequel.

Fifteen

Kamini. NOW.
2019

The phone is ringing again. This is the third time since morning. An unknown number. Truecaller says Bhai Saab. I'm too busy and agitated to take calls from unknown people. I throw my phone in my Birkin and focus on the mayhem in the room. The list of prospective candidates for the national elections is the agenda for the day. If all had gone well, I would have had nothing to worry about. But nothing is right anymore. I'm being ignored. The party that was eating out of my hand is sidelining me and this has been happening for a while now. The signs that were subtle earlier are loud and clear now.

I was unable to meet Patil when he was in town. I'm unable get an appointment with him in Delhi either. Now every request to speak with him is met with a polite excuse: 'He is tied up and will get back to you at the soonest.'

In politics, it's all about where you stand in the circle of power, how close you are to the nerve centre and what's the tone in which people speak with you. It's always the low-life parasites, the ones who hover around the source of power, the flies around the honeypot – the flunkies, yes-men and secretaries – who echo their masters' attitude and convey to you that your time is up.

I'm at the party office with fifty or more screaming men and a few women; each of them are trying to talk louder than the other. Rathod and Palgaonkar are leading the show. The fifty screaming idiots think they still have a chance at getting a party ticket. The list is already drawn up; one or two spots might be vacant.

I'm in the far corner of the room. I'm the only one who isn't contributing to the rising decibels of the room. That's not how I work. I can see Dheeraj in conversation with Rathod. He is getting agitated, I can tell. It's not very often that Dheeraj loses his cool. He seems frazzled nowadays. He should be. Nothing he does is right anymore. Maybe he's lost his mojo. Everyone has an expiration date. Maybe his is near.

Suddenly, I feel a pair of eyes on me. It's Palgaonkar. He is in conversation with a hopeful candidate; more like silently trying to pretend as though he is listening but he isn't really. He is looking at me, unblinkingly. The staring match goes on for a while and then a tiny smile breaks on his lips. With his eyes still on me, he presses a switch on the wall. A piercing sound rings through the room, silencing everyone. He keeps his finger on the switch till everyone is quiet. This isn't the first time the switch has been pressed. It's often used in meetings like these and sometimes it doesn't even work. Today it does.

Palgaonkar addresses Rathod, who doesn't bother standing on a stool. Today, the shortest man in the room is the most powerful. He has the final list of the candidates from Mumbai who have made the cut to contest in the approaching national elections. He begins calling the names. I know I'm not on that list. I didn't make it. I get up and begin walking towards the door. Just as I reach the door, I hear it.

'Kamini Pratap Singh.'

I spin around to look at Rathod and Palgaonkar in surprise. I'm not the only one in the room who is surprised. I'd been written off by everyone. Hell, I'd written off myself. All eyes turn towards me. Dheeraj is clearly stumped, almost dumbstruck. He is walking towards me, all smiles and barely able to contain his excitement. I start walking towards the podium. Palgaonkar has a strange look on his face. I don't know what it means. I want to find out how this happened. Just when I reach him, I feel the mobile vibrate inside my bag.

Who is this persistent bugger?

It will have to wait.

'Palgaonkarji, thank you. This is a huge surprise. A very pleasant one if I may add. May I have a word with you?'

'Sure, but before we speak, there's someone else who would like to have a word with you.' He signals me to follow him and hands me his mobile. I don't see the name on the screen; I'm too shaken and stirred by what just happened.

'Hello,' I sound rattled. I clear my throat and repeat myself, hoping it sounds more lucid and confident this time.

'Kamini.' A heavy and slow voice replies.

'Patilji!' I can recognize his voice even in my sleep. The slow cadence; the heavy, deep-throated, measured voice, which he knows is his signature.

'Yes, Kamini. I know the past few months have been difficult but you're an asset to the party. There's been a lot of negative media light on you but we can't forget the good work you've done. We have a long road to travel together, Kamini. Let's work towards that. See you in Delhi.' The line goes dead.

'How did this happen? I thought … thought …'

'Kaminiji, the party high command has great expectations from you. The media glare on your family because of the Asavri incident is most unfortunate. But Patilji and the party want to lay a strong foundation of governance and you are part of their plan. Just make sure nothing goes wrong from here on.'

The phone in my bag is ringing again. I fish it out, thinking it might be from the office or Tanya. It isn't. It's the same unknown number. I ignore it.

The rest of the day goes by in a blur. I'm in non-stop meetings to detail planning for campaign strategy; I barely have any time. I know for sure that while the party could do without me, they can't ignore the money I bring in. I'm dispensable, my money isn't. I plan on making myself indispensable.

I grab a very late lunch. It is almost 5 p.m. The day has left me tired but excited. Dheeraj approaches me with a 'I need to tell you something' look.

'What is it?'

'Madam, Asavri isn't in the city. They have been fooling everyone and sending us in circles about where she is. She left soon after the press meet. I've been trying to find out her current location, but no luck.'

'So not only has Elvis left the building, Elvis has left the city. With Avniel, of course.'

'No one has seen him around either. His assistant is saying that he is on holiday. A solo holiday. Rumour has it things have gone south with his live-in girlfriend. So he's on a R & R getaway.'

I push away the fresh salad that I'd ordered and was enjoying till a while ago. Till Dheeraj came and gave me the update.

'Don't give me any more bad news, Dheeraj. Why can't you handle the issue? What's the hitch here? I'm on my way to Delhi, Dheeraj. There can be no speed bumps. Where has that bitch gone? How much does Avniel know? What we have is a huge pile of only questions, Dheeraj. No answers. I want answers. I want to know where that dog took his bitch. Handle it, and this time make it go away for good. Don't show me your fucking face till you have good news for me.' I pick up my bag and walk out of the room. I can feel a migraine coming on.

Bloody Asavri. I'll kill you with my bare hands this time, bloody bitch.

It's quite late when I finally reach my bedroom. What a day it's been! A rollercoaster ride, really. Never thought the day would end on such a positive note. I throw my bag on the bed, undrape my sari, let it lie on the floor, as I do with my blouse and other pieces of clothing. I know they will be picked up and taken away while I shower. My staff is inconspicuous, smooth and quick. That's how I like it.

I stand in the bathroom and pull out the carved ivory stick that has been holding my bun in place throughout the day. My hair is still thick and lustrous. After being encased in a tight bun all day, it doesn't believe it's being offered freedom to fall. The semi-opened bun rests near the nape of my neck. I release it further and it tumbles over my naked chest, covering one breast. I fling my mane behind, raise my arms and watch my breasts heave up. I touch my nipples to wake them up. They take their time. They respond better to an unfamiliar touch. It's been a while. Quite a while, in fact. I place my hands on my waist and turn.

'Not bad for a forty-six-year-old.'

I don't admit the truth even to myself. My dark skin glistens in the light, my breasts perk up when I raise my arms. There is a slight sag. I hate to admit it, but there is. I turn to one side. My stomach is still flat-ish. My legs are toned and tapering down to slim ankles. My hips jiggle and feel fleshy. Pratap would have loved to slap them around. He liked full hips and always complained that I didn't have enough flesh on my butt. Suddenly, I miss Pratap. He was good to me; in life and in bed. I smile and think of some of the games we played together and with others. His favourite, also mine, was watching a man and a woman pleasure me. It excited him like a small boy being handed a new toy. Such a pity he met with a sudden and unexpected accident. I was sorry to see him gone, but not for long. Publicly, I mourned him for a year; a grieving widow always makes for a great start to a political story.

Dheeraj has done so much for me all these years, it's really a pity he's starting to slip up. I'd hate to have to get rid of him.

I tell myself not to think of that now and return my focus on my tummy, which, to my horror, feels a tad jiggly. 'This needs better workout, as do my hips.' Asavri has made me miss quite a few gym sessions.

Stop it! Stop it right there! No more thinking about her today. You are all set for the South Block, I reprimand and remind myself.

I decide to soak myself in a luxurious bath to wash away the day's fights. I turn on the faucet for the tub to fill up and select the essential oil that I want to add. I choose rosemary.

'Scotch on the rocks,' I pick up the phone and command. My latest poison is Japanese whisky. I've been saving my latest purchase for a special occasion. Today deserves the Yamazaki, a fifty-year-old single malt from the limited edition I procured. At $3,00,000, it certainly doesn't get any better than this. Ever since I embarked on the journey to become the champion of the aam junta, I had to stop splurging on bags and shoes. Though I can't let go of my Hermès Birkin, I most certainly can't be seen carrying the Leiber Precious Rose which has 1,016 diamonds and 1,169 pink sapphires. It's the rarest of rare bejewelled bags, the only one in the world, and I don't have it. So I've turned my focus towards whisky – the liquid gold.

The tub isn't full yet. I put on my silk gown and walk back into my room to turn on some music. I notice the mobile; it has slipped out of my Birkin. I decide to check a few messages. Also, the phone never stopped ringing after the list went out to the press.

I scroll down to see who all called. I know all of them barring one number. Eight missed calls. The last one was at 5 p.m. Someone is desperately trying to reach me.

The Yamazaki arrives along with a cheese platter, few slivers of apple, a pear chilled to perfection and two tiny squares of dark chocolate. The liquid gold in my palm swirls as I twirl the glass and bring it to my nose. Yes, there's a strong oak. *The oak grip is deep,* as the connoisseur had described it. I take a sip. I let it roll around my tongue as I taste aromatic wood after which I take it in. I close my eyes, enjoying the predominantly fruity finish. It's beyond exquisite. I lean back on the throw cushions on my bed, pick a slice of pear and a little cheese.

When the mobile vibrates on the bed, I realize the multitude of messages and calls that I need to reply to. I begin scrolling through the messages.

Among the host of congratulatory messages lies a message, unnamed and unmarked. By now I know it's from the unknown number, the person who called me eight times during the day. Curiosity makes me click on it before the others.

I open the message. It's in Hindi, typed in English.

'*Issko sunno*. Then call.' Short, cryptic and crude. Clearly a person who isn't comfortable with English and lacks phone etiquette. There's an audio clip with the message. I press on the play icon.

I go cold. The room begins to slowly swirl, gradually gaining momentum as I feel myself getting sucked into a vortex. I barely manage to put the glass on the side table as I sit up straight on the bed and listen to the audio clip again and again.

'Don't kill her. She needs to stay alive. I need Asavri to stay alive.'

Sixteen

Avniel. NOW.
2018

'Ask her about Monty,' I tell Doctor Parul before she steps into the room to start the session.

Doctor Parul is the leading clinical psychologist at Anandmay Hospital. She visits us thrice a week to conduct sessions with Asavri.

What kind of a name is Parul for a psychologist with fancy degrees and decades of experience? Such an inconsequential and secretarial kind of a name. I expected her muddle-headed secretary to be a Parul.

Doctor Parul is short, very short, but not the kind that can be ignored or missed. Very stern and official with me, she makes no bones about expressing displeasure when I press her to ask about Monty, other members of the house, the girls, etc.

'Both you and the police commissioner are making a big mistake by pushing me. The patient is in a very fragile state. If her mind snaps, she will sink further into the state she's already in. She will be of no use to anyone if she goes mad and ends up in a cell.' This Parul sure has gumption.

She doesn't mince words. I know for a fact that she has said the same to the commissioner too.

She is standing outside the door with her right hand on the door frame and her index finger drumming on it. She stares right at me. She wants to sort this out before she begins the session. She's in trousers and a linen shirt that's rolled up to her elbows. Her hair is cropped very short, but not in a fashionable way; it's just very short. Dr Parul looks like a woman who doesn't care much about the daily rigmarole of maintaining a stylish cut.

I decide to be compliant, though I'm tired of being so. 'Parul … it's critical …' She stops me before I can continue.

'Dr Parul,' she corrects me, raising one eyebrow as though to say: *Don't you dare make that mistake again.*

I correct myself. 'Dr Parul. It's critical that she talks about the people who held her and the place she was kept in. I need to be present in the sessions.'

'This goes against doctor–patient confidentiality.' I expected to lock horns on the matter and have my fail-safe ready – the commissioner on speed dial.

'If the mental doctor gives you grief, Avniel, call me.' Those were his words. So I connect the *mental doctor* with the cop head and let them fight it out.

'Dr Parul, the commissioner would like a word with you.' She gives me a look that says, *I know you are pulling rank on me and I detest it.*

I know what he's telling her. She doesn't even get past the pleasantries once I hand her the phone. She's listening intently.

'She was held captive by a gang we have been trying to break for years. She must have evidence against Bhai and his notorious Zeher gang; they're wanted for many cases. We can use whatever she tells us. Avniel will not disrupt the session.'

What he actually means, but doesn't tell her, is that the cop force has been under a lot of pressure since the girl they declared dead turned up alive and ravaged. They need to find the gang and make a parade out of it to salvage their image.

Her face looks dark as I spot a muscle in her jaw flex. I once again know what must have come from the other end. 'Avniel will sit in on every session. If you can't bend the rules to help me get the bad guys, I can find another doctor.'

I can see she is angry. Dr Parul isn't the kind of woman who likes being told what to do or pushed around.

I fear she is on the verge of picking up her bags and leaving. She seems like the kind of person who values her scruples more than anything. Before she says anything further, I add, 'Please agree. Do you want Asavri to be in the hands of some quack these cops get? Do you think they will get someone with your credentials and experience? Think of the damage that can do. Please help her. She has already been through hell, don't let it happen again. I want her to get better.'

'Really? Her well-being is the only concern you have?' She raises her eyebrows quizzically.

I reply with a sigh. I don't want to argue with her on this and nothing I say will salvage my image.

She decides not to put me through the wringer and says, 'Okay, if the patient agrees then I have no objection.'

I am not surprised with Asavri's nod of approval. She has always trusted me and, thankfully, no matter what cloud gathers over her mind, I am still the good guy. Though I don't feel like one.

As the session begins, I take my seat in the corner. We are in the study, a large room lined with bookshelves containing everything from the great masters to the bestselling pulp fiction. I can say with absolute certainty that none of them have ever been read by the visitors who have stayed here. Though they are meticulously cleaned; not a speck of dust on any of them.

'Why don't you lie back on the recliner, Asavri?' The doctor gently tries to ease her back on the soft cushion of the leather recliner.

'Why? Why do you want me to lie down? What will you do?' Asavri's retort is a scared whimper. Her lips are shivering as her hands grip the sides.

'Nothing at all, dear. We will just talk. I thought you might be more comfortable lying down. But suit yourself. Sit if that's what you prefer.'

When the doctor draws the blinds, making the room cosy, with feeble light filtering in through the sides of the blinds, Asavri speaks up again, 'Why are you making the room dark?'

'It's too sunny outside, Asavri. I'm trying to make the room cosy so that we can talk.'

'I don't like the dark. Please let the light in. Please.' She's almost pleading.

'Of course, Asavri. Whatever you are comfortable with. This is your space. Anything that you don't want, won't happen. If you want to stop, we will stop. Okay?' The doctor tilts the blinds to allow for light to come in.

'Are you sleeping well, Asavri?'

'Yes, I am.'

'Are you eating properly?' When she doesn't reply, the doctor looks at me and I shake my head.

'Avniel here tells me that you aren't. You need to eat and get strong so that you can sing. The whole country is waiting to hear you again. I know I am.' I've always found the gentle voice and I-am-your-friend tone of therapists to be bloody fake. They charge a bomb by the hour and pretend like they care. I wish she would just get on with it.

'Do you know where you are, Asavri?'

'Yes.'

'Can you tell me where we are?'

'I think … it's beyond Lonavla.'

'That's right. Do you know what month it is?'

'December.'

'You're doing good, Asavri. Today, we are going to talk about a person. Okay?'

'Who?' I can't see her face from where I'm sitting but I can tell by the tone that she is worried, tense.

'You often speak about Monty. Why don't we talk about him?'

Silence follows. I can see her pick at the design on the armchair with her nail. She is scratching the fabric and avoiding eye contact with the doctor.

The doctor pauses, waiting … observing Asavri's face.

'Take your time, Asavri.'

After what feels like a long time, she says, almost whispers, 'Can you tell him I didn't run away? I lost him in the crowd and then couldn't find him. He will be angry, thinking I ran away. I didn't.' She's gripping the armrest tightly.

'Yes, I will tell him that and he won't be angry. I promise. Does he get angry often? Asavri? Did he hurt you? You can tell me. This is a very safe place. No one will hurt you.'

'Monty got me food. Sometimes he got angry but it was my fault. He is my friend.' This is getting us nowhere. We are just going round and round in circles. I scribble something on a piece of paper and hold it up for the doctor to see. I've been told not to talk or make any noise during the session, hence the scribbled note.

Ask her about the House. Does she remember seeing the doctors and nurses there? Or any other girls? Something about the House. I underline the word *'House'* to stress its importance.

'Okay, Asavri. Let's talk about something else, shall we? Tell me something about the House. What do you remember?'

'It's always very dark inside. The windows are small and have grills. The doors have big locks. No one can leave.'

'Did you try to leave, Asavri?'

'Yes. Many times.'

'What happened?'

'Monty brought me back. He hurt someone.'

Her voice trails off and I can feel the tremor in it. I have a recorder in my pocket that the doctor knows nothing about. Even though Dr Parul has agreed to hand over the recordings of every session to the cops, the commissioner's orders were clear: 'Carry a recorder. I don't trust these mental doctors.'

'I don't want to talk about that. Please.' She is wiping her eyes with the back of her hand.

The doctor continues, 'Okay. Then tell me something else. When were you brought to the House, Asavri?'

'After the accident.'

'So you must have been badly hurt because of the accident. Were there doctors and nurses to take care of you?'

'No! NO! NO!' Asavri bolts up right on the recliner, sits on the edge and screams, 'No! Please! NO!' Then she begins to cry, choking over her words.

'Calm down, Asavri. Calm down. Nothing bad will happen to you here.' The doctor rushes to her side and puts her arms around her.

'I don't want to talk about them. I don't want to talk.' She is shivering, and suddenly I smell urine in the room. The doctor and I exchange looks. Soon Asavri realizes it too and looks ashamed. 'I'm sorry. I'll clean it up.'

'Don't worry about it.' The doctor leads her out of the room.

She peed out of sheer fright on being asked about the House! *What did you see? What happened to you in there?* As I wait for housekeeping, I remember a conversation I had with the police commissioner a few days before her release from the hospital.

I'd given him the paper napkin I'd found in her clothes. Madhubala Biryani House. His men found the restaurant in Pahargaon. It was in a slum called Zeher Gully. Many shopkeepers confirmed that Asavri was kept captive by Bhai and his men in the Ghar. Everyone calls it Ghar – the House.

He also told me, 'Monty is Bhai's younger brother of sorts. Bhai is the head of the gang, and Monty has a thing for Asavri. He is a fan; used to watch every episode of *Indian Koel*. Everyone in the slum knows how crazy he is about her. He made sure everyone voted for Asavri during the contest.

While Asavri was there, sometimes, though very rarely, the two were seen roaming the streets, going to a local fair, eating in a restaurant. They seemed to be in love.' His words seemed too incredible to believe but there might have been some truth to them.

The commissioner said, 'Ask her about Monty. She has been in the House, Avniel. Not just lived there, but survived and escaped. That's a first. Over the last few years, many girls have been kidnapped by the gang and we haven't found any traces of them or any proof to tie their disappearance to the Zeher gang. The gang sells these girls to sex cells in Dubai and Bangkok. About two years ago, about the same time as the accident, two doctors and three nurses went missing. They were never found. But they were seen in that area. I have a strong suspicion that they were hired to treat Asavri and then killed so that word about her having survived didn't leak. She must know a lot about what went on in the House. She needs to talk, Avniel. Make her talk or I will.'

I could tell he was under tremendous pressure to crack the case but his last words worried me. *Make her talk or I will.* The last thing I want is for cops to interrogate her. She's too fragile and I don't want the cops anywhere near her right now. They show no mercy. But I also know that if Asavri doesn't talk, nothing will keep the cops away and I won't be able to stop them from hurting her more.

I find Dr Parul in the living room and chat with her. I need to understand a few things.

'Why isn't she talking more clearly about the gang leader, about Monty and her time in that house? What's holding her back? Has she lost her memory?' I'm grasping at straws.

'No. There's no memory loss. She remembers her home in Shantipur, the name of her school, names of her friends, the contest and that she's the winner. She hasn't forgotten anything, Avniel. She is fully aware of where she is, which month we are in.'

'Then why isn't she telling us about the people who kept her captive? What happened there? Who were they? She should be keen to spill out everything so that the cops can get those bastards.'

'Avniel, this is a clear case of traumatic bonding, popularly known as Stockholm syndrome. Her life was in grave danger. She believed she would never be free. She had come to believe and accept that she would be abused and raped brutally till she died. In this scenario, there was one person with whom she possibly bonded emotionally. Someone who showed her kindness, even love; small acts of kindness, which to her seemed like the gift of life. He became her emergency god. She believes that if she tells on him, it would be a betrayal.'

'She believes the man who kept her captive and hurt her is her god?' There's more disbelief in my tone than on my face but I have read enough books to know this is very real.

'Don't try to see the situation from a logical or rational perspective, Avniel. When the human mind crumbles, there's no telling which direction it could go in. You've told me about her earlier life, with her parents, her marriage, getting rejected by her husband, followed by abandonment from her family and then finding out that she's an orphan. These incidents caused a lot of mental trauma and then she lands up in hell, where she's brutalized daily for months. Then comes someone who shows her a little mercy.'

'Monty.' From where I stand, I can see Asavri standing near the glass door, staring at the sprawling lawns outside.

'Yes. Monty is someone very special but she's also scared of him. She has said multiple times that Monty will be upset that she's been gone for so long. She's also asked me if I can tell him that it's not her fault. That she didn't run away. She's terrified of him but also believes that he is the one who can save her.'

'Yesterday, she asked me if she could step out into the lawn,' I tell the doctor. The puzzled look on my face says it all.

'Yes. She has been manipulated with so much fear that she asks for permission to do even the smallest of things. This is a classic abuser–abused pattern. She must have been severely punished for doing simple things like eating, drinking or even stepping out of her room without seeking permission.'

I see that she hasn't moved, unable to take a step to walk into the garden. This is the same woman who decided on her own to call for a press conference and tell the whole world about her ex-husband, Rudra, and his wrongdoings. And now she's waiting for permission to step out into the garden.

The doctor understands my confusion and adds, 'The poor girl has been raped again and again for days, months by different men. They drugged her and abused her. I'm certain she witnessed atrocities that have wrecked her mentally.'

'Then what is the way forward?'

'She has to talk about it. But it can't be rushed. You saw what happened today. When I asked about the doctors and nurses, she reacted very violently. She urinated. That was out of fear. She has certainly seen something ... maybe many horrible things and is terrified to even think of them, leave alone talk. She can't be pushed or it will cause irreparable damage to her psyche. Gradually, I will lead her to confront what happened. To be cured of it, she has to confront and accept it. But very gradually. Avniel, please don't try to play doctor in my absence. Bhaskar wants her cured fast because of reasons both you and I know. The cops want her to talk only because they need the evidence. But please, I repeat myself, please don't try to take this upon yourself ... You have no idea what you're dealing with.' She gives me a hard, unblinking stare.

I promise her I won't. This is a promise I know I will keep. Asavri's blank state terrifies me. She pissed out of fear.

I find Asavri in her room, sitting in a chair and staring at the lawns. I want to sit next to her. Will she feel better if I hold her hand? I take a step or two in her direction and then stop. She's sleeping ... maybe dozing. The doc gave her something to calm her down. I pick up a stole from the bed and place it on her. A strand of hair hangs over her eyes. I move it slowly, careful not to wake her up.

Later in the night, I check all the doors and windows. I have a word with the band of security men I have handpicked. They have been given pictures of Monty, Bhai and a few others.

'No one, I repeat, no one is to be allowed inside the resort,' I tell them again.

I go to her room to give her the night meds. She's in bed with a soft blanket pulled up to her chin. She has placed many pillows around herself, as though making a tiny island. All the lights in the room are switched on. It looks like a floodlit indoor stadium. I step in to switch them off. I barely flick one switch off and she jumps up with a start.

'Please! No. Don't switch them off. I like them on, please.' She's pleading, almost begging.

'Yes, yes. Of course, Asavri, whatever you're comfortable with.' I say hurriedly, trying not to imagine the horrors she must have experienced in the dark. I point to a tiny gadget with a button on it. I tell her what I have told her many times in the day.

'If you need anything, anything at all, press this button. If you feel scared, press this button. Okay? I'm in the next room. When you press this button, a bell will ring on my wristband. See?' I press the button to show her. I do this many times throughout the day so that she knows that I'm right next to her. She nods and pulls the tiny gadget near her pillow. I give her the medicines as per the prescription.

'If you don't mind, can you stay for a while?' This is the first time she's asked me to stay back with her.

'Sure, I will.' I pull up a chair and sit across her.

'Why didn't you look for me? After the accident.' Her voice is feeble.

'I was injured in the accident. When I woke up in the hospital, ten days had passed. They'd cremated a body. Everyone said it was you.' This was the truth … but only partly. I'd busied myself finishing the book; I'd started writing it before the finale. I wanted to finish it fast. The publisher wanted to release the book as soon as possible.

'Let's cash in on her memory while it's still fresh.' Those were his words. I'd agreed. I'd never considered the possibility of her being alive. It suited me just fine that she'd died.

'I thought you'd come looking for me. I was sure you would, but you never came.' I'm finding it difficult to face her. Thankfully, the meds take effect and she falls asleep.

I see her as a curled-up tiny bundle under the quilt, asleep with all the lights on. I think of the girl who liked to sleep in pitch-darkness. I silently tiptoe out of the room, leaving her question unanswered and my guilt hanging heavy on me.

Next morning, I find her seated in a large wing chair by the window. She's still in her night pyjamas and an oversize tee. Shefali bought some clothes for her before we left the hospital. She looks thin, almost bony. Like she needs a good meal. She doesn't eat well, only picks at her food, I've observed. I'm about to call her for breakfast when I notice something and stop.

She's lost in deep thought, her knees drawn up on one of the sofa arms. One elbow is resting on her knee and she's tapping her upper lip with two fingers – index and middle. I stand there without disturbing her, watching her make that gesture. It's not the first time I've seen her do it and she's not the only person who does it.

I call Kay. She answers after four rings. It's early for her. Her voice is still groggy from her sleep as she mumbles, 'Yes, boss.'

I get straight to the point without morning greetings.

'Kay, I need you to do something. I don't know how you'll do it. Just do it.' I know the urgency in my voice has woken up my assistant completely.

'Sure. What is it?'

When I tell her, there's silence from her end. I know she heard me. She is trying to follow my train of thought.

'Are you sure of this, boss?'

'Yes, I am. I'm not wrong on this. I just need scientific proof. That's all.'

'Won't be easy, boss, but I will do it. Don't know how I'll get it, but consider it done.'

Seventeen

Monty. THEN.
2016

It was the yelling that woke me up. Loud cursing, hurried, nervous running and then more shouting. The House was awake very early that day. Usually, people would start waking up around 10 a.m. and everyone would be up and about by 11 a.m. It wasn't an early morning kind of place.

My eyes felt heavy with sleep. But there was too much shouting going on outside my door. I wished I could sleep some more. I slept late, as always watching the latest videos on my phone. I was getting better with my angles and focus. I would watch them again and again.

Why is everyone yelling so much this early? How is Bhai okay with this?

It was coming from the room at the end of the corridor. It overlooked a gutter and the chawl. The room was being prepared for something or someone. The windows had been pulled out and new ones put. The older ones used to rattle in the wind and couldn't be shut properly, allowing the rain to come in like an uninvited guest. The new ones were firm and shut well too. A lot of lights had been fitted. I wondered what all the *chillum-chilli* was about.

Suddenly, the yelling stopped ... there was a long pause and then it started again.

I'm not going to get any sleep. Better go and see what the yelling is about.

It took me a while to get out of bed. *Saala*, my leg always feels sore in the morning. I grabbed the lathi. It was in bed with me. It always is. I never let it out of my sight. One of my legs is shorter than the other; it's always been like that. I need the lathi to support myself while walking. Many years ago, I think when I was twelve, someone played a prank and took away the lathi while I was sleeping. Bhai found the guy and struck him on his leg a few too many times with my lathi. We weren't living in the House then. That *harami* still walks using a lathi. I'd see him sometimes in the market. He'd always scurry away like a scared mouse. He probably wets his pants every time he sees Bhai.

I slowly walked down the corridor. It was usually dark. The tube lights would be switched on all night but that day the corridor was well lit. Some of the girls were scrubbing the black edges of the floor while others were sweeping with a broom. They didn't look too happy to be scrubbing and cleaning after being up all night.

Saali randiyan! *Ask them to fuck and they do so happily. But you tell them to do saaf-safai and they make a face.*

'Monty saab! If you don't mind, can you walk from the side, please?'

That was Ena. She wasn't exactly new but not too old in the House either. We were friends. She'd let me take pictures and videos of her. The latest was one of her bathing and playing with the soap on her body. She was also very flexible and could bend herself in all sorts of ways. I liked her.

Just to annoy her, I stamped around with my foot and the lathi, leaving marks on the floor she had just swept.

'I'll remember this when you want a new video, Monty. *Kutta saala.*' She stuck her tongue out. She was hunched up on the floor, sweeping and bending slightly, giving me a great view of her tight breasts that were too big for the tiny choli she had on. She knew what I was looking at. She bent further with a smile and then yelled, 'Monty, *jaa abhi. Saaf karne de.*' I smiled and moved to one side as I wobbled towards the room where the shouting was coming from.

The girls were adding lots of phenol to the water. The smell was very strong. Phenol was used in large quantities in the House. Especially in the courtyard and in the room on the ground floor after beatings and questioning. It cleans up blood, spit and urine very well.

The last time I remembered the corridor being scrubbed so clean was the day Bhai got married. That was three years prior, I think.

Is Bhai getting married again? Last time didn't end well.

A raunchy local dancing sensation had caught Bhai's eye. When Bhai entered the room after the ceremony, she laughed and called him Natu. Bhai is short. Since then, she lies on the dirty footpath, barely alive. Both her legs were chopped off just above her knees. Someone from the House would give her food. Not every day ... about once or twice a week. It was thrown on the road just a little beyond her reach. Driven crazy by hunger, she'd crawl towards it in an attempt to reach it before the stray dogs. When Bhai decides to punish, he doesn't kill. He keeps you alive and barely breathing.

I hope it's not another wedding.

It wasn't.

'Abey, chuttiye ... maine bola thaa ...'

'Kya bola thaa, saale haramkhor ...'

For the longest time, I'd thought Ramesh's name was Chuttiya. Everyone used to call him by that name so I started calling him Chuttiya bhaiyya. Everyone laughed a lot. Bhai also laughed. He doesn't often but that day he had tears in his eyes. I didn't understand why everyone found it funny. This happened a very long time ago. Everyone teased Ramesh that entire day, calling him Chuttiya bhaiyya. It was a good day. Everyone laughed, joked and then Bhai ordered biryani for everyone. Even the girls. Later that night, Bhai called me and said, 'Monty, his name is Ramesh.' After that day, no one teased Ramesh. When Bhai draws a line, no one crosses it or even dares to come close.

I stood near the door and watched the argument. Bhai was in the room too. I'd never seen him up so early. The pause between the yelling was him speaking. He never raises his voice, and when he is upset, he is barely audible. Everyone is terrified of his silence.

What I could understand was that there was some problem with the room being on the second floor.

'How will we get the stretcher up the narrow staircase?'

'I can carry her in my arms ...'

'*Suar!* Hospital bed ... how will that come up? Carry her in your arms ... *Harami, Bhagwan jab akal baat raha thaa, tu saala kya kar raha thaa ...*'

The yelling stopped suddenly. Everyone shut up. Bhai raised his hand. *Bada mazaa aata thaa* watching Bhai deal with the men.

'Let's not waste more time. It's my mistake. I chose this room. I should have known.' Bhai always takes responsibility for his decisions; right or wrong. Everyone in the room huddled up to him and started apologizing. They spoke all at once.

'*Nahin, Bhai! Nahin. Kya bol rahe ho* … This is on us.' Bhai silenced everyone with a raised hand again. 'Let's not waste time. We have three days. Room on the ground floor. Break the doorway to allow more space. Three days.'

Three days for what?

A room on the ground floor was to be turned into a hospital room. A special generator was brought in so that there would be uninterrupted electricity. The lights go off often in the House. Why did they need a generator just for one room? Who would be staying there? I didn't bother asking. Nobody ever told me anything. Most of the time they didn't even answer when I'd ask a question. They'd just pretend not to hear me. People would walk past me, pushing me as though I wasn't there. Like I was invisible. Even when I fell, no one bothered. I stumble quite often because of my leg. I lived in the House but didn't really exist.

I'd been in the House for as long as I could remember. How long? I don't know. It wasn't the kind of place where you'd count and celebrate the passing of time. You just lived one day at a time. I still remember the one-room hut next to the train line. Bhai and I used to live there. Then one day he came and said that we were leaving. I followed him to the House. In those days, Pilot was the boss. He asked him about me and Bhai replied, 'He's with me. He won't bother you. Just give him a corner and he'll be OK.'

That's where I stayed – in a corner, living on whatever little scraps I could get my hands on. I never asked Bhai, 'Why are we in the House? What next?'

I never ask Bhai any questions.

'Monty!' I almost fell as I tried to turn around in a hurry when I heard Bhai call for me. Maybe he was going to give me something to do? I wanted to do something for him. Anything.

'Stay out of everyone's way. We need to get the room ready in three days. There's not much time Monty, so don't get in anyone's way. Okay?'

He walked away before I could even answer. He knew he would be obeyed. Bhai is always obeyed. No one dares otherwise.

For the next three days everyone worked all day and night to get the room ready. I kept out of everyone's way; watching and waiting for the person to arrive who would stay in that room. It was late in the evening when I heard the ambulance. It wasn't often that an ambulance came to the House. We already had our doctor. The people he couldn't cure were usually shot dead, except when Bhai decided otherwise. That didn't happen often.

I was on the steps outside the House. It was starting to get cold soon after sunset. Diwali was long past; but some of the residents kept the string of lights hanging till after Christmas and then the New Year. Some of the bulbs weren't glowing; must've been a few years old. At least some were glowing. *Thodi si roshni toh chahiye, aur kya!*

I saw the cloud of dust before I saw the cars. I wasn't the only one; others saw it too.

Ramesh and the others rushed out. Bhai followed.

'Monty, move. Make way.' He nudged me with his feet. I hurried as fast as I could. When I stumbled, he pulled me up and pushed me aside so that I wasn't in the way.

'Who is coming, Bhai?' I asked without expecting an answer. I didn't get one. The ambulance came in slowly. People were sitting outside their huts, women standing in the balconies. Everyone went inside and shut their doors. Children took their cricket bats and went inside. Even the strays went away.

How does everyone know that they need to go away? Did someone tell them or teach them?

Bhai stood on the third step in his white kurta and pyjama. Starched and ironed. Without a crease or a spot. I don't remember seeing him in any other dress. Even on his wedding day, he wore the same ... with the addition of a thick gold chain after the men kept requesting all day.

A shiny Mercedes came in, followed by the ambulance and then a black Fortuner. Cars and mobile phones – two things I love. Bhai said that someday I would own a car dealership. The best cars in the world would be in my shop. I had the name ready – Bhai Motors.

I couldn't take my eyes off the Mercedes. It was like a huge black cat slowly creeping its way in. Soundless and gleaming in the fading light. Some men jumped out of the Fortuner as soon as it stopped. They were holding rifles. Ramesh and our men got nervous. Bhai raised his hand. It was his signal to stand down.

Who is this? Why is there so much security? Must be someone important in the ambulance. Why are they here?

I took out my mobile. The best part about being invisible was that no one noticed what I did. So my mobile phone video-recorded everything. No one had stepped out from the Mercedes yet. One of the guys with a rifle opened the ambulance door. Two doctors and three nurses – I could tell by their long white jackets – stepped out of the ambulance. Bhai walked over to the Mercedes and its window rolled down. That was strange. Bhai didn't usually do that. People walked up to him, not the other way round. But that day he did. I snuck in closer to get a better look and record whatever they were talking about. I could see a man's face hidden behind huge black goggles. Their voices were clear too.

'Take good care of her. I need her alive, Bhai. Remember that. She is very important.'

'You don't worry about anything. She's my responsibility. I will not disappoint.'

Why was Bhai speaking like that? The man in the car didn't even bother stepping out. He just stuck out his hand which Bhai clasped with both of his. This bothered me. Bhai talking like a servant, bending his head, shaking the man's hand, who didn't even fully roll down his window.

'Who is that?' The man had seen me.

Bhai turned towards me as I quickly put away my phone.

'Don't worry about him. That's Monty. He's nothing.' Bhai held and shook the man's hand, and continued, 'As I was saying, don't worry about anything. She'll be fine here. I'm here to take care of her. Don't worry. You remember …'

'Ya. You don't worry about that. You take care of the girl. I will handle the rest.' The window rolled up, and Bhai walked up to the ambulance. I didn't like the man in the Mercedes. I wished Bhai would teach him a lesson.

The men carried out a stretcher. Someone lay on it. Lots of tubes attached to bottles on stands also came out, along with the stretcher.

'Careful! Be very gentle,' one of the doctors said sternly. 'Walk very slowly.' He sounded very nervous. I couldn't see who was on the stretcher. I understood why there was so much yelling about the second-floor room. The stretcher wouldn't have made it up the narrow staircase and whoever was on it couldn't be moved. I had never seen the men walk as carefully and slowly as they did while carrying the stretcher inside. I followed them.

'Monty! Get out!' Khujli yelled when I tried to enter the room. I stood at the doorstep, watching them lift the body and place it on the bed. It was a woman, I could tell. She was covered in bandages. In no time, the room was transformed into a hospital room. There were a few monitors with a blinking line and tubes going in and out of the body. The doctors and nurses checked if everything was working fine.

'Monty! Don't go in.' Chetan pushed me roughly on his way out. I grabbed the edge of the door to avoid the fall.

I went and stood in the far corner of the room. Nobody noticed me when I came in.

Who is that?

After a very long time, I slowly walked towards the bed. The face was covered with bandages. I could tell she was going to have lots of scars. There was a tube going in through a hole that'd been made for her mouth and one for each nostril, though there was also an oxygen mask. Whoever it was had been in a very bad accident. Or beaten up. Blood, cuts and such things weren't new to me. I just wanted to know who she was.

'Who is she?'

One of the nurses started to say something but the doctor snapped, 'Please leave the room. The patient needs to rest.'

As I turned around to walk out, I heard him tell the nurse, 'Just do your job so that we can go home soon. Don't talk to these people. Please. I just want to finish the job and go home.'

'Doctor, we need to change the bandages on her face,' said one of the nurses and pointed at the body. I stood by the door and watched them unwrap the victim's face. They were blocking my view so I tiptoed closer to have a look.

The face was a bloody mess. Like she had fallen on glass. I crept in closer to get a better look. They cleaned the face and dabbed more medicine on the wounds. She made a loud moan as she opened her mouth. One of the nurses dabbed her lips with moist cotton. She tried to open her eyes but couldn't. There were just too many open wounds and blood. She moaned louder the next time. The doctors had almost finished cleaning her face when I got a good look at her, before they continued adding more medicines.

I moved away. I'd seen enough. I could recognize Asavri anywhere, in any condition.

But how did she … get so badly hurt? She just won the contest a month ago. Who did this to my Asavri? I always knew we would meet … but like this … I never imagined I would meet her like this.

I felt happy and sad at the same time. Sad, because my Asavri was in this condition; happy because she was in the House. Everyone here needs a friend. You can't survive without one in the House. I will be her friend. *Sachi wala best friend.*

Eighteen

Avniel. NOW.
2019

Three reports from three different labs. They all say the same thing. I'd suspected it the day Asavri was released from the hospital and Tanya was sitting in the front row ... lost in deep thought, making the same finger-tapping gesture under her nose. Exactly the way Asavri does it. I had a gut feeling about it and my gut is never wrong, but as the truth stares at me from the paper – the report from the lab – I feel as though someone has turned off the oxygen supply to the room. I read the report again and again.

I was on the phone with Priya, trying to placate her about my sudden disappearance, when Kay's email arrived in my mailbox. I just had to open the attachments. Priya keeps talking as I read the reports. I don't tell her where I am. The conversation isn't going too well.

'So you don't want to tell me where you are because you don't want the word to spread?'

'Something like that.' What I'm reading in the email takes my mind away from what Priya is saying.

'Are you reading something while I'm talking, Avniel?'

Shit.

'You don't even have the decency to give me your undivided attention for five minutes!'

'It's not like that, Priya. I ... I ... You ...'

'How is it, then, Avniel? You don't want to tell me where you are because you think I will go around telling others. You don't call. When I call, you are distracted. What the fuck is happening?'

'It's not like I don't trust you, Priya. It's just better this way.'

'What are you? A secret CIA agent on a covert assignment?' There's a snigger in her voice and I can see the irritated arch of her brow. I just wish she'd hang up. I need to read these reports and call Kay. But it doesn't seem like Priya is going to do that.

'Priya, just bear with me on this. Please understand. Just be with me on this ... please?' I know I sound desperate, because I am. I want to tell her but I know that she'll tell her girl gang and that's how word gets out. Right now I need to keep Asavri safe and away from everyone. I haven't even told Bhaskar where we are. I just told him that I will try to get her back to normal. He trusts me enough to pay for everything without asking any questions.

'Yes, I understand it very clearly, Avniel. What I understand is that your girlfriend isn't in your circle of trust. I understand it very clearly.' The line goes dead. I intend to call her back but Kay is calling. I tell myself that I'll take this call and then call Priya back and fix things with her. *Some phone sex should do the trick*, I tell myself as I swipe right for Kay's call.

'Boss, you were right. That bitch Kamini is the mother of both Asavri and Tanya.'

'Kay! Don't say these things out loud. We have to be careful.' Someone could have bugged her phone.

'Yes. You are right. What's next, boss?'

'We need more proof, Kay. These reports aren't enough. To go public, just these aren't enough at all. I need to think. I'll let you know the next steps.'

It seems unbelievable, but science never lies.

Kamini is Tanya's and Asavri's mother.

I take out my notepad and start scribbling. I think better and clearer when I write on paper.

I've been at it since midnight. The multiple coffee rings on the newspaper I grabbed to use as a coaster tell the tale of a caffeine-induced sleepless night. My eyes feel heavy. My head is throbbing and my morning breath mingled with coffee tastes rancid in my mouth. I should stop but I don't. I scribble on a fresh page.

So Kamini is the mother. Kamini needed a winner from a popular contest; a winner that the public voted for and one who would stand beside her and campaign for the elections. That's the reason she pushed her daughter into *Indian Koel*. But in comes Asavri from nowhere, a skeleton from her past; a skeleton that refuses to stay buried.

I don't like where my thoughts are leading me.

Did Kamini arrange for the road accident to kill Asavri? Since Tanya was already second in line? Asavri's death would make her the winner ...

My mind is racing with questions.

Is Kamini so vile that she would kill someone – her daughter – just to win an election? The question answers itself as soon as it arises.

Yes, she would. She's the kind to stop at nothing until she gets what she wants. Her life has been all about being someone important, rising up the ladder and winning. From a nobody she became the wife of one of the richest men in the country, and for the last four years she has been working hard to make a political entry. The state elections happened six months after the final round of the contest. Tanya campaigned hard with her throughout the state, and Kamini won by a huge margin.

Everything is starting to make sense.

The incident in her hotel room – rearranging things to terrify Asavri – we thought it was Rudra. It must have been Kamini. Only she could think of something like that. Rudra must have given her the pictures of his wedding. It's a pity he hung himself soon after Asavri's win. The suicide note said that he couldn't bear the public outcry anymore. I'm sure Kamini is behind his death too. Every inconvenient truth, every wrinkle has been smoothened, erased by Kamini and Dheeraj.

The fire at VT! That was also them! That's why Tanya had to make an excuse to go away. She had been instructed to do so. Kamini must have planned to burn the place down. But things didn't quite go her way because her juvenile, disobedient daughter couldn't stay away from a night of unsupervised fun! When the fire failed to take care of the Asavri problem, she had her killed in a road accident.

I can see the pattern clearly, but then ... there are two things I can't explain. I have no proof to link Kamini and Dheeraj to everything that happened, and second is, if Kamini wanted Asavri dead and out of her way, why is she still alive?

This is where I draw a blank. This has me flummoxed. Someone wanted Asavri to live. Who and why?

I shut my eyes as I massage my temples. I'm tired and wired up at the same time. Some sleep would be good but I know I won't be able to.

Since Asavri and I arrived at Scenic Valley more than a month ago, I haven't been sleeping well. I get up several times every night to check on her. I've always been a light sleeper, but now I am barely able to get some shut-eye, being constantly on guard. There's tight security at the resort and I have hired extra guards too, but I still feel unsafe and worried. I don't need a fertile imagination to arrive at the conclusion that I'm up against someone with deep pockets, loads of resources and a team of goons who will stop at nothing. This is enough to chase away my sleep. I'm just living each day expecting the worst to happen and when it doesn't, I tell myself: *Good, today is gone. Let's see what tomorrow brings.* I'm almost waiting for an attack. I know it is coming. I just don't know when, and I'm tired, exhausted from the tension of waiting for it.

The DNA reports confirmed my worst fears. Kamini will stop at nothing to keep her secret buried. Asavri is a ticking bomb that can destroy everything – Kamini's life, status, political ambition. Everything. I no longer have even a shred of doubt that Kamini is behind it all. I just don't know how to prove it. It won't take her long to find out where I'm keeping Asavri. When she does, nothing will stop her. And when she makes her final move, there's little chance of the pesky reporter being spared.

I gulp more black coffee. The mere thought of what Kamini might do is terrifying. I'm jumpy and can feel the caffeine-infused nervous excitement pulsating through me. I get out of my chair and walk towards the large glass window. I knock on the glass to feel its toughened surface. I already checked with the security detail – all the glass façades in the house are special bulletproof glass. I take little solace in knowing that this place was approved by the private security teams of the richest Sheikhs in the Middle East.

If they considered this place safe enough, I think I'm safe as long as I'm here.

Dawn is breaking over the horizon. I want to open the door to the balcony and walk out barefoot, but the doors are centrally locked and can't be opened till 9 a.m. The wounded animal is shut in a cage to safeguard it from the hunter. I don't like the way my thoughts are going. I press my forehead to the glass. It's cold. My burning skin feels good as I continue to press my face against the cold glass.

The view beyond is soothing. Certainly no Himalayas, but still so verdant and serene to the eye. Wish I could go for a run. I think better when I run. The knots just untie when I do. But I can't right now. I can't leave Asavri here alone, even with security. I can't leave her nor do I want to go out and expose myself. It's too dangerous. I don't want to go for a run and get 'run over by a drunk driver'. Anything can happen.

I stand by the glass, staring at the cliff, the rolling greens and the gentle mist that's lazily floating between the trees. I have something of a plan emerging in my head. I need details. Lot of details. Just a DNA report isn't enough. I need evidence from the orphanage where Kamini left Asavri as a baby. Surely someone must have handled the paperwork. Maybe someone remembers her? I know it's a long shot. Approximately twenty-five years have gone by but some people must remember. Maybe a maid, a sweeper, an attendant or someone …

My story will be incomplete without substantial proof. I also need more information on Monty, the place she stayed and, most importantly, what happened there.

Yes. I am writing Asavri's story. This time I'm writing it not for myself. It's for her. Everyone must know what a vile and dangerous snake Kamini is. Kamini must be exposed, and that's what the story will do.

I have been thinking about Monty a lot. As I turn around, I find Asavri in my room holding a few pages in her hand.

'These are just random thoughts, Asavri. Nothing really.' I try to sound casual, as though the scribblings mean nothing at all. I extend my hand for the sheets but she doesn't return them, instead continuing to leaf through them.

'Why are you so obsessed with Monty? Why does everyone keep asking about him?' I see the pages she is holding in her hand. I've scribbled 'Monty' in big black bold letters with impatient circles around the name.

I clear my throat before speaking. I promised the therapist I would not discuss anything with Asavri in her absence.

'Monty kept you captive, Asavri. You were his prisoner.'

'He's the one who saved me. He kept me alive. He kept me alive!' Her eyes fill up with tears as she drops the papers and starts weeping, shivering and mumbling all at once. I rush over to hold her. She is whimpering.

'He will hurt him.'

'Who will hurt whom, Asavri?'

'Bhai. He will hurt Monty.'

Nineteen

Monty. THEN.

2017

As we walked down the corridor together, I knew there would be questions. She saw the peeling paint on the walls, the small dark rooms and the windows with grills. The large doors with heavy, chunky locks on them.

'Why are there grills on the windows? Even the balconies have grills. And the doors ... why do they have such big locks? Why?' The answer lurked in her eyes as she asked, terrified that what she was suspecting might be true but she hung on to the hope that maybe she was wrong.

So that the girls don't climb out and escape. I didn't tell her that. Instead, I said something about the pigeons being a menace. She didn't buy it. I'd been told by Bhai not to say anything to her.

'I know you like her, Monty. I've seen you glued to the TV during the entire contest for months. Keep your mouth shut.' I knew better than to disobey.

It'd been three months since Asavri arrived at the House. She was fine by then, the doctors said.

'So can I go home now?' she asked, trying to sound cheerful, but I sensed fear in her voice. Bhai was also in the room. She moved to a spot behind the large hospital bed, trying to keep some space. She stood near the headboard, drumming her fingers on it and trying to smile, but I could see her gulp down her saliva and lick her lips. She used to do the same during the contest when the names of the eliminated participants were being announced. I knew her signs very well. I wanted to hold her hand and tell her that she'd be fine. But I couldn't. Bhai would never allow it. It's against the House rules. And she wouldn't be fine; girls in the House never are. Her eyes searched for me. I could feel her eyes on me. I looked at my mobile. I couldn't look at her.

'Of course you can go home,' Bhai replied in that soothing, reassuring tone of his, the true intent behind which I knew. It was common knowledge in the House – he was the nicest just before things would get worse. 'But first, let's thank the kind doctors and the nurses who took such good care of you. Shall we?' he continued.

She didn't understand what he meant but nodded her head and said, 'Can I make a call? They must be worried about me. You know, back in Mumbai.'

'Sure. Soon.'

Asavri. Don't. Please stop talking. Please. I wanted to tell her but I couldn't disobey Bhai.

When it happened, she couldn't stop throwing up. Retching, crying and then throwing up. She shut her eyes tight, as though she wanted to unsee what she just had. I wanted to hold her when Shashi fired the first bullet. The doctor wasn't expecting it either. Asavri gasped and then stood frozen, unable to believe what she'd just seen. It's never easy to see brains being blown out of their skull. The sound is awfully loud, and the sight ... The red splatter is incredibly messy. Blood and bits of brain everywhere. Sometimes you discover a tiny bit clinging to a crack on the wall or under a chipped tile several days, even weeks, later. The first one to get hit doesn't really expect it even if the gun is held to their head. They think, maybe believe, that the person holding the gun will change their mind. When the trigger is pulled, the bullet shoots out and hits the skull with a loud 'Thwang!' An awfully loud noise. The body jumps in recoil and then falls on the ground, the look of horror frozen on the face.

Bhai doesn't like bullets; he prefers poison. 'There's more drama in it,' he'd say. But every once in a while, he'd use the bullet just for the big bang or if he was in a hurry and just wanted to get it over with. That day he had an appointment with a barber to trim his beard.

Though he shot both the doctors in front of Asavri, I knew more was coming. The three nurses were dragged in as well. They were crying, almost hysterically. They had heard the shots and knew they were next. I wish they were but Bhai had other plans. He gave a sign and three men ripped off the nurses' dresses within seconds. They stood naked, trying to cover their private parts, with their arms sobbing and begging.

Even before it started, I knew which of the three wouldn't make it.

Ramesh pulled out his dagger before Bhai even signalled. He picked the short, dark one with small breasts. I was right. I knew she would be the one. Since I never got to play, I placed bets. My score was getting better. The boys owed me money; we had placed our bets the previous night. Thinking of my win made me forget Asavri. The nurse screamed with all her lung power while Ramesh slashed her with his dagger. When he sliced off one of her breasts, she fainted and Asavri started screaming.

Bhai then turned to Asavri, who stood against the wall with her arms wrapped around herself, trying not to scream. He spoke to her gently, as though he were asking her if she wanted an ice cream. 'Do you want to go home?'

She screamed and ran blindly. First, into the pillar; she stumbled and fell. Then she picked herself up and ran into the wall. By the time I caught up with her, she was gagging on her vomit and tears. I turned around and faced Bhai, who had followed us. 'She understands, Bhai. She understands,' I was almost pleading. I knew that he wouldn't hurt or kill her. All that was just a show of strength. Not just for Asavri but also the other two nurses. A clear message: fall in line or this is what awaits you.

I took her to her room. She was still retching but there was nothing left in her stomach to throw up. It was the bitter bile that came out. She had urinated. Her dress reeked. I led her to the bathroom, filled a bucket and handed her a mug.

'Take a bath. Pour cold water on your head. You will feel better.' I closed the door as I stepped out. The doors didn't have a bolt. It wasn't allowed in the House. I stood outside, waiting for the sound of water splashing. I didn't hear anything. After some time I inched the door open and peeped inside. She sat still in the same position, in the same spot, holding the cracked mug in her hand and staring at it like she didn't know what to do.

It was the shock; it had paralysed her mind. She couldn't believe what she had just seen and the possibility of the same happening to her. I went in, bent her head and poured a few mugs of water over it. I used a thin towel to dry her. She stood shivering and weeping, unable to stop. She kept muttering, 'I want to go home. Please. Someone save me. I want to go home.'

I didn't reply or say anything. I knew she could never leave. She would have to learn to accept that. They all did. I handed her the towel.

'Dry yourself. I'm outside.'

Days turned to weeks. I spent all my time with her. I told her many times, 'Don't close the door of the room.' It was not allowed. The girls weren't allowed to do that. It was a rule that was meant to be followed. In the House, everyone followed rules.

I tried to explain it to her many times but she didn't listen, so I had it pulled out from the hinges. She needed to learn to obey. She needed to learn many things. For example, she couldn't step out of the room without asking for my permission. I told her nicely, many times. When she didn't listen, she left me with no choice – I had to cuff her leg to the bed. The chain allowed her to move around in the room till as far as the toilet.

I saw the hate in her eyes as I cuffed her. But she needed to learn and obey. There wasn't any other way. I found the longest chain I could and used that so she could at least walk around in the room. Others didn't usually have that privilege. She never thanked me for that.

She remained quiet and withdrawn but I knew her spirit hadn't broken yet. I'd seen every interview of her. I especially remembered the one where she spoke about how she found out that she was an orphan, and then the one where she spoke about Rudra and how he had humiliated her. She fought through all of that to come to Mumbai, live alone and then win the contest. She was not one to give up easily. I knew she would try something. They all did.

'So you watched all the episodes of *Indian Koel*?' she asked me one morning. Dark circles lined her eyes. She seldom spoke, so when she did I was surprised, pleasantly so.

'Yes, I did.'

'Why?'

'What why?' I didn't understand her question. 'I liked hearing you sing, that's why,' I said while pretending to straighten the sheet on the bed. It didn't need straightening. It made me uncomfortable when she looked at me. She smiled. It was the first time she ever smiled at me. I could feel my heart pounding in my chest.

'Do you want me to sing for you?' She smiled some more and I felt my cheeks go red.

'If you want to.' There was nothing I wanted more but I didn't tell her that.

'Let me try. I think my broken jaw has healed and so have the wounds on my tongue … Let me try to sing.' She cleared her throat and proceeded to sing one of my favourites. I didn't care about the House rules anymore. She sounded even better in person, sitting right in front of me on the bed with a thin mattress and her leg chained. I didn't realize when she moved closer. I didn't move away. She kept singing for a long time. Bhai and the others might've heard her too but her voice was so sweet that they probably didn't want her to stop.

'Monty, you like my voice, don't you? As the winner of *Indian Koel*, I will sing many more beautiful songs. Every time I sing those songs, I will think of you, Monty. I will be singing them for you. Help me, Monty. Please.' The last few words felt like a razor slicing into my skin.

Asavri was no different from the others. I'd hoped she would be. I told her I was her biggest fan. I got everyone in the House and the neighbourhood to vote for her. I made her win. I was trying to keep her safe in the House. I even got her a long chain with the cuff so that she could walk around … and how did she repay all that? By trying to play me – pretending to care just to use me to get out of the House. I kept my eyes shut. I wished she would stop talking. It was insulting to hear her talk to me like I was a moron. The lame, diseased man who she thought was the weakest link in the chain.

It was so humiliating. Much more than the look in her eyes when she saw me for the first time. My white skin with brown spots and the long scar on my left cheek have that effect on people. They cringe. She did too. I'd expected that, but this …

I slapped her hard. She looked stunned.

'Monty? What …' I slapped her again.

Just because I have one leg shorter than the other doesn't mean I have a brain the size of a pea!

The corner of her lip bled. When I tried to wipe it with a cloth, she pushed my hand away. I slapped her hard on the other cheek. We did this for a long time till she stopped resisting. I cleaned her bleeding lip. I got ice for it. She sat quiet, not even shivering.

I dragged her to the window. 'Come here. You need to see what happens to women who think they are too smart.' She was too terrified to move. Her cheeks were bright red. They must've hurt; I hit hard.

'Look! Do you see that woman crawling on the dirty footpath? Do you see her?' I pointed to the woman outside, or whatever was left of her after Bhai chopped her legs off.

'Do you know why this happened to her? Because she laughed at Bhai and teased him for being short. She thought she was too smart. Bhai had her legs chopped off and threw her there. That's what happens when you think you are too smart.' I let her stand and watch the woman on the pavement. Nothing remained of the beauty she once was. Her hair had become a nettled mesh of dirt and other things. Flies swarmed around her. She crawled as far as she could to relieve herself, which wasn't too far. Caked in her own excreta, she could be smelt from the window. Once in a while, when the smell would become unbearable, someone would take a hose and aim it at her, leaving her gagging and gasping for air as the water hit her with force.

I noticed that the sight had had its effect. Asavri stood holding one of the bars on the window. Her knuckles turned white. She held her breath. I knew what she was thinking.

'I know what you're thinking. This isn't happening. *Yeh ek bura sapna hai. Yeh sapna nahin hai,* Asavri. This is happening. This is *sachi-sachi* real.'

It was the same with all the girls. First, they couldn't believe everything that was happening to them but then eventually they'd accept it. She would too.

'If you obey me, you'll not get hurt. And don't play games with me. Ever.' I left her near the window and walked out. I went to the kitchen to tell them to make runny khichdi for Asavri and to give it to her cold. The inside of her mouth was bruised; she couldn't have anything hot or spicy till it healed.

She would sit by the window and look out. All day. Staring and thinking ... About what? I don't know, though I wanted to know. I felt sorry about slapping her so hard but then she shouldn't have tried to play me. I couldn't be taken for a fool.

I wanted a fresh start so I helped her in the room – made the bed, tucked the bedsheet, filled the jug with clean water, got her food and on some days I even snuck in a fruit or two for her. I wanted to be her friend. I wanted her to like me. I knew that love would take some time. But I wished she'd talk more. She looked so chatty in the TV interviews. It's so boring to keep talking while the other person just mumbles. I asked her to sing. She started but then choked soon after. She began weeping so I told her to stop.

I was tired of sitting in the room, watching her stare out of the window. That's why I thought the game would be fun. The running away game. I didn't want her to get hurt the way she did. I just wanted to have some fun. It was getting so boring in the House. Nothing was happening.

So I took off the cuffs and told her that the men and Bhai were away on business. Bhai was, the others weren't. I told her I'd left the main door unlocked and about the bus that left for the city and how long it would take her to reach the bus stop if she ran non-stop. I told her all of that.

First, she didn't believe me. 'Why are you telling me all this? You said I can't leave this place ever.'

She's clever. I like that.

'I love you, Asavri. And you are a singer. You should be out there singing. I feel sorry for you. Go. This is your chance.' I've always been a very convincing liar.

She believed me. I'd never seen anyone run that fast. I had tipped off the guys about it and they were waiting in the bus and on the road. I told them not to jump out immediately.

'Let her believe she is free. Then grab her.' *This will be fun.*

It was supposed to be just a game. The men were to catch her and bring her back. I never told them to tear her clothes. That was their idea. I think they were bored, too. No new girls had come to the House in a while.

I stood in the third-floor balcony. It gave me a straight and direct view till the end of the road. I could see above the huts and past the narrow gullies. I waited to see the men appear with Asavri. But they didn't.

Why was it taking so long?

I found out soon. I spotted some commotion behind the tea stall. Someone was running. Falling over things, stumbling over potholes. It was hardly a road. More like a narrow gully with an open drain running along it. It didn't take long for me to understand what was happening.

It was Asavri. She was running. The men knew the gully well enough and were jumping in from corners she didn't know about. Whoever got to her ripped off her dress. Someone flung something white in the air. It was a bra. I didn't wait to see any more. That wasn't what I had wanted. They were hurting my Asavri. It took me quite a while to get down three floors. I cursed myself, my one short leg. I curse it often but that day I cursed it like never before. I wanted to run down the steps but could only hobble down like a dog with three legs. I stumbled many times and even hit my head on the stairs. I bled. I didn't care. I just needed to get to Asavri. They were hurting her. My Asu.

I was late. By the time I reached the courtyard, she was crouching down, all huddled up. Naked. Bleeding. The six men were waving their prizes in the air. Bits of clothing they had ripped and taken from her. She was begging to be left alone. I started yelling. Screaming at the top of my lungs. They didn't pay attention. They began tossing a coin to decide who would take her first.

'Stop it! Stop this now!' My throat hurt. I screamed but they ignored me. As always, no one heard or saw me or paid any heed to what I was saying.

Thankfully, Bhai arrived. I'd never felt so relieved on seeing him step out of the car. I began to explain. He raised a hand and they left. I took off my shirt, draped it around her and together we limped back inside. I took her into the bathroom, ran the tap and washed her. I tried to be as gentle as possible. There were deep gashes on her; the men weren't exactly gentle while tearing off her clothes. She didn't flinch when I touched her to clean the wounds. I did the best I could. I used to watch the nurses bandage her. I tried to do the same. I went to the wardrobe to fetch her a clean dress. She had none. There were only two – one was in shreds and the other hung on the rope outside the room.

'I'm going to my room to get you a shirt. Wait here.' I thought that maybe she hadn't heard me. I told her again, 'Wait here,' before realizing how stupid it was to say that. Where could she have gone?

By the time I got back, it was too late. One of them was already in. Four waited outside for their turn. I knew what was happening. Bhai was furious to see that she was outside the House. His only rule, the cardinal rule: do what you want but inside the House. But Bhai also knew that the dogs needed to be fed. He let his dogs loose.

I knew better than to try to stop them. I was neither strong nor important enough. I was a nobody, a worthless, lame man.

I sat there, outside the room, watching them go in one by one. I watched them come out pulling up their pants. I watched them waiting, massaging the bulge in their pants. Two of them went in twice. I heard her scream. After some time she didn't scream anymore. I wished she would. The silence was killing me. I stuffed the sleeve of my shirt into my mouth to stop myself from screaming.

Please don't. Please stop hurting her. Please stop hurting my Asavri.

Twenty

Kamini. NOW.

2019

'May I come in, madam?'

It seems like yesterday when he was standing at the door of my office, asking for permission to enter. It's been twenty-three years since that day.

I pick up the glass and drain whatever's left of the Yamazaki in it. The room has stopped spinning around me; it's moving in a slow swirl now. I pick up the phone and ask for the bottle of Yamazaki. I'm going to need a lot of alcohol tonight.

I walk out to the balcony. The air is salty. A fine spray washes over me as I lean over the railing. The relentless crashing of the waves against the boulders has always fascinated me. It is years of silent lashing that leads to the changed form of the boulders. Even the mighty boulder isn't immune to the determined waves; they work silently and patiently.

I step back and fall into the chair, allowing the cushions to engulf me. My head rests on the back of the chair as the cane lattice scratches my neck. A starless sky spreads out as far as the eye can see. I stare into the black night and look back at the past. Twenty-three years ago, Dheeraj stood at my door, asking for permission to enter.

'May I come in, madam?' he repeated. I gave him a questioning look.

'I'm Dheeraj Shastri. From the accounts department, madam,' he replied, still standing by the door he hadn't been granted the permission to walk through.

I signalled for him to enter, mildly annoyed with the intrusion. I had lots to do. Having resumed work after a month-long honeymoon, I was eager to dive back in. *How did Judy let him through?*

'Yes?'

'Madam, I'm here to propose you hire me as your personal assistant,' he said as he closed the door behind him, walked up to my table and stood behind a chair.

I capped the Mont Blanc I was using and looked at him. I remember thinking: *This should be an interesting conversation.* Someone was offering to be my personal assistant when I hadn't even considered having one. Judy was my secretary and was doing a good job. What exactly was this man proposing to do differently? I asked him to sit but he declined, saying he preferred to stand. I continued looking him in the eye, trying to gauge the man who stood before me.

He had a calm, soft voice. He appeared to be in his late twenties. I remembered seeing him in the accounts section. A plain, unremarkable face. The kind of face no one would notice. Hair neatly trimmed and oiled; I got a whiff of coconut oil. He wore a white shirt buttoned up till his neck and plain black trousers.

He stood in my spacious office, overlooking the bay and the curve of the Queen's Necklace. He was in the presence of the wife of the owner and MD of the company and there was not even a flicker of hesitation or nervousness on his face. It was as though he was in the right place. Dheeraj's calm and confident demeanour is what struck me the most about the man. Totally unfazed and unruffled. I liked that about him.

'I didn't know I needed one and, more importantly, didn't know I was looking for one.'

'Yes, madam, I know you aren't looking for one. But I think it's best to garner support before you need it. You'll need an extra pair of eyes and an extra pair of hands to work for you while you focus on your job.' I've always enjoyed a conversation with a sharp mind, a mind that leaps a few steps ahead of mine. Dheeraj struck me as that person. Though I needed to get back to work, the man in the starched white shirt had piqued my interest.

'Why don't you sit down, Dheeraj?' I offered him a seat again.

'I'm not here to sit, madam. I'm here to offer my services.'

'Hypothetically, suppose I do hire you. What's the first thing you'd do?'

'I would quell and erase the slow tide of dissention that a certain family member is building against you. Pardon my saying this but this isn't news to you. You are the best choice for Pratap sir, a worthy and competent ally, but according to the family you aren't. This family isn't kind to outsiders, especially those who don't have a bloodline that can be traced back at least six to seven generations.'

He certainly got my attention. Yes, it wasn't news to me that the family wasn't exactly doing cartwheels for me. I'd expected dissention but I didn't expect it to happen so soon.

'Dheeraj, I have the mega merger to focus on. I have taken over corporate affairs and PR for Pratap & Sons. We are on the cusp of collaborating with a Korean partner. I can't be bothered with annoying relatives planning a coup. Handle it. And ... think of it as your audition. Let's see how well you perform.' I waited for a smile. He didn't. I would learn soon that Dheeraj never smiled; a fact that has remained constant. He worked silently and delivered.

'You won't be disappointed, madam,' he said as he walked out of the room and into my life.

That was the start. Of course, I hired a PI to find out if he had any skeletons in his closet. He was clean. Single, a fact that didn't change in the next twenty-three years, with parents in Nashik whom he visited once a month for three days. I was careful and did a sweep on him every now and then. I didn't trust him with the really important stuff for a few years. He just managed the irritating, snooty blue-blooded family I'd married into, my PR and social work that I used to present my best image to the outside world. Then he handled some of the men and women I'd been with, when they thought they could get easy money out of me.

The Asha tai problem I handled myself. Dheeraj was too new to be trusted with it. It was after I handled Asha tai that I realized I needed an extra pair of hands and eyes.

Her letters began arriving a few years after my marriage. *How did Asha tai get my address?* I ignored the first few.

Beta, I'm all alone now. There's no one to take care of me. You are all I have. I want to live with you so that you can take care of me. After all, I am your tai. Your only family.

Did she really think I was going to let her into my new life? My new swish life that I had so carefully worked to build. She must have seen pictures of my home in a magazine or maybe the TV interview Pratap and I had done. Simi had insisted on shooting a few scenes at home. And the greedy hag was dreaming of living with me.

Her last letter was the final straw. *Beta, I have booked my tickets and I will be reaching Bombay.* She mentioned the date and the train details. She was arriving in ten days. I needed to do something to stop her. It was the fat, juicy olive in my Martini struggling to stay afloat that gave me the idea.

Tai didn't know how to swim and unless the fat bitch had taken swimming lessons – highly unlikely – she would sink faster than a stone. I told Pratap I was going for a two-day yoga camp in Rishikesh. The man never asked any questions; I loved that about him. I needed only a few hours to do what I had to but it's always nice to have some buffer, hence the extra day should I need to improvise.

Tai was surprised to see me at her door and in tears when I told her that I was there to personally take her to Mumbai. It didn't take long for me to probe her about how many people she had told about going to Mumbai. As I suspected, everyone she knew. The woman could never keep her mouth shut but I was going to silence her forever. I had arrived unannounced, so no one knew about my arrival. I had knocked on her door after ten in the night. I didn't waste any time. I wanted to get away from the shithole fast. After an hour or so of her non-stop banter that I tuned out, I suggested we take a walk towards the Ganges. It was way past midnight. She didn't refuse. It was something we used to do often when I was a kid. I knew just the place I wanted to go to. The rains had been heavy that year and the river gushed in full fury, brimming over. She was talking non-stop, tipsy with excitement and alcohol. I ensured she consumed half a bottle of vodka before stepping out.

When we got to the point where the water was deep, I called out to her, 'Tai! Come and do pranam to Ganga maa. You won't be seeing her for a while.' She could barely walk, tottering drunk.

As she stood at the edge, with her head bowed down, I pushed her hard.

'Moon! Help me ... He-lp me!' She bobbed up and down, terror in her eyes now that she'd realized what my intentions were. The current carried her out further out. I could see her head go down and come up and then no more. I wore men's shoes three sizes larger than my own, a plain, muddy-brown, shapeless kurta over baggy trousers and a cap on my head, my hair rolled and tucked inside a skullcap. It was too dark to see anything and if anyone saw, they would see a man's figure standing by the river. I stayed in the shadows for a long time to make sure she had drowned and then left. I went back to her house, picked up my small bag, wiped the door handles, the table and everything I had touched. I hadn't eaten or drunk anything in the two hours that I was there.

'I'm on a fast, tai. So no water or food' I'd told her when she inquired why I wasn't eating. I didn't want to leave any evidence of my visit. I slipped into a burkha as I left the house.

I left a note taped to the main door for her domestic help, who would come in the morning. It said: 'I'm going to Bombay. Will be gone for a long time. Money with Aruna.'

Aruna was her neighbour. I left some money in the letter box. This was for the maid's salary. No one would miss her. Asha tai wasn't exactly the favourite neighbour in the lane. Everyone disliked her. The note on the door was enough to inform that she'd left for Mumbai. Everyone would be happy to see the nosy chatterbox gone. Tai's obese body finally came to good use; she became fish feed.

I caught the first flight in the morning back to Delhi. Checked into a decent middle-class hotel, waited the day and then took the evening flight to Mumbai. I was back just in time for the dinner at the governor's bungalow.

This incident made two things very clear. I had skeletons in my past that needed to be burned, wiped out and disposed of. I couldn't go around doing this. While it was supremely exciting to plot and carry out these plans, it was risky. I could get caught. Dheeraj was slowly but steadily gaining my confidence. It was time to delegate.

I put Dheeraj through some more trial runs to test his efficiency and finally gave him the task of dealing with Mission of Mercy – the orphanage where I delivered and left my firstborn.

Dheeraj turned out to be better than what one could have hoped or imagined.

My mandate was always clear to him. I gave him a name and simply said, 'Take care of it.' I didn't ask for details of what he did, how he did it. I needed it done and he did it.

He dealt with the Mission of Mercy situation like a professional. He took seven to ten years to systematically clean it up and didn't leave a single loose thread. Clearly, this was a man who worked silently and patiently.

I click on the audio clip again and hear it. He has been working silently and patiently to destroy me.

I remember the night, a month after Asavri became the winner. Always a light sleeper, the first ring had woken me up.

'Madam, there has been an accident.'

'What? Who?' Tanya was in the bedroom down the hall. *Did she sneak out again?* I bolted up right on the bed.

'It's Asavri.'

I'd wanted to do an air punch and ask, 'Is the bitch dead?' but controlled myself. 'How bad is it?'

'Very bad, madam. Barely there.'

'Dheeraj, the accident ... did you ...'

'No. It just happened. A road mishap.'

'Please take care of it, Dheeraj. Do it now.'

It was a sleepless night after I hung up the phone. Not the bad kind of sleepless, but one fuelled by excitement. The last and final skeleton was being taken care of. Only this was no skeleton. It was alive and breathing. With her gone, nobody would know that I had an illegitimate daughter, born a year before my wedding to Pratap. It was the result of a wild, drunken night in Ooty. Any one of those three men could be her father. At the cusp of my political career, Asavri was a disaster waiting to happen. All my efforts to have her evicted from the show had failed. Food poisoning, fear psychosis; even the fire in the pub couldn't finish her. Instead, she turned into a hero when she saved my T, who blatantly disobeyed my order to stay away from the pub. What I'd been plotting to do for so long was taken care of, thanks to a road accident. I couldn't believe my luck!

I didn't have to kill her, and just like that she was gone from my life!

When Dheeraj returned after five days, all he said was, 'She is gone forever, madam. Nothing to worry about anymore.' As was the rule, I never asked about the details. I couldn't perjure myself if I knew nothing. Seeing the drama of the mangled body unfold and it being proven that it was Asavri who died in the accident almost made me congratulate him on a job well done. The ticking time bomb was gone … or so I believed. It seemed too good to be true. I forgot the cardinal rule: when something seems too good to be true, it probably isn't.

Two years later, I'm sitting with my mobile in my hand, earphones pushed deep inside, playing the audio clip again, hearing Dheeraj say, 'Don't kill her. She needs to stay alive. I need Asavri to stay alive.'

I know his voice too well. It's him.

Could it be doctored? Is someone trying to turn me against him? Everyone knows he's my right-hand man. Now is when I need him the most.

The thought crosses my mind several times. Then I think about how Asavri returned and Dheeraj has been unable to find out anything about where she was or how she survived. Nothing. He hasn't found anything because there's nothing to find. He knows it all. He said he doesn't know where she is after being discharged. I bet that's a lie too.

All these months he kept saying he's trying to find where Avniel took her. I believed him. I've wondered how she has been alive this entire time ... She never died! Dheeraj kept her alive. He lied to me, to my face; again and again. I believed him. He lied to me. So did he bring her back? What does he want?

He is the one person I trusted implicitly and now I feel like a fool. I'm a fool because I flouted all the rules and trusted a single person to handle everything in my life. I think about the number of tests I put him through to weed out any seeds of mistrust I had towards him. He came out clean every time and with every test he cleared, I trusted him more.

I got played. I've always taken enormous pride in sniffing out crooks and back-stabbers. How did I not sense Dheeraj going rogue? I'm too angry to be shocked.

Is he working with the opposing candidate to throw me off track? But he stands to gain if I win. Or maybe he shook hands with someone bigger and more powerful.

I got played. Dheeraj made a fool of me.

The realization feels like a burning iron pressing on my skin.

Twenty-One

Monty. THEN.
2017

Her body ached. I could see it in the way she walked. She limped, holding the wall for support, and took small steps as she staggered to the bathroom. There was blood.

The sound of footsteps terrified her. She would wait to hear them, wait for it to begin. They came in at all times, often many times during a day. I couldn't look her in the eye. She would lie in bed with the glassy look I'd got to know so well. Sometimes, while it was happening, she would lie still, almost limp like a rag doll. Like a body that has no life. I was always in the room. I couldn't leave her with the men, alone. It never bothered them that I was there. When they'd leave, she wouldn't move; she'd just lie on the bed, staring at the wall. I'd cover her. Pick up the clothes and help her back into them.

Julie, from the kitchen, asked me once, 'Why do you stay in the room, Monty? Are you recording her?'

I was too shocked to respond. *How could she even suggest that? How could she think I would record Asavri?*

'I can't leave her alone,' I mumbled.

She didn't understand. No one did. No one could. I didn't bother explaining.

I couldn't protect her from the men. The least I could do was be with her. How could I leave her alone? I could never leave my Asu. I'd silently tell her, 'Asu, please hang in there. This will end ... this will end soon.'

I would help her bathe and wash herself after the men. I bought Soframycin ointment for the scratches. She'd point to the spots I'd miss.

I asked Julie what to do to help ease the pain between her legs. Having entertained Ramesh and his friends quite often, sometimes all in one night, she knew well. She told me that I would need ice cubes in a plastic bag, a bucket of hot water and a towel.

I was clueless, staring at all three and wondering what to do with them. Julie had a good laugh and the other women joined her too. I tried not to blush when they teased me and said, *'Uff! Kambakht ishq.'* Julie showed me what to do. We alternated the ice pack and hot towel between her thighs. She let me place them between her legs as she lay down, a thin and hopeless stream of tears running out of her eyes and over the bridge of her nose. I sat on the floor holding her hand, letting her cry.

The men began injecting her often. Bhai's orders. Heroin. The drug is easy to control once the blood gets used to it. It was also easy for the men to abuse her while she was in a drug-induced haze. I was waiting for them to lose interest in her. How much longer would she be fresh meat to them? It was sooner than I thought. New girls arrived and the men turned their attention to the new 'toys'. New screams echoed through the House at night. It didn't bother me. It was Asavri's silence that I couldn't bear. She didn't look at me, though she did thank me every time I got her food, filled the water jug with clean water and put a new bar of soap in her bathroom. She used soap a lot; the shampoo not so much. I bought the large Liril bar. I remembered from one of the TV interviews, she'd said that she loves the smell of Liril. I had hoped she'd notice. Even if she did, she said nothing. She'd stiffen every time I'd enter the room but I knew she was glad I was there. When I'd leave, she would ask when I would be back. It felt good hearing her say that. I'd always try to hide my smile.

'I'm sorry about the noise in the House.' I don't know why I said that. She was crouching in her bed, staring at something on the floor.

'Huh?'

'I mean the screaming. One of the new girls is screaming a lot.'

'Better her than me.'

Every time she'd hear the sound of shuffling feet approaching, she would clutch the edge of the sheet that covered her. She'd wonder if someone was coming to her, for her. When the footsteps would pass the room, she'd relax. She often shivered in her sleep. Crying. I would hold her till the shivering stopped, whispering softly to her, 'I'm here. Don't worry, I will never leave.' I think she heard me in her sleep.

One night, I decided to do something. I wasn't sure if it would work but I had to try.

Next morning, I waited till Bhai was done with his bath and morning meal, which was more like a midday meal. He took stock of the consignments, the boxes that needed to go, the money that came in and the girls who were ready to leave. I waited till he was done. I just hoped he was in a good mood and everything was fine with the business so that he'd agree to what I was about to ask. He saw me hovering around; I was always hovering around but that day was different. His eyes met mine and I looked down.

'Monty!' I was surprised to hear him call me. He never allowed himself to get distracted while attending to business. I hoped I hadn't disturbed him. I didn't want him angry.

'Yes, Bhai.' My voice trembled.

'What is it that you want to say?'

'Nothing, Bhai. Nothing important. You finish your work, Bhai.' It suddenly felt like a bad idea. Because of my stupidity, Asu would get hurt again, I was sure of it. I suddenly felt the need to piss. My armpits felt cold and I started to hobble away.

'Monty!' His voice grew loud and impatient. '*Bolo kya hai?*'

Everyone in the room looked at me. It was too late to backtrack. I cleared my throat and said it.

'She is my responsibility. Tell the men to stop, Bhai. Don't hurt her, Bhai. Please. The men ... please ...' I looked at my feet. One leg dangled a few inches above the ground, the other bore my weight. My right hand held the stick firmly. What was I thinking? This was the most stupid thing I had ever done. I was certain that I would end up in the piss pit ... and Asavri ... I'd never get to see her again. Bhai could do that. The girls who came to the House left in a month's time and were never seen again.

Everyone stayed quiet and then suddenly Bhai started laughing, after which the others joined in, as if on cue.

I looked up and smiled, though I had no clue why. I was pretty sure the others didn't know either. With Bhai, you never know.

'Tujhe pyaar ho gaya, Monty! *Arre, iss langde ko pyaar ho gaya.'* Bhai almost choked with laughter. Others laughed even louder. I was the only one who wasn't laughing. I limped over to him, threw my stick down and sat near his feet.

I touched his feet. They were so clean and smooth, almost pink. I didn't want to start crying and I had a tough time holding back the tears. I hated myself for crying. I wiped my eyes hurriedly, not wanting anyone to see them.

Bhai put his hand on my head. The others stopped laughing.

'No one will touch the girl. Monty, she is yours. Take care of her. You can take care of her, okay? But she doesn't step out of the house. Remember.'

I bent my face to his feet and kissed them. Tears wet his feet as I pressed my face on them. He patted my head, like one would do to a dog. As he was walking away, his toe scratched my cheek and the nail cut across my skin. I bled but I didn't care. I felt no pain. All I could think of was that no one would hurt my Asu anymore.

Later in the night, I told her and she didn't believe me. She didn't say anything, but she wet the edge of her kurta with water and wiped the cut on my chin and applied Soframycin on it. I smiled all night. I knew she didn't believe me so the next morning I had the door brought back, put a lock on it and gave her the key. She didn't take it. She thought I was playing a game again.

Only this time I wasn't.

Twenty-Two

Avniel. NOW.
2019

It's not a request. It's an order.

'My team will reach at ten. They will speak with her. The doctor lady can be present.'

I'm being informed the night before about the team's arrival at the resort.

'The team will be there at ten sharp. Keep her ready,' I'm further told, rather directed. The tone suggests that there's no scope for any discussion. They expect to be obeyed and know they will be.

I'm not surprised. I was expecting it. Yesterday, we completed two months in the resort and Asavri still hasn't revealed anything substantial in her sessions, though the doctor feels she's made progress. Bhaskar has been calling too.

'How is she? Any progress?'

'Yes, she is making progress. She's eating better. Talks to me, looks at me while talking and the doc reduced her sleep meds. She's certainly getting better.'

What I see as progress, Bhaskar doesn't. He didn't bother trying to hide his impatience. 'I haven't sent you with her so that she eats well and sleeps better, Avniel. Can she return and face the public? Can she start singing?'

I was amazed by his questions. I didn't know how to answer. 'Do you have any idea what she has endured, Bhaskar? The woman has lived through hell and you're worried about her singing career? Are you even hearing yourself?'

'Are *you* hearing yourself, Avniel? You motherfucker! Are you fucking around with me? Do you have any idea how much is at stake here? And you're giving me details of what she ate and how much she slept?'

I disconnected the call and threw my phone on the bed. But I also knew that disconnecting the call wasn't going to stop him. Soon after, I get the call from the cops informing me about their arrival.

They get there quickly. It's a three-member team and they are in plain clothes, unusually well dressed.

'We didn't want to blow the cover, hence the fancy outfits. In case the gang is searching for her, we want to look like regular people checking into a resort,' they tell me.

One of them – the youngest, I presume – is in a low-waist denims, appropriately ripped at the knees, and tight tee with a cap on his head. Another is in a summer jacket with linen pants and the third is in a silk shirt casually hung over cream trousers. Someone sure had fun shopping!

They step out of an Audi looking like a trio on a day out in the Western Ghats.

'It's a bright and sunny day,' the younger one says as he takes a few steps forward with his hands in his trouser pockets. He looks like a real estate agent who made some fast money selling dubious property.

I ignore the comment. 'Would you like some breakfast before you begin?' They must have left by 7.30 a.m. latest. I wonder if they stopped for food en route.

'Let's finish what we are here for,' says Menon. He's the one in the silk shirt and is the one calling the shots. He doesn't wait to be ushered in. Just strides in, with the other two following him hastily. I point them towards the dining room when they ask. I'm surprised. I thought they would sit in the living room.

The doctor steps in with a last-minute effort. 'I have to repeat myself. The patient is still fragile. We need to proceed carefully. Please …' She stops as Menon turns to her.

'I'm not going to repeat myself. You're here to stand by and assist. Don't get in the way of police work. If you do, it won't be good for you.' He speaks in a flat tone with a finality that leaves no room for further debate.

Asavri is ready on time. I requested the doctor to arrive before the cops reached. I didn't want the cops to talk to her in the absence of the doctor. Asavri has bathed and changed into a pair of light blue denims and a pink top. She is in her room. I go in to check on her. She is sitting on the edge of an ornate chair near the window. She is staring out of the window, her hands tightly gripping the arms of the chair. Her wet hair, still short, is sticking to her head; drops of water trickle down to the neck of the tee. She looks like an ordinary young girl ready for a day's outing to the mall.

'Do I have to speak with them?' There's a hopeless plea in her eyes.

'I wish you didn't have to. I tried to stop them but couldn't. I really did.' I want her to know I'm on her side, unlike the previous time.

She's fine till she sees the three men. I can tell she is terrified. She starts dragging her feet.

'Asavri, they are here only to talk to you. I will be here with you and so will the doctor. See … she's also here. They will ask a few questions and you just have to answer them. okay?' I hope I sound reassuring. She looks at me, frightened. I try to smile back.

The two accompanying cops have installed a camera on a stand and a microphone for the interrogation. I now understand why they wanted the dining table. The microphone sits on the tabletop. A small pile of large white envelopes are stacked on one side. I also see a large file and a notebook with a few pens. The camera stands on a tripod, between two chairs, ready to record the conversation. There are three chairs on both sides; the rest have been removed. All the lights in the room have been switched on. The large room is swathed in bright lights, as though a banquet will begin shortly.

The cops mean business and don't want to risk missing anything.

'Good morning, Asavri. Myself Menon. These are my colleagues Sharma and Pandey. We are from the Mumbai crime branch. We just want to ask you a few questions. Please sit and be comfortable. Before we begin, could you please say your name out loud for the record?'

'Asavri.' She sits on the chair that the camera is pointing towards, looking tiny, frail and scared. She's barely audible when she speaks.

'Full name, please and kindly speak louder. We are recording the conversation so look straight at the camera.'

'Asavri Bhattacharya.' The doctor and I flank her. Menon and the others are sitting across from us, facing her directly.

'Before we begin, I want to state that you, Asavri, are speaking to us freely and we haven't forced you in any way to talk. You are doing this because you want to help the Mumbai police, am I right?' Asavri nods to Menon's statement, to which he further adds, 'Please speak up, Asavri. A nod isn't enough. Speak loud and clear.'

'Yes, I'm speaking to you of my free will and have not … haven't been forced to.' There's a tremor in her voice. It's the most farcical agreement ever issued, as though she has a choice.

'Very good. It's everyone's duty to assist the police. Thank you. Let's get started. Asavri, I'm going to show you a few pictures. Look at them very carefully and tell me if you've seen the people in them. Take your time. There's no hurry.' Menon puts one picture before her and she takes a sharp breath in. I know she recognizes him.

'He is Bhai.' She points but doesn't touch the picture.

'Look carefully and then answer,' Menon urges her, pushing the picture closer to her.

I can tell she doesn't want to look at the picture. There's nothing evil about the face that's staring out of it. It's very commonplace. A face that you are likely to pass by on the road or in the market and not give a second look to. He has the face of a nobody. Except for the hint of a smile that's almost not there. It's not nasty or dirty. It's rather unsettling. Maybe I'm imagining it because I know this is a man who runs a drug trade and a prostitution ring. He is looking straight into the camera, almost brazenly saying, 'Catch me if you can.'

Asavri repeats her answer. Menon takes out three other pictures. She identifies two of them but doesn't know their names.

Next, he shows pictures of a house taken from various angles. It's a rather large house, quite decrepit. About four floors and each has numerous windows. The windows have thick black grills. It stands in an area full of shanties.

There's some empty land around the house but no vegetation. Just a dusty patch and a few steps that lead up to a big door. There's no sign of life in the house, no faces at the window or clothes hanging. Just a big structure with peeling paint, cracks in a few places, grills on the windows and a large door. It looks like a place that doesn't welcome anyone in; a kind of place that keeps people locked in. Once in, never out.

Menon is observing Asavri closely as she picks up each photo and looks at it carefully. I'm looking at her too, unable to read her thoughts. Clearly, the house is known to her. She is looking at the five pictures again and again. Menon doesn't interrupt. After a long time, she looks up and replies, 'This is the House. I have lived here.'

Menon exchanges looks with the others. They look excited.

'Do you know this is the house from where Bhai runs his operation? You're the first person who has lived there and survived to tell us about it. You must tell us everything you know and saw. Did you see the godown where drugs are packed and dispatched? How many times in a month did the goods move?' Menon is almost frothing at the mouth. He's missing an important point. I decide to butt in.

'Asavri wasn't there as a work person. She wasn't part of the team that handles the operation. She was a captive. I really don't think she would have any information about the work that went on there.' It's important for Menon to remember that Asavri isn't one of them; she was their prisoner.

'Don't speak or interrupt. Speak only when I ask you a question. I will have you removed from the room if you speak again.' Menon glares at me. I want to glare back but nod and look down instead.

The doctor speaks up, ignoring the fact that I was just reprimanded for speaking out of turn.

'Asavri, what are you looking at?'

She is holding one picture from the small pile. It's a close-up shot of the House.

'When was this taken?' she looks at Menon and asks.

'We will come to that soon,' he says, but changes his mind as Asavri keeps staring at the picture in her hand. Maybe he thinks if he plays along, she will cooperate more.

'About three weeks ago. Why?'

'There's something at the window. Is it a person? Can you tell me what it is?'

Menon looks irritated with the divergence but complies. Pandey gets a magnifying glass and peers at where Asavri is pointing in the picture.

'Looks like someone has placed a glass jar with some kind of a plant in it. Someone has kept it on the windowsill so that it gets sunlight.'

'Can you tell me which floor it is?'

He looks at the picture intently. Pandey speaks, 'It's the second floor. Looks like the last room. The corner room.'

'This is the room where I stayed.' She doesn't look away from the picture. 'It wasn't big but it had two large windows with thick grills on them. From one of the windows I could see till the road beyond the basti. The winding road that met the highway. From the other I could see the top of the shanties, the broken-down huts.'

'Okay. Let's move on,' Menon tells her. This is of no importance to him but I understand why she used to sit and look out of the window in the hospital. The window overlooked several shanties.

She puts her hand on the picture and looks at Menon. 'May I keep the picture, please?'

'Yes, you may if you answer my questions.'

He repeats his questions about the House and the activities that went on inside. Asavri has no answer for any of them. 'I don't know anything about what work they did or how it was done.'

'You stayed in that house for almost two years, Asavri. How is it possible you know nothing?'

'I was in this room and I stayed there. I was not allowed to go out ... only when they said I could.' She is fumbling over her words. The doctor and I exchange looks.

This explains why she asks for permission to do every little thing.

'So you've seen nothing regarding their work? Nothing at all?'

Asavri shakes her head and looks at the picture in her hand. It means something to her and I make a mental note to ask her about it later.

'Okay. So let's continue,' Menon says and places four other pictures on the table. Almost instantly, Asavri closes her eyes and grips the edge of the table. I can see beads of perspiration on her forehead and a sweat patch under her arm.

'You've seen them, haven't you? Asavri, look carefully and tell me what you know.'

'Please, let me go. Yes, I've seen them but I don't know their names.' She has her eyes shut tight and the doctor has disapproval stamped all over her face and an arm wrapped around her.

'What did they do in the house? How do you know them?' Menon isn't going to give up.

She has her hands on her face and is trembling uncontrollably. She is shaking her head as though she's trying to dispel a thought.

'You need to talk, Asavri. You can't stay silent. What did these men do?'

'They came to my room night after night after night … every night.' She starts crying. The doctor pushes back her chair and goes over to Asavri, looks at Menon and says, 'Let's give her a break, shall we?' Menon glares at her as though to say: *Back off. Don't interrupt when I'm getting results.*

'Please.'

'Fine. Just a four-minute break and then we resume.'

The doctor pulls a whimpering Asavri away from the table. I can hear her mutter, 'I don't want to talk. I don't want to remember. I just want to forget. I want to forget.' She's clutching the picture tight in her hand.

I offer to accompany her along with the doctor but the latter refuses. 'Let me take care of her.'

I decide to chit-chat with Menon.

'Who do you think is behind this? Why did the gang keep her alive?'

'Someone very important and with lots of money.'

'How did she get away? This doesn't seem like an easy place to escape from.'

'Someone must have helped her. Someone on the inside.'

'Why would one of Bhai's gang do something like this? This is outright betrayal and would result in severe punishment. Has anyone from the gang turned up dead … killed after Asavri's departure?'

'No. Not as far as we know. Nobody from the gang has been found dead.'

This is strange indeed. Asavri, who was closely guarded and held captive, escapes and no one is punished. It just doesn't add up. I can tell Menon is thinking along the same lines. He is staring at me. I decide to ask him another question.

'Who do you think is responsible for all this? Is there a person of interest?'

'Mr Avniel, I think you should stop watching cop serials.' Menon smiles at my question. 'You can hold off on writing the next book on her life for a while.'

'What do you mean?' I start to say but am silenced by the smile on his face.

'You've got no one fooled, writer saab, especially not me. Don't tell me you're in love with her or that you're doing this for some higher purpose. Reporters like you love only one thing. A good story. And isn't she a great one? A young girl from nowhere, abandoned by her family, wins a singing contest, dies soon after and is found alive after almost two years. Moreover, she's been in the devil's lair and survived to tell the story. I'm no writer or reader, but it's a bestselling story just waiting to be written; maybe a movie deal will also follow. So help me get to the bottom of this. I want nothing more than to bust the ring and their operation. You help us and you can then write your next bestseller. It's a win-win for both of us. Now go get her back. I said four minutes; it's been almost seven.'

I don't try to debate with Menon. No point in telling him or Bhaskar that Asavri's not just a story to me anymore. I really want to help her. But I lied and spun a yarn for so long that no one believes me anymore.

I get Asavri back in the room for questioning.

The doctor looks at me as though it's my fault that the cops are grilling her. She hisses, 'This will do far more damage than you can imagine.'

'It's out of my hands, in case you didn't notice,' I hiss back.

'I thought you were friends with the commissioner.'

I don't know what gives her the impression that I have a backslapping-buddy relationship with the cop head. I just ignore her taunt.

We take our places at the table. I can see Asavri's face is puffy. The tip of her nose has become a flaming red. She looks anything but okay for further questioning but I think she knows there's no other way. They won't stop till she tells it all.

Menon is ready with his next set of questions.

'I have to tell you something before I show you the next bunch of pictures.'

She looks at him and nods quietly.

'You must have realized that the gang that held you is involved in many illegal activities. They deal in drugs and selling girls. Many of those girls have gone missing, Asavri, in the last few years. We suspect they are being sold to prostitution rings around the country and maybe in Dubai and Bangkok too. Did you interact with any of the girls? Did you see any of them?' Menon places ten or more pictures of girls on the table.

Asavri can't recollect having seen any of them.

He clears his throat before continuing, 'You were brought into the House after the accident. You must have been badly hurt. Who took care of you? Were there doctors who attended to you?' He ends his question by placing five pictures on the table. Two doctors and three nurses.

'Yes. They took care of me. A hospital room was set up for me.'

'How long were they all there?'

'For a few months.'

'Are they still there? Do you know what happened to them? Because they are missing ...'

'They are dead. The doctors are.'

Menon and his men exchange looks. 'How can you be sure they are dead?'

'It happened before my eyes. Bhai shot the doctors.'

'And the women ... I mean the nurses ... what about them? Were they killed too?'

She begins shifting in her chair and looks away from Menon. I can see the tremor in her lower lip as she bites it hard to try and stop it from trembling.

'I don't remember.' She is looking at her lap. I'm no interrogator but I can tell she is trying to hide something. She doesn't want to talk about what I'm assuming is a horrifying memory. I know Menon isn't going to stop till he gets it out of her.

'Tell him, Asavri. Tell him what you've seen and be done with it. These aren't good people. So just tell him everything.' Menon is about to stop me but after hearing what I have to say, he stays silent and then nods.

'One of them is dead. This one.' She points to the picture. 'The other two I don't know about.'

'Was she also shot like the doctors?'

What she tells us next chills everyone to the bone. 'No. She was cut to pieces.'

Hearing about it makes me want to throw up. I can't even imagine what it must have been like to watch it happen. There's silence in the room. Everyone is trying to absorb what Asavri just said. Finally, Menon finds his voice and speaks.

'Who did it? Was it Bhai? Or was it Monty?'

'NO! It wasn't Monty. Monty never hurt anyone. Monty has never hurt anyone. Please listen to me. Monty never hurt anyone. He isn't bad.'

It's like the raw, live end of a wire. The name Monty. The moment she hears it, she spirals out of control. She starts rambling and talking in hurried sentences again and again, repeating the same thing, 'Monty isn't bad. He never hurt anyone.'

What is it about this guy that has her in such a grip?

'Okay, okay, Asavri. Calm down.' Menon realizes that a hysterical Asavri would be of no help.

'Do you know what happened to the bodies of the doctors and the dead nurse? Were they buried somewhere? There's just no trace of them.'

Asavri is silent and looks at the five pictures laid on the tabletop. When she speaks it's almost a whisper.

'The men cut up the bodies and threw them in an acid tank. It was there at the back of the House.'

'How do you … Did you see …' Menon is stalling.

'They did it in front of me. Bhai made sure I watched. Said that this is what happens to those who try to run.' For a while there's silence in the room. All of us are just trying to absorb what she said.

'Can I go now? Please …' She is trying to hold back her tears.

It's almost late afternoon by the time Menon, his team and the doctor leave.

'It was a good day. We've got a lot of information. Boss will be happy.' That's Menon's parting shot. By boss, he means the police commissioner.

The doctor also leaves and we are alone in the sprawling house surrounded by rolling greens and a dense jungle beyond. It's amazing how nature goes from looking beautiful in daylight to extremely creepy at night. As the sun wanes, having done it's day of work, the fading light gives way to darkness. The familiar feeling of unease sets in. No place is unbreachable, especially for monsters who cut up bodies and dissolve them in acid.

I grab a chilled beer and down a long sip as I start writing down all the details from the session. I remember everything. I press the cold bottle against my face. It feels good. I continue writing but my fingers are sluggish on the keyboard, as though they have turned to lead.

I'm exhausted by the day's events, by everything that's been happening since she returned. I've put my life on hold for her. Correction: I have ruined my personal life for her. Priya and I are now beyond repair. I know that well enough.

Suddenly, I miss her. Priya. I want to go out for a nice meal. Maybe to Olive; that's an all-time favourite. Just a normal evening without having to think about men who rape, drug and chop human bodies into pieces.

I finish keying in all the details. I go over them and think hard in case I've missed something. I think I've got it all.

I walk towards Asavri's room, hoping she hasn't slept off. It's not even close to dinner time but then again she looked physically and emotionally drained by the time Menon finished his verbal grilling.

She is awake and, as I suspected, looking at the picture with the window.

I walk in and sit away from her on the bed.

'It's the picture you took from Menon?'

'Yes. It is.' She has placed it on a huge white fluffy pillow and is touching the picture with her finger, almost caressing it.

'What is it in this picture, Asavri? I would think you'd never want to see the House ever again.' I tread gently with my question.

'It's not the House I see. It's something else.' She proceeds to point at something in the picture. 'You see the plant in the glass bottle, Avniel?'

I walk around the bed and sit closer to the pillow to get a better look.

'Yes, it's definitely a glass jar with something leafy in it. Yes, that's what it is.'

'He said the picture was taken three weeks ago. That's what he said, right?' I didn't realize it was a question for me so I stay quiet.

She's staring at the picture, touching it with her finger as though she wants to reach something … maybe someone. After what seems like a long pause, she speaks.

'He's alive. He hasn't killed him. He's alive, and he's taking care of the plant for me.'

'Who is alive, Asavri?' I'm scared of breaking the spell. I whisper my question.

'Monty.'

Twenty-Three

Monty. THEN.
2018

She was adding water to a plant in a glass jar. She saw it in a broken, almost smashed pot behind the building. The leaves were yellow and withered. No one bothered to water it, though some of the men often piddled on it. She asked for a twig. I laughed. 'It's dead. What's the point?'

She didn't persist; just kept quiet and bent her head. I could see she really wanted a twig from the plant so I got her one. Her eyes lit up when I handed it to her.

'You'll see, new leaves will grow.' She took it to the bathroom and washed it tenderly, as though she were bathing a child, skimming her fingers along the stem, rubbing it gently. Unable to find anything to put it in, she placed it in a steel glass that she used to drink water. Later, I got her a glass jar. Bhai loved pineapple jam and cartons of pineapple jam were brought in every month. One of the empty jam jars was what I got for her.

No new leaves sprouted for a long time but that didn't stop her from changing the water every second day and placing the jar in the sun for a few hours every day. On a few occasions, I heard her sing to the plant. I laughed my head off! Who sings to a plant?

'What's the date today?'

'What did you say?' I didn't hear her. I was looking out of the window, watching the men unload pots of plants from a truck. Three men were unloading a big red rug from another mini truck. There had been a lot of commotion in the House since early that morning. Someone was coming. Someone important. I wondered who it was.

'The date. What date is it?' she repeated.

'15 April.'

'You mean 15 April 2018,' she said. 'The finale of *Indian Koel* was on 20 November 2016. I left for the road after a month. The accident happened on the night of 22 December. I've been here for almost a year and a half now,' she said with a sigh, like it was the worst thing to have happened in her life. I felt angry. Nothing I ever did was enough to make her happy. What had I not done for her? I spoke to Bhai and stopped the men for her. No one even looked at her after that, leave alone coming to the room. How did that happen? Did she ever think of how risky it was to ask that of Bhai? No one in the House had ever asked Bhai for a woman to be left alone. I did it. I did it for her.

'Maybe I should ask one of the men to give you company tonight?' I spit my words out. 'You sound very bored. I think some company is what you need. Some new men have joined us, maybe you'd like to get to know them, huh?'

I kept standing near the window. I knew I had frightened her. Good. She needed to know that I was the best person for her in the House. I was the one who stood between her and the nightmares that could start anytime.

'I'm sorry, Monty. I didn't mean to be ungrateful. You … you have kept me safe.' She was standing with her back against the wall, staring at the floor. She was terrified. I had no intention of letting the men back in the room but I left her with that thought. I was more interested in the activities happening outside the House. I decided to go down to find out more.

I had already forgiven her but still walked out without saying a word. *Let her worry for a few hours. It will keep her in line.* She followed me till the door and then stopped. She wasn't allowed past the threshold. I was happy to see that she was being obedient.

I walked out of the room and tried to stay out of everyone's path. They were rushing around, doing something. I was never given any task, any responsibility. I didn't feel bad about it anymore. I was taking care of Asavri and she was very important to Bhai.

I wanted to find out what the commotion was about. Who was this important person for whom the House was being cleaned and prepared?

Bhai had been screaming at everyone since the morning. He found faults in everything. The line of potted plants wasn't straight; he thought some of them looked wilted. They looked pretty fine to me. The long red rug was rolled out in a straight line from the steps, with the plants placed alongside it. I wondered why the red rug was needed.

The house smelt of biryani, kebabs and many other things. Cooks from Madhubala Biryani House were out in the backyard cooking. Plants in different pots sat in the room and near the entrance. I entered the room next to the main hall. There was a large table I'd never seen before. The table had a white cloth. It was a white bed sheet and it was almost touching the floor. Why did we need to cover the table? We'd never done that. Bhai was screaming about the plates and glasses. Apparently we didn't have the right ones. What we had were either stained or chipped. The women scuttled away, terrified to be within his earshot, leaving the men to deal with his ire. They were almost pissing in their pants. It was nobody's fault. The House never has any guests or parties. We'd celebrate, but on those occasions Bhai would sit on the table without any cloth covering it and eat from the usual steel thali. Rest of us would squat on the floor. The stained and chipped glasses never bothered us or Bhai and neither did the steel thalis, some of which had dents.

But that day they did bother him.

He was late. Someone mentioned 'he' was supposed to reach by noon but it was almost three.

Who is this he?

This was the first time Bhai had been kept waiting and I knew it was making him angry. He paced down the corridor with his hands tucked behind him and head bent down. Suddenly he turned around and looked at me.

'Monty!' It was the first time I heard him scream, 'Where is she? Your girl.'

I got so nervous that I could barely speak. I bit my tongue and spit spluttered out.

'What's the matter with you, idiot? Have you become dumb now? I asked you where's the girl.' He started walking towards me and I didn't know why I couldn't get the words out of my mouth.

Ramesh came to help. 'She's in the room, Bhai. Should I get her?'

'No. That's not needed. Is she okay?' Bhai asked.

Ramesh and I didn't know whom the question was addressed to, so we both stayed silent.

'What's the matter with everyone? Do I have an army of dumb men?' He looked at Ramesh.

'Bhai, I've not seen her or been in the room since you ordered. Should I go?'

'I can go.' I found my voice with great difficulty. I didn't want Ramesh to go there. Asavri would think I sent him because I was angry.

'You're with her all day and night. Still you need to go see her to tell me if she's okay? What kind of a special moron are you, Monty?' Bhai barked at me.

'She's ... she's fine, Bhai. She's okay. She never steps out of the room, like you said,' I managed to say.

I was terrified when he asked about her. He came to the room twice, sometimes thrice, a week to check on her, but just then I feared that he would hurt her because whoever he was waiting for was late and he was probably frustrated. He walked out to the courtyard as I quietly left the room and found Ena. Though I didn't spend time with her or record videos of her anymore, she still liked me. She was the one who got sanitary pads for Asu.

'Ena, go to Asavri. Now. Stay with her. Don't leave till I'm back.' I wanted to tell Ena to tell her that I wasn't angry anymore. I knew that would be pointless. She wouldn't believe it. She thought the worst of me. I thought of something else and yelled out to stop Ena.

'Give her an injection.' She knew how to inject. If Bhai broke down the door and found her drugged up then maybe he wouldn't hurt her, and even if he did, she would be unconscious and wouldn't feel it. 'Ena! Stay with her.' I was going mad thinking of what to do. I couldn't think of anything. I just wanted Asu to be safe. That was all that mattered.

Of course she will know. Even if she's unconscious, she'll wake up and feel the bruises. What an idiot I am! I was sick with worry. I wished I could take her to some safe place, far away from everything, but I knew that could never happen.

'The car's arrived,' someone yelled, breaking my chain of thoughts. It was past four. I expected Bhai to be fuming but instead he was smiling. He patted his kurta, rubbed his hands and walked out as others made way for him. I dragged my feet behind and followed slowly.

He was such a plain-looking man. I'd seen him before, it'd been a while. He was the one sitting inside that shiny Mercedes that followed the ambulance when Asavri arrived at the House. He hadn't even bothered stepping out of the car that day. The door of his car opened right next to the red carpet and he stepped on it. He looked bored. In a white shirt and black pants, he looked like one of those so-called lawyers who sit outside the courthouse with a typewriter on a rickety table. Why was there so much fuss for this man? Why did the House need to be cleaned and prepared?

I'd seen Bhai with many visitors but it was different with this man. He was leading the way and Bhai walked a step behind him. It was very odd. Bhai always led. Another thing I noticed was that Bhai was bending, leaning towards the man as they spoke quietly. I wanted to get near them. I had my mobile phone ready. Luckily, I had a very good one.

Bhai followed him into the living room where the sofas awaited. White curtains hung at the windows. There was a low table near the sofa with a flower arrangement. I'd never seen the room look that pretty.

'Oh! I forgot,' the plain-looking man said. 'It's in the boot. The money.'

'Dheeraj bhai, don't be so formal with me. I'm your humble servant.' Bhai held the man's hand with both his palms and shook them. When he signalled with his eye, three men left the room. I couldn't believe my eyes. *Why is Bhai behaving like this? Who is this man and what hold does he have on Bhai?*

I inched closer. I switched on the video recorder on my phone and tucked it in my shirt's chest pocket. I'd cut a small hole on the pocket square so that the camera lens could record without anyone seeing the phone.

The man refused to eat or drink.

'I'm not here to eat. I'm here to deliver the money and check on the girl. How is she? Are you taking care of her? Is she unhurt? I need her alive and well.'

'Don't worry, Dheeraj bhai. She is being taken care of. You have nothing to worry about.'

'I hope you've kept your dogs away from her?' The man pointed at the men. 'Nobody should touch her, I hope you understand that. I need her untouched and unharmed.'

I wasn't surprised by the ease with which Bhai lied without batting an eyelid. 'Nothing to worry about. She's absolutely safe. Nobody touches her. She is now Monty's wife-to-be.'

'Monty? Who is that? What wife?' The man bolted upright and his leg knocked over the flower vase on the table, spilling the water. The wet patch grew in size. 'What the fuck are you talking about?' he began yelling. 'Who is Monty?'

Bhai cleared his throat and pointed at me; all eyes turned towards me.

The slap sounded like thunder, after which there was silence. 'Your half-psychotic, lame brother! You motherfucker! Are you mad? Do you know who that girl is? She is Kamini Pratap Singh's illegitimate child. She is worth her weight in gold. Take very good care of her, you fucking idiot. Not a scratch on the girl. Am I making myself clear, you idiot? I'm bleeding money, more than what you asked for, so that the girl is kept here, and you are planning a wedding! What are you, bharatmatrimony.com?' He poked Bhai in the chest.

What Bhai said next shocked me even more than the slap. 'Don't worry, nothing will happen to her. No one is getting married. I have eyes on Monty and the girl. She's fine. Do you want to see her?'

'No. I don't want to. I have no desire to see her and, more than that, I don't want her to see me. There's a reason why I chose this gutter. So that she can't be seen or found, you *maderchod*. Just keep her safe. She must never leave this place till I say so. Just do what I say. That's all.'

'I understand, Dheeraj bhai. Worry not. Let's have some food, shall we? We have the best biryani you'd have ever tasted. And then maybe some of the girls can entertain you?'

'*Tum log saala gully ka kutta ho, mujhe bhi wohi samjha hai*. Gully ka kutta; that I sleep with the keeda-makoda you keep here and sell God knows where?' I can't imagine anyone speaking with Bhai like this and Bhai listening silently.

It was well past midnight when I turned the key in the lock. I entered quietly and shut the door behind me.

'It's me,' I whispered. I knew she was awake. I could see her body stiffen with fright. When she heard a step outside the door, she must have thought it was one of the men.

Ena quietly left after I stepped in.

It was hot and stuffy inside. No fans in the rooms was another rule. It was common for the girls to loop a bedsheet around them to try and hang themselves. So no fans. I could've slept in my room that had a fan but I didn't want to leave her alone, and taking her to my room … that wasn't an option. Didn't want to risk making another request to Bhai.

There was hardly any breeze; it was going to be a severe summer. I hung my shirt on a nail behind the door. I'd had a few too many that night; I could smell it on my breath. I knew she could too and didn't like it but didn't say anything. *Well, she needs to get used to it. What's a man who doesn't drink?*

Was Bhai serious when he said that she's my wife-to-be? Is it possible that he's thinking of getting me married? The thought made me happy but I wondered if it would make Asavri happy. Would she want that too?

'Who had come today?'

'Someone called Dheeraj.'

'Dheeraj! Did you say Dheeraj?' She sat up in her cot and stared at me in the dark. 'He was here?'

'Yes. He was here to check on you. You're Kamini Pratap Singh's daughter, he said. Did you know that? You said your parents got you from … somewhere … where was it … Shillong …'

Twenty-Four

Avniel. NOW.

2019

I've not seen her all day. When I stand outside her door, I can hear the nasal chant.

'So … hum-m-m …'

At different times of the day I can hear Asavri chanting. This is the latest from Dr Parul.

'I'm a certified Art of Living instructor and have found the breathing exercises to be very helpful for my patients. Asavri needs to find the power that is in us to deal with the trauma and the backlash of it all,' Dr Parul said.

The slow, sonorous hum is annoying; it gives me a headache. How does this even help? What does the word even mean and how does chanting 'sohum' solve a problem? Doctor Parul started this soon after Menon's visit; it's been a month and a since Menon and his guys met her.

'She has endured enormous mental and physical trauma. Medicines can only do so much. She needs to heal from within, and Sudarshan Kriya will help.'

The cynic in me shrugged but I can see that it does work. I can see the change in Asavri.

She is improving by leaps and bounds. The breathing exercises seem to be working like magic. She walks around in the lawn by herself, talks to me and doesn't refrain from making eye contact while speaking as against staring at the ground. She's now speaking in full sentences and initiating conversations.

She walks out of her room after finishing the chanting and says, 'I want to speak with Menon. The cop.' There's a strange shine on her face. Maybe it's sweat. But then the rooms are centrally air-conditioned.

'Sure. What do you want to say to him? I can pass on the message.' I'm taken aback by her direct ask; it's almost an order.

'No. I want to speak to him.' She takes the phone from my hand.

'Yes, Mr Menon. Yes, I'm fine. I'm doing better. I remembered something so I wanted to tell you personally. Outside the House there is a woman. Without legs. Bhai had her legs chopped off because she laughed at him. She knows a lot about the men, Bhai and the business they did. She used to be a dancing girl. She can tell you a lot about what went on in the House.'

I'm looking at her as she runs her fingers through her hair, sighs and walks around the other side of the table and sits across me. She pours herself a tall glass of chilled water, gulps it down and then presses the glass to her cheek. I'm looking at her, almost waiting for something … I don't know what but I find out soon enough.

'You aren't with *Filmfare* anymore, are you?' I put down the lid of my laptop; looks like we're going to have a talk about something. The conversation I've been dreading since she was found – the one I knew would happen – is unfurling. I'm not prepared but one can't be prepared for something like this.

'No, I freelance now.' I'm not ready to tell her about the book yet. I open the laptop again and pretend to be busy looking at the opened page.

'What do you do? What kind of freelance work?' She isn't going to let go of it. I'm sure of that.

'This, that and the other.' I shrug my shoulders and pick up the papers on the table like they need my attention ASAP. They don't. All the mock conversations I had in my head with her about this has just vaporized.

'Like what? What did you work on after you finished *I'm Nobody's Child*?'

It hits me like a ton of bricks. I begin to stammer. I never imagined she would talk about the book in such a matter-of-fact manner.

'I … uh … I can explain, Asavri … It's …' How did she even get to know about the book? How long has she known?

'I've known about the book for a long time, Avniel. Someone got me a newspaper clipping of your interview.'

I can't meet her gaze, leave alone answer her question. Nothing I say is a good enough reason to have betrayed her trust.

'You used me. You used my life, every detail, every little thing that I told you; you used it for a book.'

How could she know so much from just an article?

'I couldn't sleep last night so I went into the library and found your book. *I'm Nobody's Child*. You couldn't even think of a title on your own. You had to use my words. The owner of this house must be one of your fans if there's a copy in the library. I was up all night reading. I'm not upset that you didn't tell me about the book. I'm upset that *you* wrote it, Avniel. I trusted you, one friend to another. You used me and my life.'

'Let me explain it to you, Asavri,' I begin.

'Yes, please do that, Avniel.' She cups her face with her palms. The ragged scar and puckered skin is towards me. I can barely look at it, leave alone imagine how it happened. She continues with her eyes fixed on me, 'How could you go and write about the things Baba said to me after Rudra brought me back to Shantipur? Those hurtful words uttered by the man I loved and adored. He called me the scum of the gutter, which he shouldn't have ever picked up and brought home. The delirium my Maa lapsed into after Baba had a stroke and the things she said. What the neighbours and my other family members said – I told you everything in my moments of despair and weakness. I thought I was showing my scars to a friend. I didn't know he was keeping a record of it to use in a book.' She angrily brushes away a tear that slipped out, as though telling herself, 'Don't you dare cry.' If she cries, it will be easier for me. Tears I can handle. Not the hard, cold truth.

I don't know how to justify what I have done. There is no justification. It was a bloody good story but it wasn't mine to tell. It was my chance to get out of the rut I was stuck in but I never had her consent. I never thought about her consent.

'And you thought, "She's dead so who is going to question me now?" Isn't that so? My return from the dead was bad news for you, but then I didn't just come back, I returned with an even more juicy and interesting story. You aren't the only one who reads other people's diaries. I read your notes that are lying around in your room. Seems like I returned from hell with a sequel for you!'

'Listen, Asavri. You can get back at the people who did this to you through the book. I can help you. What these monsters did to you, they need to pay! I'm doing this for you, Asavri.' It sounds like a weak defence but surely she will see the truth in it. I want to help her for real this time. Together, we can nail Kamini and face the consequences.

'You don't do anything for anyone. The only person you serve is yourself. It's always the story that matters to you. People don't matter, only the story. I don't matter. I never did. I'm just a story for you. You're sick.'

'Asavri, listen to me. I know what I did was wrong. Please let me make it up to you.' She's getting up and walking towards her room. I follow her. She shrugs me away, walks back into her room and shuts the door in my face.

I want to tell her about Kamini, the DNA report and how I've been working tirelessly to find out the truth about what happened and who is responsible. Yes, I've been a nosy, opportunistic bastard, but I want to help her now. I really do. But I also know trust is like fragile porcelain; once broken, it can't be mended. When our nightmares become a reality, it's devastating. My worst nightmare just played out.

It's dinner time and I can hear her do the Sohum chanting again. How many times does she do this every day? I walk into the dining room and see that the table is laid only for one person.

The server tells me, 'She wants to have her meal in the room. Madam said she'll ask for it when she is ready.' I'm okay with that. Seeing her is like staring at the writing on the wall, written in large bold print: YOU USED HER

SHAMELESSLY. When she was a psychotic mess and didn't look at me with accusing eyes, it was easier. Not anymore.

I spend the rest of the evening unable to do anything, listless and restless. Kay hasn't called yet. I try Priya's number. She doesn't pick up.

I almost jump out of my skin when my phone rings. It's not Kay. It's Menon.

'I wanted to give you the news myself. We cracked down hard on the gang. Most of his key men have been arrested. Though Bhai and his two men absconded, their network has been busted. The House has been seized, the residents taken in for questioning and the place is under lock and key. We will get the man soon. Nothing to worry about.' I could hear his voice brimming with pride at his achievement.

'What about that Monty fellow? Have you got him?'

'No, we haven't. But his picture is with every cop in the state. He will be caught. He can't escape.' I want to point out to Menon that Bhai and his two flunkies are still out there and so is Monty. What the fuck is he celebrating? But I stay silent.

'Another thing. Thank Asavri on my behalf. Based on what she said, local cops picked up the legless woman from the area. She had very valuable information about Bhai, his men and what went on in the House.' I can tell by the sound of his voice that he is jubilant. He is mighty pleased with the outcome and is surely on his way to a promotion and another star on his collar. His excited voice depresses me even further.

Blinding lights illuminate only a part of the surrounding garden that looks so serene by day and creepy at night; the rest is ominous darkness. What if someone is hiding in the shadows? Waiting to strike. I think of something and call up the security guard again. Menon is celebrating in Mumbai but Bhai and Monty are still at large. It is not comforting to know that. Asavri is far from safe, as am I, since I'm with her.

As I walk to my room, my mobile hums. I've been waiting for this call. It's Kay. I sent her on an important mission.

'Yes, Kay. Tell me what you've found.'

'Some good and some bad news. Which one you want to hear first?'

'Cut the drama and just tell me all of it, Kay.' I'm impatient and tired. I don't want theatrics. Just facts and details.

'OK. So here it is,' Kay says. 'The document room with all the paper proofs of women who willingly left their children, adopted babies from the home and those who have been there for their delivery – that document room caught fire about fifteen years ago and almost everything was destroyed.'

'And, of course, they are too archaic to have computer records.'

'Yes, boss. No computers. Even today there's just one computer, which looks like a relic. It's a place that's stuck in time. Way back in time.' Kay sounds tired. I know she has been working round the clock on this.

'Have you had food, Kay?' Sometimes I forget to be human in pursuit of a story.

'No. Should I hang up, have dinner and then call you back?' She has that tone which says, 'Stop fucking around. You don't care a fig about me and whether I've had dinner. So cut the bullshit.'

I laugh and say, 'No. Keep talking. Were you able to find someone, anyone who may have seen Kamini there? Could be a janitor, receptionist, anyone?' I'm grasping at straws.

'No. But I found something interesting. That's the good news.'

'What is it? If you haven't found anyone, what else could be interesting?' Disappointment rings loud in my tone.

'Boss, hear me out. About twenty years ago, sisters and other people in the missionary started dying. Yes, you heard me right. Some who were very old died of heart attacks. One died after she consumed a bottle of pineapple juice and went into a diabetic coma from which she never recovered. Some others died in a road accident, one of them drowned in the bathtub, one died due to a gas cylinder bursting, another had a very bad fall and died. It's really weird. The deaths are spread out over the years. In the last seven to nine years, no such accident has happened.'

I know what Kay is thinking. I'm thinking the same thing and we both speak at the same time. 'Someone very carefully and meticulously wiped away all those who may have seen or known someone or something.'

'Yes, boss. It's really eerie. Whoever this person is, the mastermind behind this, is a careful planner and very patient. I know this isn't really good news but it's good because we know Kamini had someone erase her past. Someone has been cleaning up the mess of her past and that can be only one person.'

'Yes. So basically anyone who may have seen her there twenty-three years ago is dead. This is getting more and more murky, Kay. Be very careful.' I don't need to tell her what we are dealing with. She isn't used to words of concern from me. I'm always only about work, deadlines and meeting those deadlines, so she ignores what I just said.

I hang up without a word. Just the DNA report isn't enough. Does Asavri know something more about this? After today's conversation, I doubt if I'll get anything out of her. She could very well call Bhaskar and tell him that she doesn't want me around. Bhaskar is my friend till it suits him. I will be asked to go if he thinks I'm an impediment to Asavri's recovery and she doesn't want me here. The BBC documentary didn't quite impress them as I'd hoped it would. I couldn't give it the time it needed and deserved. Priya is gone. Asavri can't stand the sight of me despite the fact I that want to help her now. I'm back where I began – in the rut. I put my head on the table and before I know it, I'm asleep.

I'm tumbling into a dark pit. I hit something hard. My head is spinning.

'I'm going to chop you into pieces and throw you in the acid tank.'

It's Bhai. He's coming towards me with a huge chopper in hand.

Someone is laughing. Really loud. It's Kamini. 'You poor, pathetic fucker. You really thought you could beat me?'

Someone is shaking me. The ground is shaking. Suddenly, I can't breathe.

'Avniel, wake up!' I can barely open my eyes. When I do, I see Asavri near me. I bolt out of the chair.

'What! What happened?'

'Nothing happened. You fell asleep on your laptop. You had a dream.'

My neck hurts, as does my back. I feel dizzy and unsteady. It felt so real and so horrible. My head hurts. I stagger to my room, badly in need of a cold shower and a strong cup of coffee. I stand under the shower for a very long time, letting the cold water assault my skin and senses. Finally when I feel cleansed of the frightful dream, the dark pit and everything else, I walk out. When I re-emerge from my room, fully woken up and freshened, I see Asavri with my laptop.

'You're the only person I know who has his own name as his password. You haven't changed.' A wry smile on her lips, she continues reading. I know what she's reading. It's too late to stop her. She had almost an hour to read.

'Delete everything, Avniel.' She points towards the laptop. 'Every note, synopsis, summary, chapter outline. Everything. I know you keep backup. Delete everything. If a single word about me goes out to the press or anywhere, Avniel, it won't be good for you.' I know it's pointless trying to tell her I'm doing this for her.

She walks towards the door and I make one last effort. 'Do you know Kamini is your mother? She left you in Shillong after giving birth to you and she's behind all this.'

'Yes, I know Kamini is my mother, have known it for a while now. I also know that Dheeraj is the one who threw me in that hole. I know everything.'

Twenty-Five

Monty. THEN.
2018

I couldn't remember how long it had been. Being chained to a pillar, left in the sun with no food and only some water. I lost track of the days. The sun was very strong; I could feel my skin burn. It felt like someone was slowly peeling it off with a pair of sharp tweezers. I knew I wouldn't die. That's why the water. Bhai wanted me alive. One can go on for days without food but not without water. I would've preferred death. Now that she was no more, what did I have to look forward to in life? There was too much blood around her for her to survive. I could see that through my alcohol haze and sleepy eyes.

I must have passed out while talking to her. I remember telling her that she is Kamini Pratap's daughter. I drank a lot that evening so that I could keep sitting there with Bhai, Dheeraj and the others.

When I got back to the room, I could barely walk. I collapsed. I woke up sometime later, feeling as though my tongue was stuck to the back of my throat. I was so thirsty. Alcohol does that. I was almost choking. I knocked over the water jug trying to grab it. My fingers felt tingly and my hands seemed to have left my body. Then I walked to the bathroom, hoping to drink some from the tap. I just needed to drink something. I almost slipped and fell. The bathroom was almost always wet but it felt more slippery and slimy than water. I felt a leg as I slipped and fell. I could barely lift my head, it felt as though someone had tied an iron ball to my neck.

I couldn't stop screaming. They had to break down the door and drag me out.

'What did you do, Monty? What did you do? You killed her! You pig!' I'd never heard Bhai yell so much. I was bathed in her blood. It was on my face, my hands, all my clothes … drenched in her blood. Bhai was thinking I'd done it. That I'd killed her.

'I didn't do anything. I found her like this.' I could taste her blood on my lips.

Some of the women dragged me away. I wanted to stay but I could barely stand. I wanted to hold her for the last time before they took her away, but I knew that was impossible so I walked away with Ena as Ramesh carried her lifeless body out of the pool of blood she lay in.

'She used the nail behind the door. The one on which you hang your clothes, Monty. She used that rusty nail to slice her wrists,' I was told the next day. The nail had a blunt, almost flat end; it must have been so painful to slice through layers of skin to get to the vein. She really wanted to die. Why? Why did she endure so much pain? The women refused to let me out of their room. Later, I learnt it was on Bhai's orders.

'Keep him here. I will deal with him later.'

Four days later he came for me. I let him kick and stamp on me. There was little I could have done to stop him and I didn't care. It didn't hurt. What hurt more was that she was gone. She hurt herself slowly so that she could leave me. How did I think anyone could love me? A white-skinned, ugly man with one leg shorter than the other.

'I should have left you to rot in that garbage bin where our mother tossed you after you were born! You filthy rat. You're just like her. Filthy, dirty scum. Nothing. You can do nothing right.' I don't know who stopped Bhai from kicking me but I wish they hadn't.

'Bring him out.'

When Ramesh tied me to the pole, I knew it then. I wish Bhai had killed me in the room. I didn't want to go out like that.

'He stays here. Like this till I say otherwise. And this is your piss pit. Come and relieve yourself on this *suar* whenever you want to. He doesn't deserve to be treated any differently.' To inaugurate the new piss pit, my brother stood there and urinated on me as every member of the House looked on, some of the women stood at the window and watched, some people from the gully came to see what the commotion was all about. After all, it's not every day that the leader of the gang decides to tie his younger brother to a pole on the road and invites everyone to take a leak on him.

I knew Bhai had no intention of killing me. When he wants to kill, he does it and when he wants to torment, he chops off legs and throws them on the pavement or ties them to a pole and has the neighbourhood piss on them. The woman with chopped legs looks at me and seems to say, 'Welcome to my world.'

Seven days passed. Rashes and boils covered my skin in places. The acid of urine, my vomit and the sun made for an obnoxious combination. It'd been a while since someone got me some water. I couldn't remember when was the last time I had eaten. I was seeing and hearing things. The previous night I'd heard Asavri singing. My mind was playing games. I wanted it to be over but I knew that it would end only when Bhai decided it.

Is that Ramesh and Ena I see? Why are they walking towards me? I didn't trust my eyes. *Must be seeing things again.* But when Ramesh unlocked the chains and I fell into Ena's arms, her eyes looked red and puffy. Bhai had finally relented. The question was why.

'You are standing in my shit, Ena.' I looked at her face. She looked like she'd been weeping.

'Things I do for you! Such a *harami* you are.' I passed out and felt Ramesh pick me up.

When I woke up, I found myself in the room that we all knew as the medical centre. There was a doctor in the House and a room with a few beds. There were enough medicines for the doctor to use. Felt nice to be in a clean bed and it felt as though I'd been bathed in some medicine. I was surprised that Bhai allowed me to live and get treated. I was responsible for Asavri's death. He was supposed to keep her safe and alive. I remembered Dheeraj saying that again and again: 'Take good care of her. Nothing must happen to her.'

And she died. She killed herself. Sliced her wrists with a nail. I failed to take care of her. I failed Bhai, yet he let me live and I was in the medical room with the doctor applying cream on my boils and rashes. It didn't add up. Something didn't add up.

The sullen-faced doctor was of no help. He was too much of a loyalist to tell me anything. I waited for Ena or one of the women to visit me. I knew they'd come. They always did. Meanwhile I had nothing to do but sleep and count the cracks on the ceiling. The paint was peeling and often chunks of cement fell out. No one wanted to be there and it wasn't because of the doctor and his medical abilities. It was that one never knew where a cement chunk would fall from.

I must have drifted off to sleep. I was given something that reduced the pain of the burn on my skin. I woke up when I felt a hand on my knee. There was a shape ... someone sitting at the foot of my bed. I was still groggy because of the medicine and it was very dark in the room. No moon that night either.

'Who's that?' I was barely audible and didn't really care. What was the worst that could have happened after being tied to a pole and being pissed on for seven days?

'It's me.' The shape moved in closer.

'Asavri?' I saw the familiar face in the dark. Her oval face and hair that was now till her neck. *Am I dead? Is that why I'm seeing her – another dead person?*

'Yes. It's me.' She raised her arm to push away a strand of hair and I saw the white bandage on her wrist.

'Asavri!' I tried to get up but couldn't. They'd pumped in too many medicines in me. *Is this really true? Or is this another dream?*

'Monty. Don't try to get up. Please, you need to rest.' Her voice sounded weepy. Raspy, as if she had a bad throat. She cleared her voice and moved in closer. She touched my face. Her fingers almost scalded me; they were burning hot. It was too real to be a dream. But I still didn't dare to believe in anything.

'You are not dead, Asu? I thought … you died.' My eyelids felt so heavy. I wanted to stay awake and talk to her but I sank into a deep sleep once again.

'I'm here, Monty. I'm here with you. I'll never leave. I promise.'

I felt her lie next to me. I heard her; like a whisper in the wind somewhere far away. I sank deeper in sleep and saw her face drift in and out of my sight. In the end, I just gave up and allowed myself to drown.

Next morning, I woke up wondering if it was a dream. It did feel like one. I was alone in the bed … so it was a dream. The bright sunlight that streamed in and the blue sky beyond looked happy, but they did nothing for me. It was just another miserable day for me without her. If I could see her only in my dreams then I would never wake up. I pulled the sheets on the bed, pounded the pillow and looked under the bed. I didn't even know what I was hoping to find. Some trace that the previous night hadn't been a dream. There was nothing in my bed or in the room to tell me that she was there. I know she wasn't.

'It was a dream, Monty. Just a dream. She's gone,' I told myself, though I didn't believe it. I didn't want to believe it.

As I was telling myself again and again that it was only a dream, she walked in. Just like that. Wearing a cream salwar with a tee. She walked in with Ena. I stared at her, not believing my eyes. *What am I seeing? Maybe I'm still asleep. Maybe the drugs the doc gave me are very strong and they're making me see things*. Only this time, it wasn't a dream. She was alive and came up to the bed and sat near me. Very near. I could see she was trying not to cry, biting her lower lip hard as her shoulders trembled. She raised her hand to wipe away a tear that'd broken free. There were thick bandages on her wrists. Both of them.

'It wasn't a dream. Last night. I didn't dream it, did I?'

'No. You didn't. I was here and I slept next to you. Ena took me away before the doctor arrived. I'm sorry, Monty. It's my fault. It's all my fault.' She was choking, crying and trying to talk at the same time. I stopped her.

'It doesn't matter, Asu. You're alive and that's all that matters.' I pulled her into my arms and felt her arms go around me. When she pulled me closer – tight and close – I didn't try to stop my tears.

I was in her arms, she was in mine. Suddenly, the day looked beautiful to me.

Twenty-Six

Kamini. NOW.
2019

I drain three cups of tea, gulping it hot and letting it scald my tongue and mouth as it slithers down. It burns. Hurts. Betrayal burns and hurts more. I stand under the shower longer than usual, hoping to calm my head. It doesn't. Finally, I make the call.

'Yes, Kaminiji. You are not easy to get a hold of.' He takes the call on the third ring but doesn't sound surprised to hear my voice. He addresses me by my name.

He knows my name and about me. I don't even know his name. That needs to change fast.

The fact that he addresses me by my name tells me that he was waiting for the call but is smart enough not to take it after the first ring. I'm dealing with someone who knows the game and is prepared. His voice is heavy but clear. This isn't a man who drinks all night and is hungover in the morning. His English has a Hindi accent; he is probably more comfortable in the vernacular, which is why I stick to English.

'What you sent me yesterday, how do I know it's not doctored?'

'Doctored? *Matlab?*'

'I mean how do I know you haven't created it with help from some technical guy? How do I know it's true?'

'Wait.'

My phone makes the near silent chime that indicates the arrival of a new message. I plug in my earphones and listen to it.

'You motherfucker! Are you mad? Do you know who that girl is? She is Kamini Pratap Singh's illegitimate child. She is worth her weight in gold. Take very good care of her, you fucking idiot.'

'I have lots more. Some video recordings too. *Bhejun kya?*'

This conversation can't happen on the phone anymore. It's not safe. We need to meet and discuss. We agree on 2.30 p.m. at the art gallery on Peddar Road. Post-lunch, mid-week, it will almost be empty.

'You'll be able to recognize me?'

'Yes.' The line goes dead.

I reach an hour before the decided time and sit in the coffee lounge across the road. I sit near the window, open my laptop, all the while keeping my eyes on the door of the art gallery across the street. I come to this café often, so the staff knows that I like to be left alone. My usual café Americano with hot milk on the side and a sealed bottle of water is placed on the table without having to ask for it. Both are left untouched. Since morning I've waited to arrive at the art gallery and meet the man. All through the morning meeting at the office, followed by the party meeting, I have been moving from one hour to another mechanically. Hearing but not listening. Nothing is making sense anymore. I let go of the reins and allowed someone else to have control over them. Dheeraj holds the reins of my life, of me. The reality of it all sits on me like a gigantic boulder. He knows everything and is plotting against me. I don't know what hurts more – the fact the he has gone rogue or that I didn't catch it. That he has been getting away with making an ass of me.

How could I have been so blind, so foolish and so trusting? When Asavri returned, even then I didn't suspect it! What does he want now that she is back? What will be his next move?

My eyes dart up from the computer screen to the entrance door of the gallery. Right next door is Mora Taara. Women walk in and out. There aren't any other shops, not even a paan shop, where men can idle away time. I'm sure he arrived early too and is waiting in advance. I don't see anyone who could be the man I'm meeting. It could be anyone. A man with a laptop bag slung around his shoulder approaches. He stops to light a cigarette. Is that him? I get a good look at him from my seat in the café. He doesn't look like a person Dheeraj would seek help from to keep Asavri captive. But then Dheeraj doesn't look like a man who would stab me in the back. Dheeraj doesn't look like a man who can do any of the stuff he has done for me in the last twenty-three years. I shake my head and focus on the man standing across the street. He looks left, then right and crosses over to my side of the street and walks away.

When it is twenty-five minutes past 2 p.m., I see a short, bulky man in a white kurta-pajama walk towards the door.

This must be him. He certainly doesn't fit the profile of someone who would visit a gallery.

I get a good look at him before he disappears inside.

Short, bulky frame, squareish face and thinning hairline. He has a lower-management kind of face, the kind that belongs to the peon in any office. Not a man of any significance or power.

When it's 2.45 p.m., I get up to leave. I put a 500-rupee note under the untouched coffee and make my way towards the gallery door. Once inside, the attending lady nods in my direction. I selected this time because I know the manager is out for lunch from 2 to 3.30 p.m. Not that the manager would disturb me in anyway; they know me too well to hover. I just like being left alone. I come here often, just to walk around and gaze at the paintings. This is one of my thinking zones. I gaze at art and think. It's always the bizarre ones that I'm drawn to. I'm skimming past the artworks till I see him standing before a canvas. I walk over and stand a few feet away.

'Do you like it?'

'What is it? It's just the reflection of the light on the paper.'

'No. It's not. Look carefully. The artist has painted the falling of light on the canvas.'

'Arre, wah! Kya photu banaya hai.'

I continue strolling. To anyone walking into the room, we would look like two random strangers appreciating the works of art. We walk around but never too close for anyone to see and know that we are meeting, yet close enough to hear each other.

I begin. 'How long have you known him?' I don't want to take names and he doesn't need clarification.

'I did a job for him in Shillong ten years ago. Since then, on and off, small jobs. He told me in November 2016 that there would soon be a big job.'

'Show me the video recordings you spoke about.'

Dheeraj in a car that accompanies an ambulance. Dheeraj standing over an unconscious Asavri in a hospital room, talking. 'She needs to get well soon and be here. I will need her soon.' Dheeraj delivering money. 'I'm paying you very well. Keep her here. No one must know.' And then the final straw: 'The bitch is Kamini Pratap's illegitimate daughter. She paid me to erase all evidence of her past and I did it. Asavri is the only living proof of what a snake Kamini really is. No one must know about Asavri till I decide it's time.'

I have seen more than I need to.

We are standing on either side of a grotesque bronze statue – half-man, half-snake. It's breathtakingly beautiful. Painfully and brutally beautiful. Agony frozen on the man's face as scales grow on him, his limbs dissolving into a slithery, tube-like snake's form. A fang sticks out of where there should be a tongue. One eye is glassy and still, while the other emits a final cry of pain. I'm almost transfixed by the sheer magic of the artist and the brilliant portrayal of terror and pain.

'You like it?' I look at the man; a commonplace face, the kind that walks the streets in thousands, lakhs. Is he a cop in plain clothes? The thought has already crossed my mind but I haven't said or done anything that would look bad.

He ignores my question and says, 'I am not police, madam. *Yeh sab baatein chodo*, madam. *Asli baat karo*.' He is standing close enough for me to smell his tea-laced foul breath. As he speaks, I turn my head away. I hired Dheeraj so that I wouldn't have to deal with men with foul breath and now it's because of him that I have to. The man pops a chewing gum in his mouth as though he understands why I turned my head away.

'So how is she out here now? She escaped out of your clutches, huh?'

'No one leaves my House without my *marzi*, madam. *Ladki toh door ki baat hai, hawa bhi nahin nikalti mere marzi ke bina.*'

'What do you want?' I allow him to speak and he does. If he were a cop, he would want me to talk, which he doesn't. I stand facing him so that the tiny but very powerful camera hidden in my locket captures his face clearly. Now that I have his picture, it won't be long before I know everything about him. He tells me everything I want to know and also what he wants. I hear him out and tell him that I will contact him soon. As I leave, I ask him his name.

'Everyone calls me Bhai.'

I don't make the call from the car. I don't want the driver to overhear. Dheeraj may have his ears everywhere. I wait till I reach the office and tell my secretary to hold all calls for half an hour. I'm not to be disturbed.

He picks up the call on the first ring.

'Madamji, long time.'

'Yes. I need information on someone. I only have a picture.' I skip the pleasantries. 'You will call back and report only to me. Is that clear? No one else, only me.'

I send him the picture. We don't discuss time frame or money. He knows he needs to get on the job ASAP and leave everything else. The remuneration will be more than adequate. I haven't used him in a while but the terms of engagement haven't changed.

The door to my room opens and Dheeraj walks in. The secretary didn't stop him. He has an all-access pass to me and I'm not going to take it away, yet. I need him to think that nothing has changed.

'Madam, I couldn't reach you.'

'Yes, Dheeraj. I'd gone to the art shop.' In case he checks with the driver, he would tell him the same.

'We need to go over the details of your campaign.'

Twenty-Seven

Monty. THEN.
2019

Bhai allowed us to move into my room. I didn't have the courage to face him and he stayed away too. Maybe he doesn't trust himself to let me live if we came face-to-face. I didn't want to die anymore. She was alive.

Mina told me about everything that led to me being freed from the pole.

'She'd bled a lot, Monty. She was sitting in the bathroom bleeding for a very long time. When she was taken to the hospital, she was just a breath away from death. On waking up, she asked for you. The first thing she uttered after waking up was your name, Monty. Of course, no one told her that you were chained in the courtyard with everyone pissing on you. That you were just a few feet away from her room. They fed her all kinds of tales about you being on a trip. When she was able to get out of bed, she saw you from the window. She begged me to take her to Bhai. I did. She fell at his feet, apologizing for what she did, promised she would never try to kill herself or run away and made him grant your release.'

I couldn't believe what I was hearing. Asavri spoke with Bhai about letting me go and he agreed. How? Why?

I got to know more later. Since Bhai had been instructed not to touch or hurt Asavri, he told her, 'Every time you try to run away, someone innocent will get hurt. Badly hurt. I will find you, Asavri. Then I will make you watch, and if I don't find you, know this that every day I will pick one unsuspecting person, someone who has nothing to do with you, and hurt that person brutally. So for every day that you enjoy your freedom, someone will be in hell.'

Ena also told me that Bhai made her watch while he picked a random girl from the village and had her plundered by the men before throwing her to his pack of hungry dogs who hadn't been fed for over a week.

'Don't shut your eyes, Asavri. If you do, I'll get another girl. Watch and learn. Don't try to run. Don't try to kill yourself. Others will get hurt if you do. I punished Monty because he is your friend and, also, he failed to take care of you. Anything you do, Monty gets hurt. Remember.'

We are in my room and Asu is once again playing with the plant in the jam jar. 'See, Monty, I told you the twig isn't dead. Look! A tiny leaf has grown.' She liked my room better. It was larger and had a fan. The window overlooked the cluster of shanties, unlike the one in her earlier room, which looked out to a rotting canal clogged with waste plastic, carcasses of dead rats and filth. The stench was so overpowering that often we had to keep the window shut. My room had two large windows and from one of them you could see all the way till the road. The main highway that winds its way around the Western Ghats and towards Pune city.

She brought the jar near me. I almost didn't see it, it was so tiny. Just a green dot on the twig. But, yes, it was a leaf.

'Life finds a way, Monty. It always does.' She took it back from me and kept it on the table next to the window. She looked so happy to see the tiny leaf. I wanted to do more to see that smile again and again.

I decide to ask the question that's been on my mind. 'Why did you do it, Asu? Why did you try to kill yourself?'

She fell silent. The smile gone, she looked at her feet. She rubbed a spot on the floor with her big toe. She was in a cream salwar and tee again; they hung on her, too large for her bony frame. I needed to buy her some clothes.

When she spoke, I could barely hear her. 'I'm really nobody's child. Nobody wants me, Monty. Nobody. My real mother wants me dead and those who picked me up from the adoption home threw me away like I'm a dirty rag. Rudra left me. Maa and Baba left me. The family that I grew up with, whom I loved so much and thought they loved me too, asked me to leave after the Rudra incident. Nobody cares about me. What do I have to live for, Monty, when nobody wants me?'

'I do. Please don't die, Asavri; I have nobody in my life. Nobody cares whether I live or die. My brother pissed on me and told everyone to do the same just to teach me a lesson. My mother threw me in a garbage dump. Do you know why I'm called Monty? Bhai found me in a plastic bag with 'Monty Fashion' written on it. He decided to name me after the name on the bag he found me in, tossed in the garbage dump. Nobody wants me.'

She came over and sat next to me and slid her hand into mine. I could feel the crumpled skin on her wrist. I turned her hand around to see it. Whoever stitched her up did a hurried job, without bothering to think it would leave a scar. I touched the skin there, allowing my thumb to roam the spot. Suddenly I saw a pool of blood. I shook my head and looked at her.

'You don't know how scared I was when I saw you covered in blood that night.'

'I'm sorry, Monty. It will never happen again. I promise.' She smiled through her tears. To me the smile looked like a rainbow in the sky after a stormy night.

That night, I told her about how Bhai lined Pilot's glasses with poison. It was years ago, when Bhai was Pilot's right-hand man.

'It took months for the poison to slowly seep into Pilot's body through the corner of his eyes. At first the signs were few and barely noticeable, then he started getting muscular seizures. In the end, he could barely move and had to be fed through a pipe. Bhai woke up as usual one morning, bathed, changed into a white kurta and walked into Pilot's room. He always began the day by kissing his palm. He did so that day as well. Held the man's hand, kissed him, spoke with him and then took out his revolver and shot him twice in the forehead.'

I could tell she didn't like hearing about Bhai and the things he did. But she didn't say anything; she stayed quiet and stared at the ground when I talked about him. I was always very proud of being his brother, though I knew I was an embarrassment to him. But ten years prior, when he shot Pilot and sat in his chair, I couldn't have been more proud. I knew I would never sit in that chair but at least my older brother did.

'I've learnt a lot from Bhai. About poison, where to get it, how to make it. Everything I know is from Bhai.' I don't know if I'm really his brother but for me, he is my brother, my everything.

I got an apple for her from the kitchen. Already sliced into pieces. Knives aren't allowed in the rooms. Though I trusted her, I still kept an eye out for sharp things that could be used to slit skin. Anyhow, she enjoyed the apple.

'Don't chew the seeds. They are poisonous,' I told her as she swallowed one. She tried to spit it out but it had gone too deep into her throat. She looked worried as she stared at me with the half-eaten apple in her hand.

'Don't worry, nothing will happen if you chew a few but a whole bunch together is deadly cyanide. Bhai taught me that. Once he bought five dozen apples, powdered the seeds and mixed it in the food that was served to a business guy who refused to pay him money. Now that man can only sip water through a pipe, can't move a muscle at all.' I tried to impress her with the stories. I wanted her to know that she was with a man who knew a lot. But she stayed quiet when I told her the stories. I also told her about what I did to Rudra. After she won, I had a few men visit him and they hanged him by the neck till he died.

'I did that for you, Asu. He was bad, and mean to you and deserved to die. Aren't you happy he is dead?'

'Thank you, Monty,' she replied, but I could tell she was scared. I didn't want her to be scared. There was nothing to be scared of. I was there to take care of her.

To make her feel better, I took her to a shop in the village and bought her some clothes. Bhai gave us permission.

'Pick whatever you like,' I told her. She selected a pair of denim trousers and two tops.

'Take more, Asu,' I urged her and she selected some more. I told her to buy some bras. She had only two. I wanted to buy everything in the shop for her. It felt so nice sitting at the entrance, watching her select clothes and go into the the little makeshift trial room behind a curtain to wear them. She wore each dress and took the ones I liked.

I was thinking of the bra she bought. I wanted to see her in it. I knew she would show me if I asked her to but that wasn't how I wanted it to be. I wanted her to want me; the way I felt. I was prepared to wait.

After shopping, we went for a meal to Madhubala Biryani House. Everyone knew who I was and by then they knew that she was someone who stayed in the House. Someone they'd see but never talk about. I felt very important when tables were vacated as we entered and people picked up their plates and moved away. It wasn't because of me. Everyone feared Bhai, and because I'm his brother they feared me. They didn't want me to complain to Bhai that I was treated badly.

It wasn't much of a restaurant, really. Just a small hut with few plastic chairs and scratched-up tables. Couples had scribbled all over the tables' surface. There was a Mohit and Ameena. Then there was a Raj and Simran. Someone watched DDLJ too many times. We laughed while trying to read the names. A couple were scratched out. Maybe a jilted lover returned and couldn't bear to be reminded of the happy past, so he decided to scratch it out. On the walls were posters of Bollywood heroines. Amir bhai loved the beauties of the past. I'd learnt their names over my visits in the past.' There's Madhubala, who looks like Madhuri Dixit.' I remember telling Amir bhai that and getting a scolding: 'Madhuri looks like Madhubala, not the other way round!' No one liked to argue with Amir bhai. He'd refuse to serve you if you crossed him, and the biryani he cooked was simply too good to be missed. He was a Madhubala fan, hence the name Madhubala Biryani House. Once, someone painted a moustache on Madhubala. Amir bhai wasn't amused at all. A full-scale investigation was pursued to nab the person responsible and when he was eventually found, he was forbidden entry forever. Amir bhai was very touchy about Madhubala and the biryani he cooked.

I could tell Asavri liked the biryani and mutton sheekh kebab. She polished off everything on her plate and grinned at me. Seeing her happy made me happy. I made up my mind to speak to Bhai about allowing us out once a month. Before leaving, she picked up a fistful of saunf with some misri and wrapped it in a paper napkin. 'I like eating these.' She stuffed the napkin in her trouser pocket.

We walked back to the House, strolling through the lanes, in no hurry to return. I'd never felt so happy around the dirty shanties as I did that day. It was a perfect day. The rains had just got over and the ground was still damp and soft. Our feet sank in some places as we walked. My walking stick was sinking deeper into the moist ground and slowing me down further. She pulled the stick out of the soft mud and put my hand on her shoulder. I leaned on her till we got to firm ground where the stick didn't sink. I would have liked to keep walking on soft ground if that meant holding her shoulder.

She matched my pace as I hobbled along. Somehow it didn't bother me that much.

We passed a stage that was being built. We stood by and watched the boys tie ropes to long bamboo poles that would be hoisted up to form the exterior cover. Some were busy tying the poles while others hammered away to make a steady platform.

'What's that for?'

'That's for Ganpati puja. It will start soon. This is the first time Bhai has given permission so everyone is very excited. You must have seen Ganesh puja in Mumbai.'

'Oh yes, I have. Ganpati visarjan at Chowpatty is a scene to watch. The idols are like mountains. People dance and sing like crazy. I saw it once. Such large crowds! It's like a sea of people chanting, "Ganpathy Bappa". The city comes to a grinding halt on the final day of visarjan. It's so crazy that it's almost scary, Monty.'

Twenty-Eight

Asavri. NOW.
2019

'Asavri! Asavri!' I hear Avniel scream out from the library. We haven't spoken much since I confronted him about the book. I don't even want to look at his face but his shouting makes me jump out of my skin. I run out, my heart pounding. What has happened?

'Come to the library.' He is standing at the door. He runs back and I follow him. I can't really tell by the look on his face what all this is about. He looks like he has seen an alien. Excited, scared and hassled – all at once.

'What is it?' I'm irritated. I've been thinking about returning to Mumbai all morning. I can call Bhaskar and he can take me back. I don't need or want to be around Avniel. As I walk into the room, the huge TV screen that almost covers the wall is showing the news. I freeze in my tracks.

It can't be.

Kamini is on the 8 p.m. news. 'Distraught, wild-eyed and hysterical, she seems to have been assaulted.' She is bleeding and screaming while being pushed through the hospital in a wheelchair.

'He killed him! That man ... that man shot Dheeraj.'

The police commissioner's face appears. 'Around 4 p.m., we received a frantic call from Kaminiji saying that she had been attacked and was in danger. Lonavla police force reached her within minutes and we found her bleeding profusely near the road. We have also found two dead bodies. Dheeraj Shastri, and the other one has been identified as the wanted gang leader who goes by the name Bhai. We will get more details when Kaminiji regains consciousness and is able to talk. We are happy that we were able to reach on time and save her.'

The news clip is played on loop, again and again. I see her hysterical face screaming. The face of the woman who gave birth to me, then threw me away like the day's garbage and then didn't hesitate to have me thrown into a hellhole. I can't breathe. I want to see Dheeraj's corpse. But there's cloth covering the dead bodies. I want to see him dead. A bullet to the head. That's what the news said killed him. That's too easy and quick a death. In my mind I've killed him a thousand times over and none of them are easy and quick. And Bhai … Bhai … I shut my eyes. I still hear his voice, sometimes. Low, steady and so easy, as though he's reading the weather.

You want to run away? Go. Every day that you aren't here, I will hurt someone. A young innocent girl from the village.

I need water. The walls of the room are closing in. I can't speak … it's as though my tongue has retreated into my throat and is choking me.

'I … uh … water ...'

Avniel rushes to pour me a glass and I gulp it down. More. He gets the bottle and starts to pour me another glass.

I grab the bottle and empty it into my mouth, letting a lot of it flow all over, drenching my face.

We don't speak. Just sit together, watching the same news again and again, waiting for more. It comes after an hour. Kamini has given her statement from the hospital room. She speaks into the camera for less than a minute. 'I've told everything to the commissioner. It's the love and prayers from all of you that saved me today.' Half-sitting, half-lying on the hospital bed, she looks pale. An ashen-faced Tanya sits next to her, holding her mother's hand. My half-sister. Does she know what her mother ... our mother did to me? Was she in on it?

How would it be if Tanya landed up in that hole with Bhai and his men? Did Kamini know where Dheeraj had kept me? It didn't matter that her daughter was there ...

The mother–daughter image freezes on the TV screen as her statement, in script, scrolls up for everyone to read.

'Dheeraj and I were headed to Khandala for a campaign planning meeting. We stopped for coffee and out of nowhere this man appears and starts screaming at Dheeraj. Something about getting a party ticket Dheeraj had promised him but didn't give. He shoots Dheeraj in the head, between his eyes. I pick up a big stone and throw it at the man. It hits him on the face and he falls. The gun slips out of his hand. I try to grab it but he is quicker than me. He grabs it. I try to wrestle the gun out of his hand and my finger presses the trigger. It hits him somewhere, he falls, but the gun is in his hand and he presses the trigger. The bullet hits me in the thigh. I'm terrified. I kick him hard and the gun drops from his hand. I don't think. I pick it up and empty it all on him. I was so scared and in so much pain, I didn't know what

I was doing. Then I limp away to the car, get my mobile. I somehow manage to make a call and tell the commissioner I need help. I pass out in pain.'

'How does this woman do this?' asks Avniel.

'Do what?'

'Get this lucky and dispose of everyone who crosses her path.' He has a look that I don't understand. 'There must be some way … something … to stop her from getting her way all the time. Every time.' He is now pacing around in the room.

'You do know you are next?' He spins around and faces me.

'Huh?'

'Yes, Asavri. Kamini Pratap Singh has successfully eliminated everyone in her path. Dheeraj, that Bhai character, and now the only remaining obstacle in her path is you. It's you who is next.' If he's trying to scare me, he is doing a good job of it.

'I think it's time we returned to Mumbai. Let me talk with Bhaskar.' Avniel starts punching numbers on his mobile and walks out.

I don't know what to think or do. There was a time when all I wanted was to get married and be a wife. That didn't happen the way I thought it would. Then I wanted to sing. I won the contest and thought everything would be fine. Then the accident happened and I almost died. I survived only to live a nightmare during which I wanted to die every day. I just wished I could stop breathing. Then in Mumbai … the hospital, and all this … I don't know what I want anymore. Whatever I want never really turns out as planned.

I press my head on the glass door. It feels cool on my hot skin. I wish I could step out. I know I can't. It's a dark, moonless night. I think it's the clouds that hide the moon. From where I stand, there's a narrow but long sit-out that overlooks a cliff. This part has fewer lights than the main garden. Monkeys jump on the branches, which hit the bulbs, shattering them. I have seen the workers clean the shards often. During the day, the sit-out is a pleasant place to be but right now it doesn't look inviting in the dark.

I'm thinking of everything and nothing, all at the same time. That's when I see it. At first, I almost miss it. Avniel must have had a beer in the evening; it's still there, along with a bowl. The cleaners must have missed clearing the table. It is standing next to the beer bottle, almost hidden. From where I stand, I can't see it well. I move to the other glass door, hoping to get a better view.

It can't be. It's not possible.

I finally get a clear view from the last door. Yes. It is. A little while back I was feeling hot, almost sweating with worry. Now, I'm shivering. I go cold as I see what's next to the beer bottle on the table right outside the library.

It's a small glass jar and it holds the twig of a money plant.

Twenty-Nine

Kamini. NOW.

2019

I spit out the sleeping pill. I pretended to swallow it but didn't. I want to be awake. I need to plan out the rest of it and this time there will be no mistakes. I haven't quite figured how to take care of Asavri but I will think of something soon. I lie back and think of everything that happened today.

It didn't take me long to find out everything about the man I had met in the art gallery. He was a wanted criminal. They were suspecting him to be the person who kept Asavri captive. Dheeraj had promised him a party ticket. He seemed very pissed with Dheeraj. I'm sure Dheeraj must have humiliated him or done something. It doesn't matter. He let Asavri go. It was his idea to upset Dheeraj's plan by sending Asavri back to Mumbai. He wanted to join hands with me, get back at Dheeraj and get that party ticket he had been lusting after.

I had a plan of my own and this time I intended to carry it out myself.

I told him that Dheeraj and I would be going to Khandala for a meeting and gave him the exact location of where I would stop the car and step out for coffee. Dheeraj didn't suspect anything. Not even when I told him that I didn't want to take the driver. Besides, it wasn't unusual for just the two of us to be in the car. We did that quite often when we needed to discuss sensitive agenda. We were talking about all things politics – future plans, campaigns, etc. The man truly had some great ideas. It's a pity I had to kill him today.

Everything went exactly according to my plan. We stopped for coffee in a desolate spot as always. Crowded food courts aren't my thing. My staff had packed a coffee-and-breakfast basket, as always. Dheeraj poured me a cup. I walked ahead a few steps. A twig snapped. I didn't bother to turn around. Dheeraj did. A muffled sound followed and the cup fell and shattered on the ground. What a pity. Murano cups lying shattered. I stood near enough to see the look of shock and surprise on Dheeraj's face. It was all over in a flash. I hate drama, and I had told that Bhai fellow; I refuse to call him Bhai. It disgusts me to have to deal with the likes of him. Anyway I told him clearly that I wanted no conversation or explanation from Dheeraj.

It's so unnecessary; explanations and apologies. I didn't want any explanation about why he kept Asavri alive when the deal was to finish her. He told me she was dead. That was a lie. He had kept her alive with Bhai, hoping to use her against me for God knows what. Good thing Bhai got fed up with Dheeraj and decided to take things in his hands.

When I turned around, the man had his mouth on my flask, sipping my coffee. Uncouth! I threw a rock at him. It hit him hard. I've always had a good aim. As he fell, I grabbed the gun, shot him in the hand, then the groin … a few I shot here and there, before plugging two more in the chest. That finished the job.

What did he think, I'm going to give him the party ticket Dheeraj promised but bailed out on? I'm done dealing with pigs who know all about me.

I had one bullet left and needed to use that well. I walked over to him and used his fingers to scratch my face and arms. I felt for his pulse just to be sure. There was none. I pointed the gun to my right thigh and pulled the trigger. The impact almost threw me off. I fell to the ground. I managed to get up; the pain was killing me as I staggered towards the car. I needed to make the call to the commissioner.

Now I lie in the hospital room, listening to the slow hum of the AC. The large window gives me a view of the city I came to and where I made a life for myself. The girl from the dirty *gully* of Varanasi has come a long way. Now all I need to do is take care of Asavri. She doesn't worry me at all. I allow myself to fall asleep.

Thirty

Asavri. NOW.
2019

It can't be. I don't know how long I've been standing by the glass door, staring at the tiny sprig of the money plant. It must have been one of the workers or the guards. That's ridiculous. Why would the guards or the servants in the resort place a tiny plant in a jar and place it on a table just outside my room? The jar looks dirty, stained ... like something picked out of the trash.

How is this even possible? I turn around. Avniel isn't in the room. I can hear him on his phone. I turn back towards the glass panel and squint my eyes. It's dark and there are no lights on the balcony. The glow of lights from the front lawn lends some brightness to a part of the porch. The monkeys are back to being mischievous again, breaking the bulbs. I need to go out and see it for myself. I don't want Avniel to find out. He has told me many times never to step out of the house at night. So far I have obeyed but now I need to go out and see. I'm sure it's nothing but something tells me it's not just nothing.

I walk towards my room and shut the bedroom door. Avniel turns to see me close the door. He is on the phone.

It's not unusual for me to close the door. I see him walk farther away from my room. I rush towards the glass door, which allows entry to the porch. The door isn't closed. There's a pebble wedged on the channel to stop it from closing fully. All the doors are centrally locked from the guard-room but this one isn't because of the pebble. I slide it open. It's heavy and moves slowly, grudgingly, as though telling me that it's a mistake to go out.

I step out and hug myself. My thin t-shirt makes me shiver. It's a cold night. It rained last evening and all morning. Inside the house, I hardly felt it but outside I'm shivering. My bedroom slippers feel slippery as they squish wet leaves strewn by the rain. I don't know what I'm hoping to see or find. I reach the table and pick up the jar. As I thought, it's dirty, stained and a crack runs diagonally across it. Someone must have picked it up from the trash pile. I say his name without thinking anymore. I know he's around.

'Monty.' It's barely a whisper. I'm shivering in the cold. 'Monty. I know it's you.' This time my voice is a bit louder. I hear a rustle near the railing. I put the jar back on the table and walk over to the edge. His white face is visible in the dark. I gasp and lean over. He is holding on to the last rod, his feet on a slim stony ledge. I reach out and he grabs my hand. I pull him up with ease. He was never very heavy. His clothes are sodden with dirt, leaves and the rain. His hair is plastered to his skull. He doesn't have his stick. He is holding on to the railing for support.

'Why are you here, Monty?' I just blurt it out and then see the hurt on his face. He'd hoped for a different response; a better, warmer welcome.

'I needed to see you. I couldn't just stay away.'

'If the guards see you ... How did you get in?'

'There's a narrow path up the cliff. It's not easy but one can walk on it and come up to this side. I came for you, Asu.'

'I'm fine, Monty. People are taking care of me. I'm okay.' I don't realize it but I have taken a few steps away from him as he hobbles closer.

'Everything is over, Asu. The cops raided the House. There was no warning. They just came. I wasn't there. Mina told me. Bhai and some others barely managed to run. All the others were caught. Everything is finished.'

'Yes. I saw that on TV. You are free now, Monty.'

'How can I be okay when you are in danger, Asu? Don't you know Kamini has killed Bhai? She shot him. Didn't you see it on TV? She will now come for you, Asu. She will kill you.'

I grab the back of the chair to stop myself from falling. 'I don't know what to do, Monty. I don't want to die.'

'Silly Asu.' Monty smiles. The scar on his face looks deeper. He wipes his face with his wet palm and hobbles to the table on one foot. 'Why do you think I'm here? What I have will finish that bloody bitch.' He holds the chair with one hand and pushes the other into his trouser pocket. He pulls out a tightly wrapped plastic bag. He hands it to me. There's something inside it. 'I did it to protect it from rain or if I fell.'

It's so tightly packed that I have to use my teeth to rip it. A mobile.

'There are so many videos in it. All of them are my recordings. Here, let me show you,' he says as he takes it from my hand and punches in his passcode.

I ask him, 'Still the same password? My name?'

'*Hamesha*. I will never change the code. Now see.' He moves in closer.

For the first time I see a glimmer of hope. These videos will finish Kamini. Every time Dheeraj visited the House, he spoke about me or Kamini, Monty recorded it all. 'Bhai took these recordings too. He used them to get to Kamini but that bitch killed him. What she doesn't know is that I have the originals!' He looks and sounds happy with himself. This is indeed great. Just what I needed.

I'm thinking of what to do next and he is still talking. Wish he would just keep quiet for a while. I look towards my room – the open glass door. I hope Avniel doesn't decide to come in looking for me.

Monty continues speaking. 'What we will do first is upload all these videos on YouTube. Then we can be safe together. I have taken a lot of money from the House. We can be fine for months. No need to worry. We will live in Goa, just the way we discussed.' He is looking at me, waiting for a reply.

'What will we do to survive, Monty? How long will the money last? And then what? You'll be a sweeper and I will wash dirty dishes in people's houses ... Is that your plan for our life together?' He is such a hopeless romantic.

Monty looks shocked. He has never heard me speak like this. Well, I'm not in the House anymore. 'Are you angry with me, Asu? You know I love you.'

'Love me?' I put the mobile on the table and move away. 'If you loved me, you would have helped me when I was in the House. You could have called for help and got me out. Instead, you sat in the room like an idiot, watching me get raped. What did you think ... seeing you gave me peace?

A familiar face sitting by quietly while your brother's men raped me all night long. I will never forget those nights. Ever in my life. I will never be normal again, Monty. And you could have stopped it. You could have saved me but you didn't.'

'What could I do?' He is stammering and fumbling for words. 'You saw what Bhai did to people who went against him.'

'You bloody coward, Monty! You are your brother's pet dog.' I almost spit out the words.

'I didn't hurt you. I protected you in the House.'

'Didn't hurt me? Protected me? Is that why you injected me with herion once a week? You wanted me to be your pet slave.' I feel like scratching his face as the memory of it all rushes back.

Anger flashes in his eyes. 'I took you to Mumbai to let you go. I helped you get away. You have any idea how dangerous that was?'

It occurs to me at that moment, something I had never thought of earlier.

'You went back to the House later, right? After Mumbai. You went back?'

'Yes. Where else would I go?'

'And Bhai didn't do anything to you? You helped me escape. You left me in Mumbai and Bhai allowed you back into the House. When I tried to kill myself, he had you chained in the courtyard and made people piss on you. It wasn't even your fault. And you take me to Mumbai, I get away and he does nothing.' I move near him and stare at him hard.

He is quiet and is looks away.

'What aren't you telling me, Monty? You think I'm an idiot? That all of you can play games with this idiot? Huh? I want you to say it, Monty. It was his plan, wasn't it? He told you to take me to Mumbai, didn't he? And you, his obedient servant, carried out his order. You weren't helping me. You just did what that brother of yours told you to do!'

'I love you, Asavri. I just did what Bhai asked me to do; he was sick of Dheeraj. But I always wanted to help you and I did, didn't I? Kamini has killed them all. She will kill you now. I'm the only one who can keep you safe. Come with me.' He holds my hand and pulls me closer. It was a mistake to stand near him. His wet and cold hands feel like a grip I can't free myself from.

'*You* can't keep me safe! You can barely walk on one leg. You need help to stand up … and you think you can take care of me?' I try to wrench my arm free.

He tries to slap me. 'Come with me. You and I are meant to be together.'

I catch his palm before it hits me and push him away. 'I don't want to go with you.' I start screaming. He grabs me with both hands. No longer near the table, he is holding me for support but I can't free myself from the vice-like grip.

'I'm not leaving without you, Asu. You are coming with me.' He starts dragging me to the railing.

'I'd rather die than go with you!' I'm screaming so loud that my throat hurts.

'What! What … is …' Avniel has heard the scream. He looks horrified to see the two of us struggle.

'Let go of her, you bastard!' He presses a button on the wall. A piercing siren begins to howl. He runs towards me.

'Monty, go away. The guards will be here any minute. Go away, Monty.' I don't want him to get caught.

'I will not go without you, Asu.' Monty has his grip on me and pulls out a gun from his pocket.

'Leave her alone, you swine!' Avniel takes a step closer and the bang of the gun reverberates, shattering the calm of the dark night. The sleeping birds wake up and start a frightened chattering. Some monkeys begin to jump from one branch to another.

'Avniel!' He has buckled down. I can see a red patch growing on his shoulder. He is on the floor.

'We are leaving now. There's a path over the edge. It's difficult but we can get away. No one can hurt us now, Asu. We will be together and we will be safe. Just what we spoke about, remember?' His eyes look soft with the anger diminished. He has put the gun back in his pocket.

We are near the railing and I dig in my heels on the slippery porch. 'I don't want to spend my life with you, Monty. I want my life back. You need to go away.'

I look at him in the eye and then kick him on the leg he is standing on. He buckles, giving me a surprised look. He can't believe what is happening. I push him with all the strength I have. I can feel tears in my eyes. He tries to grab me as he topples over. I push him harder. His body is dangling over the railing. I give him a final push and say it.

'I don't love you. I never have. I don't want to be with you, Monty. I want my life back.'

I step back as he makes a last desperate attempt to grab my hand. I watch his face as he mouths the words, 'I love you, Asu. I always did.' And then he falls into the dark green abyss. I stand there leaning, trying to listen. I hear branches break and then a muffled thud. Then I let myself weep.

I love you too, Monty. I lied. I love you too, but I can't give up my life for you. I just can't.

The guards arrive. Two of them pick up Avniel from the pool of blood. From where he lay, he saw it all. He is looking at me while I look away. I'm not ready to face him after what I just did. I pick up the mobile from the table and go inside.

Thirty-One

Asavri. NOW.
2019

I'm in a suite at the Marriott. A month has passed since that rainy, dark night on the slippery porch. The guards searched the grounds but couldn't find Monty or a body. I didn't tell them it was Monty; just said someone sneaked in and tried to shoot me; Avniel tried to save me and got shot. Avniel kept quiet and went with my story. I sat indoors with him; the wound wasn't deep. The bullet grazed past him. He wanted to talk. I said no. There was something more important that needed to be done. At first he was reluctant to help. He knew he could no longer write the book. I didn't need to threaten him. He did it, although reluctantly. I think what he saw me do on the porch scared him. Good. He should be scared. I'm done being used.

With his help, I uploaded all the videos from Monty's mobile on YouTube. The DNA report he showed me, we posted on Twitter. After doing all that, we just sat and waited for the morning.

As expected, the videos went viral. By the time I returned to Mumbai, there were cops trying to manage the mob outside the hotel. I tweeted the hotel's name. I wanted hell to break loose.

In less than twenty-four hours, the entire country found out that I'm Kamini Pratap's illegitimate daughter. That Dheeraj paid money to Bhai to keep me in the House. That he visited the House four times in two years to check on me. Though I didn't have proof that Dheeraj acted at Kamini's behest, that was taken care of soon, too.

The cops arrested Kamini from the hospital. I would have given anything to be there when they handcuffed her. Meanwhile, something else was revealed that added more fuel to the already raging fire. A lawyer released more videos and audio tapes on YouTube. These are recordings of conversations between Kamini and Dheeraj.

'I was hired by Dheeraj. I have recordings and paper proof of everything he did for Kamini Pratap Singh in the last twenty years. I was directed to release these if he went missing or died under mysterious circumstances.' The lawyer said it all on TV.

I watch the YouTube videos sitting in my hotel room. She really hated me. Or is it her past that she hated? She seemed desperate to get away from it and was ready to erase everyone and everything from that life.

'Finish her off, Dheeraj. Finish Asavri. I don't want to see her or hear her name ever again.' This was on the night of the accident when I was lying half-dead on the road.

'I had a daughter. A long time ago. I delivered in the Home of Mercy in Shillong. I want all records erased. All the women who saw me there three to four years ago – I want them gone. Make sure no one is suspicious. Take your time in erasing the evidence.' This was years ago, after her marriage to Pratap, when Kamini realized she needed to wipe her slate clean.

'Remember the baby I told you about? The one I threw away. She is back. She is Asavri. We need to finish her, Dheeraj.' This was after the orphanage scandal happened during the contest.

Not that I ever had any feelings about her, but we did meet a few times during the contest and she seemed so normal. What a snake she turned out to be! No wonder Dheeraj had been compiling video evidence and phone conversations so meticulously over the years. When you work for a snake, you learn to become one, too. He probably knew that he would need them. Though he got killed, he got his sweet revenge after all.

The TV channels can't stop talking about Kamini. I sit glued to the TV in my hotel room. It feels good to see Kamini with matted hair, a hastily tied bun and in a wrinkled sari. The blue-blooded family that had been waiting for decades to strike finally got their chance. A distraught Tanya left the country with her relatives.

The party that had been her dream – the AJP – withdrew all support from her. She does have a lawyer to fight her case but there's just too much evidence against her.

The cops are now looking into how Bhai was shot. They are almost certain she did that too. A murder charge isn't far away. She's going to be locked up for a very long time.

I pass my time in sessions with Dr Parul, meditating and trying to sing. It's not easy. I thought it would be, but every time I sing, the past just comes rushing back. Everything

... Baba, Shantipur, Rudra ... then Mumbai, the contest, my accident, then the House and finally Monty. Will I ever forget all of that? Is it possible to unsee what I've seen?

Today there's a press conference. I'm getting ready for it. It's a bright, sunny afternoon. I can see the sea glistening till the horizon. I know I'm late. I should hurry up, but I sit gazing at the mass of water spread out before me. It's not the kind of day that would remind me of the past. I'm standing in a large, plush room in one of the best, probably most expensive hotels in the city. I'm staring at a beautiful sight.

And just like that, without any warning, I'm back in the room. The room in the House. The clammy, musty smell. The smell of sweat, rotting gutters, heat and fear. I will never forget that smell. I see Monty's white face, with a deep scar running from his left eye to the corner of his lip. He is standing with his weight on his good foot, looking at me and smiling. I shut my eyes tight. I'm sweating and breathing as though my heart will burst out. I can feel a tightening sensation in my chest, as though someone has tied a band around me and is tightening it. I can't breathe. My hands shake and my legs can't hold me anymore. I fall. I grab whatever is near me. It's the curtain I grab. My fingers curl around it tight, my nails dig into my palm.

'No. NO. Stop this. Stop thinking about it. Stop thinking about him!' I scream at myself. I try to steady my breathing. It's a panic attack again. *Just count backwards as the doctor told you to,* I remind myself. *Ten, nine, eight, seven, six* ... I'm breathing better now. I keep counting.

My cheeks feel wet. I didn't realize I was weeping. I don't have the courage to admit it to myself yet.

A soft knock on the door breaks my thoughts. I know who that is. I need to go down. They are waiting.

I open the door and rush to the bathroom. I don't want anyone to see my tears. 'Just a minute and then I'm ready.'

The cameras and the lights almost blind me. Now I know why celebrities wear goggles even at night. It hurts the eye. Avniel isn't there. I told him to stay away and also warned him not to utter a word.

'I don't want to sue you for your first book. Whatever happened in the resort, erase it from your mind.' I think he understood. He's stayed away, though I know he will make an appearance maybe after months or even later. But I'm done with him.

I look at the gathered crowd in the room and smile.

The questions hit me like a tornado. Rather, a series of tornados.

'How are you feeling now? Tell us about the House and what you saw?'

'When will you start singing?'

'When did you know you were Kamini's daughter? Did she visit you?'

'When did you realize that you were a prisoner?'

'How did you survive, Asavri? All that has happened, everything that you saw, how did you live through that?'

I touch the puckered skin on my wrists. It's covered under the long sleeves of my kurta.

How did I survive? I survived because of the one-legged man with spotted white skin, who hurt me, tormented me, sat in the room while gloom descended on me only to tell me that I wasn't alone. I never told him but his being there, in the far corner, made it bearable for me. I survived being raped again and again because he never left me alone. I never told him but I fell in love with him and then I killed him. I killed him so that I could live my own life.

I don't tell them any of that. I'm not ready yet.

'How did I survive? Well … life always finds a way. Have you seen *Jurassic Park*? It's true that life always finds a way. Even when you lose all hope, it finds you.'

Someone asks, 'What happened, Asavri? Will the world ever know what happened?'

'Yes, they will. Someday, maybe I'll write a book about what happened. If you know a publisher, please tell me about them.'

Epilogue

Holi was just a week ago but for the kids in the building, it's not over. They are busy pelting water balloons at each other. It's a war zone. No number of angry stares or warning notices put up by the building society members is going to quell their enthusiasm. Little monsters armed with backpacks filled with water balloons are perched on their balconies, hidden behind pillars and cars to aim at unsuspecting passers-by. As I look down from my tenth-floor bedroom window, happy squeals and shouts float up. Looks like kids from different towers are at war over who hits the most! I can't tell who is winning. I'm not familiar with the faces, yet, but everyone is having fun.

The flat on the tenth floor of Empress Towers in Lokhandwala has been given to me by IKA TV. This was part of the prize. There's also a car that sits in the basement parking bay. This flat is mine. The owner of Flat Number 1002 is Asavri Bhattacharya, the sale deed says. It feels good to know that I have a house of my own. My own place; no one can ask me to leave it. No one can throw me out of this place. It's mine and I earned it. IKA TV has also given me a lot of money, more than what was supposed to be the cash prize for the winner. Bhaskar handed me the cheque, saying, 'I know there can be no compensation for what you have undergone ... or for what has happened to you. This is just a token ... a goodwill gesture.' I think they are worried that I will sue them and wrench out more money. People are worried, in fact, scared, that I will sue. Bhaskar, Avniel. I have no such plans but I will take the money. I certainly deserve it.

I enjoy sitting on the windowsill in my bedroom and looking down and beyond. A marble slab extends out, enabling me to sit and look out. A metal grill cage surrounds the window. I don't like the grill on the window; it reminds me of the House.

Don't fight the bad memories. Allow them to come and go. The more you resist, the more they will persist.

I remember Dr Parul's words. I'm continuing my sessions with her and the Art of Living breathing exercises. I enjoy both a lot. I've hung a small pot which holds a money plant; a cord is tied to one twig and it will start loping itself on the grill soon. Sometimes a little support is all one needs.

I see the kids running zig-zag around parked cars, ducking from the watery emissaries, screaming in glee when one of their balloons hits the target. The balloon war is being taken very seriously. The egg delivery man comes in on his cycle. The kids stay clear of him. They know if his box of eggs falls and breaks, their parents will have to compensate. That wouldn't go down well. So they halt for him to pass. The dog walkers are walking the animals, who don't seem too happy with the ensuing balloon war. Their tails are drooping. They'd rather be indoors than be the targets of water-filled balloons.

I like seeing the children, the normal lives the neighbours lead – going to the office and walking with shopping bags. Normal is nice. I still need sleeping pills to sleep. I often wake up screaming in the dark. There's a trained helper who lives with me. I can't live alone. I don't like the darkness. I keep all the lights switched on after sunset. I often hear their screams. I see their horror-filled eyes. I see death, pain and terror.

Will I ever be normal again?

'Will I ever forget all those things?' I asked Dr Parul in our last session.

'No, you won't forget but you'll learn to manage the memories and thoughts better.'

It's almost dusk. I don't like this time of the day. It makes me feel lonely. So this is the time I sing. Singing has become easier now. I was worried if the neighbours would complain. When I asked them, they couldn't stop laughing.

'The winner of *Indian Koel*, the one who sings like a nightingale, is asking for permission to sing! We wait for you to start singing.' It made me smile when they said it. So I sing whenever I feel like. I have accepted a few commitments, though I have refused public appearances. I can do playback singing but I'm not ready to sing in front of an audience.

There's a small function in the building in a few days. They are calling it Spring Fun. Mumbai has very few days of good weather so I guess people just want to make the most of it. The neighbours requested me to attend it. They assured me there won't be any press. I'm thinking of going. I need to get out more often. It takes a lot of effort to do so but it's important.

'Didi.' My domestic help enters.

'There's something on TV about that Kamini.' She watches TV all day long on her mobile while working.

'What is it, Jyoti?' I'm annoyed to be disturbed just when I am about to start singing. I'm trying to get into a regular routine.

'Please watch, didi.' She takes the remote and switches the TV on.

The news makes me forget my music, and I grab the remote.

'KAMINI PRATAP SINGH POISONED AND FEARED DEAD!'

The warden of the prison Kamini was being kept in is speaking. 'She's had quite a few rough run-ins with the other inmates. She's in prison for conspiracy to kill her daughter, and such prisoners always have a very tough time. We had to keep her away from the others. She was in solitary after a violent fight broke out last week. Today morning, she was given her breakfast. She was fine then. When the attendant went to collect her plate after an hour as is the norm, she was found paralysed, her body twisted and distorted. She was rushed to the hospital but it looks bleak for her.'

I keep watching. I can't believe what I'm seeing and hearing.

A doctor of the hospital she's in speaks to reporters. 'Even if we are able to save her, she will be a vegetable for the rest of her life. She can't move or talk. Her mouth is twisted, the muscles rigid because of the poison. It was a very heavy dose. This is a case of cyanide poisoning.'

I continue watching the news, switching channels to know more. Jyoti enters the room holding a small basket.

'Didi, this was just outside the door.'

I barely glance at what she is holding. I'm more interested in the news. 'Keep it on the table.'

I sit glued for a long time. It's almost dinner time. I tell Jyoti to serve it. She is efficient. She has switched on all the lights in the rooms.

I remember the basket on the table.

Wonder who sent it and what's in it. I untie the cord that holds the cover on the basket. About half a dozen apples, all of them red, shining and juicy, stare back at me.

Why would someone send me apples? I'm about to call for Jyoti and tell her to keep them in the fridge when I notice a note almost hidden under the fruits. I pick it up.

Don't chew the seeds. They are poisonous.

The handwriting is unsteady, almost a scribble. Someone who isn't used to writing in English has written it. There's something else in the basket, nestled between the fruit. It's a tiny twig of a money plant with a few young sprigs of leaves.

I stare at the small plant and the note. I don't know how long I stand there. I let my finger touch the writing and then fold the note. Then I pick up a glass, pour water into it and put the plant in it. I walk into my bedroom and place the glass on my dressing table. I fold the note neatly and slide it into my wallet.

Life finds a way. Always.

Acknowledgements

There's a voice in each of us; sometimes it stops us from making a mistake and sometimes it tells us: *Just do it*!

This book happened because I listened to the voice in my head which refused to stop telling me to rewrite the story. What began as a whisper but grew into a scream; one that refused to die down or quieten.

An earlier version was written, submitted to the publisher and they rejected it, much to my chagrin and utter dismay. Around the same time, another reputed publisher showed interest in the story and they wanted to take it to their edit meeting. But the murmur in my head had, by then, turned into a full-throated scream. *Rewrite the story.* A new version had begun taking shape and I just couldn't shake it off. It was bright sunny January morning when I told the senior editor to not take it to their edit meeting. I said that I wanted to rewrite the story in a different way. She agreed. Come back when you've finished writing it, she told me.

As I stepped out of their office, I asked myself whether what I'd done was the most foolish thing one could do or the bravest?

As they say, you need to be a little foolish to be brave. I followed the voice in my head, trashed 80,000-odd words and rewrote the entire story in a completely new way, keeping barely a skeleton of the former. My publisher who had rejected the earlier version, fell in love with the new story and here you are with the book in your hands.

So yes, it's correct to dedicate the book to my crazy head, my stubborn self, the voices in my head (thank god for them!) and the editors of HarperCollins India. If they hadn't refused the earlier version, I would have never pushed myself to write this amazing story. So thank you. All of you.

So please never ignore that tiny little whisper in your head when it nudges you the other way; even if it seems bizarre.

A big thank you to Arcopol, for being my biggest ally, friend and for being there to assuage my hassled and fried nerves. Swati, thanks for your sharp eye and astute editing skills. The entire HarperCollins India team – you all are really the best thing that can happen to an author.

Suhail Mathur, my literary agent – thank you for your help. Sidharth Jain of Story Ink, thank you for telling me the story is fabulous even before the publisher gave it a nod.

Special thanks to Rickie Khosla and C. V. Lakshmi for reading the manuscript and giving valuable feedback. And do Priyanka Sarkar, who proofread the MS before I submitted it and suggested the title.

Sandeep , thank you for being the sane, solid rock in my life and for keeping me rooted. Rohan, thank you for reading the first version and telling me without mincing words that it was very ordinary and I could do better. My girl friends, you know who you are; thank you for your love, unflinching support, your hugs, and just for being a part of my life.

Bapi and Ma, thank you for introducing me to the amazing world of books and encouraging me to follow my dream. A big tight hug to my mother-in-law who is eagerly waiting to see one of my books into a movie. Writing a book is a solitary journey taken by an author, but there are so many people who aid and assist in that journey. Thank you all for being in my life, inspiring me, motivating me and loving me.

And thank you to my readers. I hope you enjoyed reading the book as much as I enjoyed writing it!

About the Author

Kanchana Banerjee lives in Gurgaon with her husband Sandeep and her three boys Rohan, Archie & Casper. In another life she used to write for various publications and companies, now she is a full time author. When not writing, she enjoys gardening and playing with her dogs. *Nobody's Child* is her second book.